Praise for the

"Engaging characters and a stirring mystery kept me captivated from the first page to the last."
—Dollycas, Amazon Vine Voice, on *Divide and Concord*

"Well-crafted sleuth, enjoyable supporting characters. This is a series not to be missed."
—*Cozy Cat Reviews* on *Death, Dismay and Rosé*

"A sparkling addition to the Wine Trail Mystery series. A toast to protagonist Norrie and Two Witches Winery, where the characters shine and the mystery flows. This novel is a perfect blend of suspense and fun!"
—Carlene O'Neil, author of the Cypress Cove Mysteries, on *Chardonnayed to Rest*

"A thoroughly entertaining series debut, with enjoyable yet realistic characters and enough plot twists—and dead ends—to appeal from beginning to end."
—*Booklist*, starred review, on *Booked 4 Murder*

"Filled with clues that make you go 'Huh?' and a list of potential subjects that range from the charming to the witty to the intense. Readers root for Phee as she goes up against a killer who may not stop until Phee is taken out well before her time. Enjoy this laugh-out-loud funny mystery that will make you scream for the authors to get busy on the next one."
—*Suspense Magazine* on *Molded 4 Murder*

Books by J. C. Eaton

The Wine Trail Mysteries

A Riesling to Die
Chardonnayed to Rest
Pinot Red or Dead?
Sauvigone for Good
Divide and Concord
Death, Dismay and Rosé
From Port to Rigor Morte
Mischief, Murder and Merlot
Caught in the Traminette

The Sophie Kimball Mysteries

Booked 4 Murder
Ditched 4 Murder
Staged 4 Murder
Botched 4 Murder
Molded 4 Murder
Dressed Up 4 Murder
Broadcast 4 Murder
Railroaded 4 Murder
Saddled Up 4 Murder
Grilled 4 Murder
Strike Out 4 Murder

The Marcie Rayner Mysteries

Murder in the Crooked Eye Brewery
Murder at the Mystery Castle
Murder at Classy Kitchens

The Charcuterie Shop Mysteries

Laid Out to Rest
Sliced, Diced and Dead

Caught
in the
Traminette

J. C. Eaton

BEYOND THE PAGE
PUBLISHING

Caught in the Traminette
J. C. Eaton
Copyright © 2023 J. C. Eaton
Cover design and illustration by Dar Albert, Wicked Smart Designs

Beyond the Page Books
are published by
Beyond the Page Publishing
www.beyondthepagepub.com

ISBN: 978-1-960511-36-2

For Carolyn Vetro, an amazing woman who epitomizes the words *courage, decency, and optimism.* Your spirit shines for all of us!

Acknowledgments

Thank you, Gale Leach and Susan Schwartz, for all you do for us! You are wonderful and amazing!

And to Pam Niequist Wehbi, we cannot thank you enough for telling us about a cockroach DNA gift that left us wide-eyed and eager to share it in our own way!

None of this would be possible without our incredible agent, Dawn Dowdle, from Blue Ridge Literary Agency. We are so blessed.

To our editor, Bill Harris, and the phenomenal staff at Beyond the Page Publishing, we are genuinely appreciative of all you do.

Finally, we thank you, our readers, for bringing our acerbic and quirky characters into your lives!

Chapter 1

Two Witches Winery
Penn Yan, New York

I tugged my turtleneck and pulled it up to the bottom of my ears. Then I yanked down on my hat. So what if it meant a bad hair day? Every winter day is a bad hair day in New York's Finger Lakes. And those cute little snowflakes weren't as adorable as they were back in November. By the beginning of January with the holiday decorations down, the dreariest part of the season was about to unfold.

Theo Buchman, part owner of the Grey Egret Winery down the road from us, opened his car door and shouted, "Get a move on, Norrie, we're going to be late. You know how Madeline gets when people trickle in for our Wineries of the West meetings."

"Not as bad as Rosalee." I raced down our winery steps and got in his car, slamming the door behind me. "Sorry. Got stuck at our own monthly winery meeting. Worst part was having to conduct it. Francine never mentioned that when she talked me into the never-ending babysitting job."

"Yeah, speaking of which, when are she and Jason returning from the Philippines?"

"Not soon enough. First, Cornell's Experiment Station sent him to track down some new grasshopper, and would you believe it? My brother-in-law spotted another variety—a rare rainbow-colored one. That meant a new entry into the Global Species database and an extended return date in early April. April! It was supposed to be February. Then March. Now April. Why on earth did my sister have to marry an entomologist?"

"You're a trooper, Norrie. You'll skate through it."

Not when the ice starts to melt.

Theo turned north on Route 14 and headed up the lake to

1

Billsburrow Winery. "At least Madeline always has great refreshments. That's something to look forward to."

"I suppose. But honestly, I hope she doesn't go on and on at the meeting. It was bad enough having to listen to Franz for almost an hour. He wouldn't stop talking about the new traminette wine they plan to introduce this fall."

"Um, that's kind of understandable. I mean, he *is* the winemaker and you know how they get."

"Cammy had to kick my ankles twice during his dissertation. My mind sort of wandered. First when he went on and on about the blending of Gewurztraminer and Joannes Seyval and then later when he couldn't stop himself from babbling about the characteristics. "Dry, off-dry, spicey, floral . . ." I felt like saying, 'Make up your mind,' but that would have meant another half hour at least."

"Good thing your tasting room manager kept you from falling asleep."

"Yeah, I really owe Cammy. Anyway, Franz intends to produce an ice wine as well."

By now, we were only a few yards from the turnoff to Billsburrow Winery. "Oh, and did I mention our vineyard manager was really jazzed about it, too. Almost as over-the-top as Franz. Seems the vines like the cold and are pretty disease-resistant. It was John's dream grape, I suppose."

We parked in front of Madeline's house and saw that we were the last car to arrive. "Yeesh. Usually it's Rosalee who straggles in but everyone gives her a pass since she's in her eighties."

"Just walk fast."

"About time you two got here." Stephanie Ipswich brushed a long blond strand of hair from her face and took a sip of coffee. For a mother of two twin first-graders and the owner/manager of Gable Hills Winery, she looked younger than most eighteen-year-olds, and had the figure of a supermodel to boot.

"I got held up at our winery meeting. Sorry, guys." I helped myself to coffee and grabbed a chocolate-filled scone. "What did we miss,

Madeline?" *Please tell me ninety percent of the meeting.*

"We're just about to start. Normally, I would circle around the room and ask everyone for a quick update on what's new at their wineries, but something has just come to my attention and we need to act fast."

"I'm eighty-six years old. I don't act fast," Rosalee said. "I only move at two speeds—slow and slower. Like the time it takes for our grapes to ferment at Terrace Wineries."

Theo nudged my elbow and I tried not to laugh. Every month, the six wineries in our close-knit klatch met to share information and insights so we could support each other. But usually we met so we didn't lose any ground in the Penn Yan and Geneva gossip chains.

"What's so pressing?" Catherine Trobert, the owner of Lake View Winery, refilled her coffee and took a small sugar cookie from the tray. "If it's a legal matter, I can call my son in Maine. Steven is a wealth of information." Then she glanced my way and I was certain the cream in my coffee had curdled in my stomach. It was only a matter of time before she mentioned the prospect of me dating her son.

"Take a look out the window, ladies." Madeline pointed to Seneca Lake and we all squinted to see what we had missed.

"Looks like the same body of water to me," Rosalee said. "Don't tell me some idiot plans to dredge it."

Madeline shook her head. "No, worse. Much worse."

"Get to the point. I'd like to turn eighty-seven in my own winery, not sitting around this table." Rosalee chugged her coffee as if it was something stronger.

"Fine. Brace yourselves. The Tomson Brothers, who own the lakefront land stretching from the Geneva city limits to five miles south of us, plan to sell it to a developer from Syracuse. I'll never look at the color orange the same way again."

"And how exactly do you know that?" Theo asked. "Don and I haven't heard a word of it at the Grey Egret and believe me, he's all over the latest gossip."

3

Madeline shifted in her chair and sighed. "Because we've been looking for extra acreage. Like Two Witches, we're introducing traminette wine this fall, too, but in limited quantities since we could only spare a small swath of land. When our realtor mentioned the lakefront property would be for sale, we jumped all over it. Then, poof! A developer swooped in and outbid us."

"Wow. Lakefront land with a natural slope to the water. Perfect for a vineyard," I said, "but I bet that developer isn't thinking grapes."

"Hardly." Madeline scoffed. "From what the realtor told us, the company plans to build a high-rise complex with million-dollar lakefront views. We can all kiss the Finger Lakes ambience goodbye if we don't act fast. Tourists won't be looking at our vineyards and the lake, they'll be staring into someone's living room complete with a wide-screen TV."

"What do you mean 'act fast'?" I'd had my dealings with developers and this was one snare I wasn't about to step in.

"Approval for the project is needed by the Town of Benton Planning Board. Their next meeting is in two weeks and we need to show up in force. And this isn't just sour grapes, no pun intended, because we lost out on some decent property. All of our wineries are going to lose out on this one. Trust me, Seneca Lake will become unrecognizable. First a high-rise complex, and then another. And another. It will never end."

"Madeline's got a good point," Stephanie said. "We've already seen how so many of the tiny cottages have been razed so that million-dollar homes can be built. Now those sellers won't settle for millions, they'll want lots more and only developers can offer that. Certainly not us."

"What about the local property owners?" Stephanie perused the sugar cookies as if she was selecting an answer for the SATs.

"I'm sure they'll be there as well," Madeline went on, "but we need to be the backbone for a no vote or life on Seneca Lake as we know it will disappear within five years."

I kicked Theo in the shin and whispered, "Like the dinosaurs."

Catherine arched her back and stretched. "What do you say, everyone? We can meet a few days before at my place and practice our spiels. I'm not great at public speaking, but I'll manage."

I kicked Theo again and pointed to my phone, not wanting to risk saying it out loud—*the only speaking she's good at is about Steven. Still trying to fix us up.* Then I added the vomit emoji.

Theo texted back, *Did you tell her you had a boyfriend?*

I responded, *At least a zillion times.*

Yep, I had a boyfriend, all right. My own Geneva lawyer, sweet and hunky Bradley Jamison, who worked for the well-known family law firm owned by Marvin Souza, a name as familiar in the Hamptons as it was locally. Of course, along with that familiarity, it meant Bradley was often on the road in New York dealing with high-profile cases and high-paying ones. Hey, who says you can't have it both ways?

"So are we done?" Rosalee's voice woke me from my revery and I jumped.

"I suppose. Sorry, everyone," Madeline said. "Next time we'll catch up on our own winery business, but now we have to ensure we'll have one. Be sure to mark your calendars to meet at Catherine's place."

This time Theo texted me, *And be sure to rehearse your lines for the show.*

I laughed and grabbed another scone for the road.

"That wasn't so bad," Theo said when he started the engine. I was already bone-chilled walking from Madeline's house to the car.

"No, I suppose not for the first Thursday in January. At least we got the bad news out of the way."

"Yeah, I mean, what else can cloud up the start to the new year?"

"Don't say that! It will jinx things!"

But it was already too late and the first jinx happened within minutes of my arrival back at Two Witches Winery.

Chapter 2

Judging from the parking lot, with only six or seven cars, I knew it was going to be a slow day. Not that we couldn't use the winddown after the holiday rush, but still, when minutes seem like hours, the day really drags on.

Only Cammy, Glenda, and Lizzie, our accountant/cashier, were working, along with Fred and Emma in the bistro. Tomorrow would bring in a larger crowd so Roger and Sam were also scheduled to conduct tastings.

I greeted everyone as soon as I got in, then kicked off my boots and swapped them for a pair of mules that I kept in my office. Well, my sister Francine's office to be accurate, but since I was the one who seemed to be its only occupant, I felt I deserved to call it my own until my temporary servitude ended.

I'm Norrie Ellington, a twentysomething screenwriter with a real residence near Little Italy in Manhattan, thanks to my great-aunt Tessie's will. If you're one of those Hallmark Channel viewers, chances are you've seen my screenplays. Mostly romance and some mystery-romance.

When my sister first approached me about overseeing the family winery while she and her husband chased after some elusive, and most likely disgusting, insect in Costa Rica, I couldn't say no. But then, Jason found more insects and the Global Database found him. End of story. Now, whenever a hideous bug is discovered, guess who winds up here? Uh-huh. And this particular sojourn had better end on schedule.

• • •

I booted up the computer and was about to grab a bite to eat at our bistro when I heard a rap on my doorframe and looked up. It was Godfrey Klein, my brother-in-law's coworker at the Experiment

Station and the only one who could reach him via a satellite phone from Cornell.

With his cherubic round face and wispy light brown hair, there was something endearing about Godfrey. There had to be. Because, for some reason still unbeknownst to me, I kissed him full on the mouth for no apparent reason and am still trying to get that scenario out of my mind. Granted, it was months ago, but still . . . awkward is awkward and that was about as awkward as anything I've ever done. Thankfully, Godfrey put it behind him. I only wish I could.

"Hey, Norrie, sorry to barge in but I'm on my way back from a winery near Watkins Glen with a pill bug infestation. I have something for you and wanted to deliver it in person."

"A pill bug?" Like Jason, Godfrey was captivated by crawly things too.

"No, something really special. Something you'll treasure."

Oh no. Maybe he hadn't put the kiss behind him.

Godfrey reached in his jacket pocket and handed me a box.

Now what do I do?

"Go on. Open it."

"I'm not sure I should accept—"

"Just open it."

I lifted the lid and was petrified I'd see a ring. Instead, I looked at a small glass vial with some sort of liquid. "I don't understand. What is this?"

"Cockroach DNA! You remember my partner, Alex Bollinger, who got a grant to research cockroaches? Well, a geneticist in our lab was able to extract DNA! Isn't this exciting?"

Like stepping in manure.

"I don't know what to say."

"The department felt you should have it since you've been such a sport covering for Francine and Jason."

"Uh-oh. I know what's next. Don't tell me they're not coming back in April. They promised they'd be done by then."

7

"The study should only last two more months. Three, tops."

"Three more months? That's June!"

"I knew you'd understand."

"Understand? I'm ready to fly to the Philippines with a case of Raid!"

Godfrey's cell phone pinged and he glanced at it. "Got to go. Look, how about we talk over pizza this week? You pick the time and the place. My treat."

"They're staying longer than three months, aren't they?"

"You can pick the toppings, too! Got to run! Oh, and by the way, the DNA needs to be kept in a cool climate-controlled environment. Not necessarily refrigerated but highly recommended. I'd put it in your fridge when you get home. Meantime, you can use the winery refrigerator."

And with that, Godfrey set the record for the twenty-five-meter dash.

I stared at the roach DNA before sticking it in a drawer. Cockroach DNA. You'd think Cornell could spring for chocolate and flowers. Then again, this was the entomology department and that was the best way they could thank me for keeping them afloat by babysitting the winery.

"You okay?" Cammy asked as she peered into the office. "I thought I heard you talking to yourself."

"Not to myself. To generations of cockroaches."

"Huh?"

I opened the drawer and waved the vial at her. "Look! Cockroach DNA! A gift from the entomology department."

Cammy grinned. "How many more months did they spring on you?"

"At least two or three."

"Look on the bright side, not much happens in the doldrums of winter. You'll have lots of time to work on your screenplays."

If only Cammy could have taken back those words!

"I suppose. Anyway, it seems we're starting the new year with a contentious issue. Madeline was all over it at our Wineries of the West meeting. In fact, it was the *only* topic at the meeting."

"What topic?"

"Some Syracuse developer bought the acreage across from her and plans to build a luxury high-rise. Talk about kissing the view goodbye. And if that wasn't bad enough, she and her husband had made an offer so they could plant traminette grapes there. Right now they only have a tiny parcel of land for that grape."

"Yeesh. I'm still wrapping my head around the high-rise. It'll force lakefront property owners to sell and soon all we'll have are high-rises and vacation-home city folks. If that doesn't drive prices up around here, nothing will."

"I know. That's why Madeline wants all of us to attend the Benton Town Hall meeting in two weeks to hopefully compel the board to nix the project. All those meetings have a public session. I think it's required."

"It is. And by *all of us*, I suppose each of those women in your group will make daytime soap operas pale in comparison. All that sobbing. That pathos. That—Oh my gosh—Rosalee Marbleton will speak, won't she?"

"Uh-huh."

"You may want to give a heads-up to the local sheriff's office. You weren't around four years ago when someone suggested a leash law for all private property that wasn't fenced in. Heard she went ballistic."

"Charlie, my sister's silly Plott hound, runs free around here until it's hunting season, so I take it that law never passed."

"Got that right. Maybe Rosalee will get the board to vote no and prevent the developer from building that high-rise."

• • •

Lamentably, that didn't happen. Two weeks flew by, and next thing I knew it was time for that meeting in Benton. We never did get to practice "our spiels" at Catherine's because everyone got too busy preparing for the January wine sale. Our way of clearing the wine and merchandise racks so we could fill them up again, only with higher prices while bringing more visitors to the wine trail.

The town hall meeting, as publicized in the *Penn Yan Chronicle* and the *Finger Lakes Times*, was scheduled for seven p.m. on a Tuesday night. Bradley, who had to attend his own meeting that night, told me to state the facts and back it up with evidence.

"Keep your voice clear and steady," he said, "and don't get overemotional."

I laughed. "Overemotional? After Madeline, Catherine, and Rosalee get done, there'll be enough emotion in the room to garner them Academy Awards."

"What about Stephanie, Theo and Don?"

"Stephanie will bat her eyelashes and flip her hair. This may sound sexist, but let's hope the majority of board members are men."

"And the guys from the Grey Egret?"

"When have you ever known those two to be emotional? No worries there."

It didn't take a soothsayer to predict the dynamics of that public hearing, but nevertheless, that's exactly what happened. Zenora, whose last name I don't know, blew into the winery like an ill wind at a little past five on the night of the town hall meeting. Before Lizzie could announce her arrival, Zenora splayed her bright red nails against my desktop and took a deep breath.

Her real name was Mabel Ann, and she was a close friend of Glenda's, one of our tasting room employees. When not conducting seances, conjuring the spirits, or purifying the air with horrible smelling sage sticks, Zenora worked at Cornell University's Uris Library. She was a research assistant whose skills were so over-the-top, along with her persona, that she had her own office. Granted, it was in the basement, but still it was all her own.

According to Glenda, who doesn't make a move without consulting her horoscope and tracking celestial bodies, Zenora's reputation as a psychic was unmatched, along with her penchant for scaring the daylights out of people. Myself included. In fact, that's why I think she got her own office in the first place.

True, the women were both sweet, harmless souls, but the alternate universe they inhabited was a tad too off-kilter for me.

"Norrie!" she gasped as she stepped back and pulled her green parka over a loosely flowing flower skirt that came down to her knees, "I drove here the second my shift at the library ended."

"Uh, hi, Zenora! Did I miss something?"

"I had the most unsettling premonition. You and those close to you in the winery are surrounded by dark spirits." Then she reached in her coat and dumped a pile of sticks and dried purple herbs on my desk. "Sage and lavender. You need to cleanse your winery now. I would offer to do it for you but I have to pick up Glenda. We have a special meeting at our—"

"Coven?" The word just slipped out.

"No. Our spiritual enlightening group."

Coven.

"Um, sure. We're closing in less than a half hour but our bistro would be happy to get you something, my compliments."

"Maybe an herbal tea. I'll go find Glenda. Burn those sage sticks as soon as you close!"

Or toss them in the nearest trash bin.

"Thanks, Zenora. Much appreciated."

In retrospect, I should have burned those sage sticks and anything else that would ignite. Unfortunately, I didn't, and according to Zenora and Glenda, that mere act opened the door to a cascading series of events that added a new blemish to "the growing number of bodies" found on the wine trail.

Chapter 3

The Benton Town Hall on Route 14A near Havens Corners was a large white-framed building that looked like a combination farmhouse and barn. White clapboard and a semicircular roof line. Set back from the road, and surrounded by mature trees, it looked like one of those postcard photos of the Finger Lakes.

When Theo and I arrived at six forty-five, there were over thirty cars in the parking lot.

"I doubt they even get ten cars at most meetings," Theo said as he looked for a spot to park. "And that includes the seven board members."

"Yeah, word travels fast. Look—there's Rosalee's car. Hard to miss that relic."

"I imagine the whole crew is here. Come on, let's hope we can get seats."

The board room was straight ahead as we entered the building. Uncomfortable-looking fold-up wooden chairs and a raised stage with a podium and seven slightly more comfortable cushioned chairs behind it. Other than the flag off to the right, it was as bland as Francine's organic cereals.

None of the board members had made their appearance but the room was pretty well packed, including our little Wineries of the West group. Madeline waved us over and pointed to two seats that she had saved. "I knew you and Theo would be straggling in," she said. "Quick, sit down before anyone takes them."

Theo elbow bumped me. "Straggling in? This is early for you."

I elbowed back and moved into the row to take a seat, forcing two people to tuck their feet in and another one to stand.

"Excuse me, sorry," I muttered before plunking myself down.

At that moment, all seven board members walked onto the stage and sat in what I assumed to be their assigned seats. Five men and two women. Theo must have had the same idea I did because he kicked my ankle and whispered, "Five men. Good odds for Stephanie."

A tall, lanky gentleman in his fifties greeted the audience and led us in the pledge to the flag. Then, he introduced himself as well as the other board members and explained the first thirty minutes were reserved for public comment before the actual meeting would begin. "Comments are limited to three minutes in order to be fair for our audience. Remember, be courteous and respectful."

Rosalee, who was seated behind us, leaned forward and said, "Good. Five minutes in this chair and my sciatica is already killing me."

I nodded and smiled.

The gentleman turned out to be Avery Pullman, the board president. He asked if there was anyone in the audience who cared to make a comment. Hands flew in the air as if we were requesting free tickets to a rock concert.

The first person to be acknowledged was an average-looking man in his late forties or fifties, clean-shaven with a brush cut that helped to minimize any gray hairs he might have had. With his black shirt and tan khakis, he had "corporate management" written all over him.

"Not any of the winery owners I recognize," Theo said. "Unless it's one of the new ones."

"Shh, we'll find out in a second."

The man approached the podium, thanked the president, and cleared his throat. "Good evening. I'm Stanley Hurst, from Diamante Developers in Syracuse. I'm sure that name is familiar to most of you since we've been in your local papers for the past two weeks as well as in the online news. I'm here tonight to reiterate what I've said during prior interviews. Your region, as lovely as it is, has not kept up with the growing cities of Canandaigua and Skaneateles."

A series of groans followed and Avery, who sat behind Stanley on the stage, motioned for quiet.

Stanley took a quick breath and continued to speak. "What I'm referring to is the development of the lakefront south of Geneva. My company is proposing to build a luxury high-rise that will make this area a beacon for expansion and entertainment. The specs can be found on our website for this eight-story structure with wraparound lake views and every possible amenity."

Again the groans continued, only louder. This time it was Stanley who faced his palms to the audience and asked for quiet.

"I'll be brief," he continued. "The tax revenues alone should be a boon to all of you. Not to mention the number of new residents who will frequent your establishments and keep your businesses afloat."

"We're floating fine as it is," Rosalee said in a voice that carried across the room.

At that point, the board president stood and responded, "Everyone in our audience will get the chance to add his or her comments. Remember, courtesy."

I rolled my eyes and listened as Stanley went on. "We will add an access road to the new building and cultivate the lawn. Everyone driving by will know in no uncertain terms that luxury is spelled DIAMANTE."

With that, he took a seat and a zillion hands went up in the air. Waving and gesturing. In some cases with both hands.

"Looks like we're in for a fun night," Theo chuckled.

"Give it ten minutes and fun will become contentious. And I don't need Zenora to predict that."

Sure enough, I was right. I'd heard about school board meetings that were one step away from Armageddon, including one that my parents attended where a woman threw her house keys at the superintendent of schools and said, "If you raise the taxes, you might as well have the keys to my house. You'll be the only one who can afford the payments."

I perused the room and watched to see who would be up at bat next. But before anyone could reach the podium, Rosalee stood and shouted, "It's a good thing sewage flows downhill to the lake!"

And that's when things took a turn for the worse.

Greg Baker, the owner of Port of Call, a fabulous restaurant on

Seneca Lake located within spitting distance of the proposed high-rise, stood up and walked to the podium. A tall, clean-shaven guy in his late thirties who always had a smile on his face, wasn't smiling now.

He took the mic, looked at Stanley, and then stepped sideways so he could address the board and the audience.

"I'm Greg Baker, the owner of Port of Call, and I am registering my objection to the proposed high-rise on Seneca Lake."

At that moment, Rosalee spoke up again, "You tell 'em! If their pipes back up, the only aroma will be muck, mire, and manure, not roasted game hens or shrimp scampi."

Greg stifled a laugh and went on. "One of the wonderful things about our lake is the fact that our visitors can enjoy the views and get away from the city. That high-rise would not only block the northern view from our wraparound deck, but it would defeat the whole premise of visiting the Finger Lakes. Many of our guests come from New York City to get away from high-rise buildings. Last thing they need to see is another one staring them in the face. It's bad for business and it's bad for our region."

With that he went back to his seat and Audrey Killion, owner of a small bakery on the lake, took his place at the podium. Petite with reddish-brown hair and freckles, she looked to be seventeen, but Theo told me she was in her seventies.

Audrey introduced herself and continued with the same breath. "That building would be the first step to changing the ambiance of our area from vineyard beauty to city sprawl. And don't tell me it would only be one building. I'm not that naïve and neither are my neighbors. Soon, we won't have an idyllic wine region, we'll be the mini-mall of the Finger Lakes. And my business will get squeezed out. I run a specialized bakery where customers can enjoy my tasty creations on a lovely porch while gazing at the lake. If this horrid high-rise is built, they'll be staring at a large edifice while sampling my shish kabob mini-cupcakes. It's an outrage!"

Theo poked me and whispered, "What's a shish kabob mini-cupcake?"

I whispered back, "Lots of little cupcakes on a shish kabob stick. Very trendy."

"Hmm. Surprised Don didn't mention it. He's usually up on those sorts of things."

Then, someone else chimed in from the back of the room, most likely beating Rosalee by a nanosecond. It was a man's voice but I couldn't see who it was.

"Did anyone think about water usage? Utilities? Fire and medical response? And trash removal? I'd like to know what studies have been done!"

Stanley stood, hands on his hips and chest puffed out. "You can access the feasibility study from the town board secretary during regular business hours."

Then the man spoke again. I twisted my head but still couldn't see him since he remained seated. "Copies should have been provided for this meeting. What information are you hiding?"

"We are completely transparent," Stanley said. Followed by Rosalee, "Yep, and that includes their brains."

On no. This might be worse than that proposed leash law.

At that point, the board president took the mic and directed his comment at Rosalee. "One more outburst and our sergeant at arms will need to remove you."

"I didn't know we were in the service," I said to Theo, making sure to keep my voice low.

He moved closer so no one would hear him. "I think it's Robert's Rules of Order but I'm not sure."

Next to the podium was our very own Madeline Martinez. She held a manila folder and placed it in front of her.

Yikes! This could be worse than our monthly wine meetings.

She opened the folder and looked straight at the audience. "I'm Madeline Martinez, owner of Billsburrow Winery on Seneca Lake, and I'd like to add my objection to the proposed development."

A different voice from nowhere but it was impossible to see who it was. "That's three against one and we're only getting started."

Madeline gave a quick nod and continued. "Our patrons come not only for the wine, but for the spectacular views. Frankly, there's nothing spectacular about a high-rise, even if it does come with amenities for the tenants. Our landscape will be forever changed and we will never to be able to recoup the regional atmosphere that we've been known for. I say nix the proposal."

Then, Catherine. She approached the podium as if it were a guillotine and dabbed her eyes.

"Oh no." Theo nudged me. "Are we in for one of her performances?"

"I'm afraid so. Just be glad you didn't pay for a ticket."

He took out his cell phone and aimed it her way. "Got to record this for Don."

Catherine inhaled and placed a hand on her chest. "When I was a young child—"

"Oh, hell no!" Rosalee shouted. "Not that story again. Cut to the chase. My back is seizing up already!"

At that moment, Avery, who was seated off to the side of the stage, nodded to the sergeant at arms. He, in turn, walked over to Rosalee and motioned for her to leave. Not a particularly good move. At least for anyone who knew Rosalee.

"Make one move toward me and I'll slap you into next week!"

And then, voices from the crowd. And lots of them.

"Leave the woman alone. If you want to remove anyone, start with Stanley and his high-rise."

"Elder abuse!"

"You just want an excuse to end the public session!"

"End the high-rise."

"I say the woman stays put!"

And on and on it went. More comments. Louder. Angrier.

Finally, the sergeant at arms stepped back and the next to approach the podium was Stephanie.

17

Theo shook my arm and grinned. "Here it comes. If you can't win them with logic, go for sex appeal."

"Oh, she's going, all right. If she tosses her long blond hair one more time, I might retch."

"I'll get you a bucket."

Chapter 4

Stephanie sashayed to the podium and turned to the board. "I'm Stephanie Ipswich. My husband and I own Gable Hills Winery in Penn Yan and have prided ourselves on maintaining that small, welcoming community touch. Right down to our white picket fence and our lovely flower gardens."

"What do you know?" This time I nudged Theo. "An advertisement for her winery as well as voicing her complaint."

"Yeah. Who says blonds aren't smart?"

This time I gave him a stronger kick in the ankle.

Stephanie leaned forward and I saw a few of the men open their eyes even wider as she spoke. "The view from the top of Gable Hill is spectacular and visitors come to take photos as well as taste our wines. When that new high-rise is built, the view will be partially obscured and Gable Hills will lose its many visitors and customers. Our business will suffer along with many other wineries known for their scenery as well as their spirits. I ask that you reconsider and vote no on this proposal." Then she stepped back, brushed her hair from her cheek, and either widened her eyes or batted them. I couldn't tell because I only saw the side of her face, but whatever it was, it gave pause to a few of the men, who turned to look at each other.

"Think that means anything?" I asked Theo.

"It does, but not necessarily a no vote."

I was about to wave my hand and put in my two cents when someone else beat me to it. It was a large-framed woman in her late fifties or sixties with curly brown hair that matched her rust cardigan and slacks. She walked straight to the podium, nodded at the board and proceeded to speak.

"I'm Martha Buell and I live directly across from Billsburrow Winery. My family has owned our home for over sixty years on the lake. And tonight, I'm not just speaking for myself." She motioned her hand upward and within seconds, at least fifteen to twenty other people stood. "I'm speaking for my neighbors and friends on Seneca Lake who are adamantly opposed to having a high-rise built on the lakeshore. It will alter our landscape, our community, and the wonderful lifestyle we have known and enjoyed. We've paid our taxes, supported our schools, and worked to make this a desirable place for residents and tourists alike. A high-rise will jeopardize all of that. We can say goodbye to country living as we know it. We implore you. Vote no."

A hearty round of applause followed Martha. Then Avery asked if there were any other speakers.

"It's now or never," Theo said.

Reluctantly, I waved my hand and wondered why on earth I did that. After all, what more could I say that wasn't already said?

"Hi! I'm Norrie Ellington, co-owner of Two Witches Winery on Two Witches Hill."

"We know it!" someone yelled. "The epicenter of Seneca Lake's murders."

I pinched my shoulders back, took a deep breath, and looked directly at the audience. "The only thing about to be murdered is the beauty of the Finger Lakes along with our burgeoning vineyards. Why? Because developers like Diamante have the capital to buy the land. Capital that we don't have because we're basically farmers who develop, produce, and market a product that requires us to take out loans for equipment as well as everything else. If you're looking for the real murderer, I think all of you know who that is. But trust me, it won't be a single act. If the Benton Town Board votes yes, they, too, will carry that moniker." Then I turned to the board. "If businesses don't develop, they languish and die. And wineries need more land for that development. Like the Martinezes who want to introduce a wonderful new variety by planting traminette grapes. This area has always been about farming. Don't make our landscape a cityscape."

And then, something I didn't expect—I got a round of applause. I hustled back to my seat and told Theo it was his turn, but I was too late. Avery approached the microphone and said, "Thank you, ladies and gentlemen. Tonight's public session is now closed and we will move to our regular agenda, beginning with the treasurer's report."

Just then, a good-looking man in his twenties raised a hand and said, "I'm with the *Finger Lakes Times*. Can you tell us when we can expect your vote?"

"We will go into executive session at the close of our meeting. Attendees are more than welcome to remain for the duration of the meeting."

"And risk deep vein thrombosis?" Rosalee shouted. "Besides, since when does a discussion about approving a development need to go into executive session?"

"It's a sensitive matter and all sensitive matters belong in executive session."

I watched as the reporter tapped his iPhone and figured he was probably getting all of this down for future reference. Then, as the audience began to leave, someone in the crowd shouted, "It's not over yet!"

Wonderful. Nothing like ending a meeting with a threat. Unfortunately, it was only the beginning.

Theo took my elbow and directed me out the door, when I realized something. "Give me a second. I'll be right back."

He stood off to the side of the room while I raced to the reporter who had just taken a seat down in front.

"Excuse me, I'm Norrie Ellington from—"

"I know. Two Witches. Nice commentary, by the way."

"Thanks." I reached in my bag, grabbed a winery business card and wrote my cell number on it. Then I handed it to him.

"Here's my number," I said.

He looked at the card, then at me and grinned. Big brown eyes, dark hair, and dimples. Yep, twenties for sure. There was a moment of awkward silence but I spoke up as soon as I saw the perplexed look on his face.

"I can't stay for the rest of the meeting. Can you please text me the decision on the high-rise? I gave you my cell number. It's not as if it's a trade secret. It's going to be announced in a public meeting and it will be on your online news tomorrow and in the paper the next day, right?"

"Sure, if you'll consider having lunch with me sometime this week."

I looked at those dreamy brown eyes but Bradley's were dreamy, too. "Love to, but I'm seeing someone."

Just then Theo approached us and the reporter glanced his way. "So sorry. I didn't realize you were a couple."

"Us?" Theo burst out laughing. "No, we are definitely not a couple. Norrie's winery is next to ours, the Grey Egret. We're just friends. Good friends. Really good friends. Nothing more. Good friends."

"I understand." Then he looked at me. "No problem. I'll text you as soon as the meeting ends. Oh, I'm Joel Margolis, been with the *Finger Lakes Times* just over a year."

"No wonder you get stuck with these kinds of meetings. I've been with the winery my whole life but not living here. Until recently myself. But it's temporary. Really temporary."

Thankfully Avery chose that second to speak into the mic and announce that the regular meeting was about to begin. I thanked Joel again and raced out of there before I gave him my life history.

"What was that all about?" Theo asked as we approached his car. "I thought you'd never stop yammering."

I shrugged. "I'm not sure. Besides, you didn't *have* to go overboard telling him we were friends. One more adjective and he'd question the whole thing."

"Just didn't want to give him the wrong idea."

"Maybe I should have taken him up on the lunch offer. I would have been able to convince him to keep me posted on any developments about that high-rise."

"You would have been over your head and given him the wrong

idea. Best to keep your life as uncomplicated as possible. Oh, what am I saying? That will never happen. Come on, it's getting really cold. I want to start up the car."

"I'll text you as soon as Joel lets me know the outcome. Actually, I'll make it a group text and let the WOW women know."

"I don't think Rosalee texts. Or does email for that matter."

"Don't worry. Gossip mail goes faster. She'll know before her coffee gets cold tomorrow morning."

As we walked to Theo's car, we noticed Madeline speaking with Stanley Hurst in front of her car. Their voices carried in the crisp snowless air and we heard every word. Stanley pretty much told Madeline that vineyards were a dime a dozen in the Finger Lakes and what the area really needed was a luxury development to reflect the twenty-first century.

Then Madeline told him what he could reflect and where. Not pretty. She got in her car, slammed the door, and started the engine just as Theo and I got into his car.

I turned my head to see Madeline tearing out of the parking lot and a heavyset man in jeans and a beige jacket grab Stanley by the arm.

"We may want to stick around for this," I said to Theo.

"Geez, Norrie, it's like twenty below in the car already. I'm starting the engine."

"I'm curious. Shh. I'm rolling my window down so we can hear their voices."

Theo shot me a look and rolled down his window, too. Then he cut the engine. Sure enough, we heard every single syllable. The only trouble was we had no idea who uttered half of them.

"I'd like to know how you found out what my offer was and then upped it. Forget unethical. It was downright illegal and you won't hear the last of it." The man let go of Stanley's arm and crossed his own.

"I don't know what you're talking about. An offer is an offer."

"I'd heard you'd walk over bodies to get what you want, but this time you stepped on the wrong one."

"Get over it."

I leaned forward, expecting to see an altercation, but instead the man left without saying a word.

Theo rolled up our windows and started up the car again. "Looks like Madeline wasn't the only one who got burned. Wish I knew who that was."

"Anyone's guess but I didn't recognize him from the wineries."

"Me either, but that doesn't mean anything. His vineyards could be on the east side of the lake and maybe he wants to expand on our side. He wouldn't be the first one."

"Or maybe it's a competing business."

"Hey, all they did was blow off steam, and give Madeline high blood pressure. At least everyone left in one piece."

"You think the proposal will pass?" I bit my lower lip and watched Theo pull onto Route 14A.

"You heard that audience. The board would need to have its collective head examined if they vote yes."

"And if they do?"

"We steer clear of Madeline until the snow melts."

Theo dropped me off in front of the house and Charlie was all over me the second I opened the door. I motioned him outside and waited while he did his business. Then, I hurried him inside before he decided to take off for the woods. Usually he goes out his doggie door into the fenced-in yard, but I had the door closed since it let in a cold draft.

"Now we play a waiting game, Charlie," I said. "And I plan to wait in my sweats with a cup of hot chocolate."

I gave him a dog biscuit and retreated upstairs to change clothes. Then I put a hot chocolate K-cup into the Keurig and took out a small bag of mini-marshmallows from the pantry. That's when a text came in from Joel—*Regular meeting over. Snooze fest. In exec session now. Will let you know.*

I looked at the time and it was a little past nine. I figured the executive session would last maybe a half hour, but it wasn't until ten fifteen when the second text came in.

Approved 4–3. Going to get some sleep.

I texted back, *Tks. I owe you. Maybe coffee.* Then I pushed the Send arrow before I thought it through. Theo would have a field day.

I quickly sent a group text out but the only one who responded was Stephanie.

Derek pitched a fit. Will call u tomorrow. Tks.

I'm sure Rosalee would have pitched, thrown, and *had* a fit if she used technology. As for everyone else, they were just getting started.

Chapter 5

I was about to turn in for the night when I realized something. I needed to know who those yes votes were. I quickly texted Joel back and he responded, *Diane Oftspringer, Victor Dahl, Michael Antonacci, Avery Pullman.* Then a few minutes later he added, *In case u were wondering. Here are the no votes: Mavis Willington, Richard Hochstatter, Craig Fleck. Btw, coffee sounds good.*

My stomach churned as I read the last sentence three times. What the heck had I done? I rationalized that this would be a business relationship and not interfere with my current relationship, but I know how those things go. One minute it's all on the up-and-up and the next thing you know, you're making out in the back of someone's car. I had to remind myself that I was no longer eighteen and as an adult, I would be making adult choices. Still, my stomach tightened and held its grip.

It was a fitful night as far as sleep was concerned but surprisingly, I was pretty focused when I woke up. I fed Charlie, let him out, made coffee and set out to google Diane, Victor, Michael and Avery, the illustrious board president. Who were these insensitive buffoons who voted to destroy our lakefront?

I got as far as Diane when the first of three phone calls came in and all thoughts of Diane evaporated for the time being.

"Norrie, it's Madeline. Great job last night. Got your text. That son of a gun Avery voted yes. I wonder if he got paid off and strong-armed the other three so the proposal would go through."

"I think that would be kind of hard to prove but we should poke around. You know, find out as much as we can about them."

"Already on it."

"Hey, Theo and I couldn't help but overhear you and Stanley in the parking lot."

"Bad enough he snuck in an underhanded bid but he had to rub it in. I told him where he could go."

"We know. I think the whole county knows. Voices really carry on those cold, clear winter nights."

"I don't care. What's the worst that could happen?"

Oh no. The "kiss of death" sentence.

"Anyway, I think we should look into that board for any hanky-panky."

"I already called our attorney."

"Sounds like a sensible plan." As opposed to some wacko thing the WOW group comes up with.

Then Don called. "Theo told me about the meeting. *And* the reporter. You were right to nix the lunch. No sense getting caught in a web."

Does coffee count as a web?

"Uh, yeah," I said. Then Don continued. "When we catch a break, we'll start googling the folks who voted yes. How about we take Diane and Victor and you can have Michael and Avery? Makes for easier work. Then we can talk later."

"Add Madeline. She's googling too. Or doing something."

"Call us after six. Better yet, come over at seven for leftover pot roast. Charlie, too. Isolde loves to see him. Once she's done hissing at him."

I laughed. "Sounds great. I'll bring one of Francine's frozen pumpkin breads."

Then the last call—Catherine.

"Of all things. Don't tell me that board president wasn't on the take. I just wonder how much he took!"

"It's not something we can prove, Catherine."

"We'll see about that. I'm calling my son Steven right now. I refuse to sit idly by and watch the pleasant view from our winery turn into an advertisement for city living."

"One can never have too many lawyers on the case."

"What do you mean?"

"Madeline is calling hers."

"Good. We'll be bound to get some results."

Or legal fees.

When I got to the winery at a little before eleven, everyone had already heard the bad news. I was greeted by Lizzie at the front door, who slid her glasses farther down her nose and said, "First a high-rise, then another and another. Wouldn't surprise me if those greedy land developers decide to add a business complex for good measure!"

"I know. I'm not sure what we can do about it, but we'll certainly try."

Glenda came rushing over next. Her long celestial-sphered earrings bounced back and forth on her neck and I noticed that today her hair was back to its holographic colors.

"Norrie! Zenora had a premonition of death hovering in our midst. She called me right before she drove to work. Did you burn the sage? Use the chant she wrote?"

Tossed the sage and gave up singing in ninth grade.

"More or less. Tell Zenora not to worry. The only death was to a future production of traminette from Billsburrow Winery. The Martinezes will need to scout around for a different opportunity to purchase land. But maybe they won't have to. She's got an attorney on it. Plus, those homeowners were pretty adamant about not having a high-rise in their vicinity. Wouldn't surprise me if they hired a lawyer as well and fought it."

"On what grounds?"

"I'm not sure, but those lawyers always manage to find something."

I made a mental note to ask Bradley when I saw him, even though he was in family law and not legal matters pertaining to real estate. But then I thought of something and went straight to the kitchen, where I knew I'd find Cammy.

Sure enough, she had just loaded the dishwasher and was about to bring a new rack of glasses to the tasting room when I stopped her. "Cammy, isn't it illegal for a school or town board to go into executive session if they're not discussing personnel? I mean, isn't it an open agenda? You must know. You've gone to enough school board meetings in Geneva."

"Only because my aunts dragged me along when it came to athletic decisions that involved my cousins. And believe me, between Marc and Enzo, that covered football, lacrosse, and tennis."

"Tennis?"

"Yeah, well, the aunts thought the boys needed something more refined for their college résumés."

I laughed. "So yes or no? Can they do it? Go into executive session without discussing something of a personal nature?"

"I don't think so, but I'm not an attorney. Ask Bradley when you see him."

"*If* I get to see him. Marvin's keeping him so busy he hardly has a minute to himself."

Just then, Lizzie opened the door. "You've got a phone call, Norrie. Joel Margolis from the *Finger Lakes Times*. Are they going to be doing an article about us? Let me know in advance, will you? Last time they sent a photographer and my hair was simply dreadful. Dreadful."

"Uh, sure."

Maybe he can write an article about sneaking out on my boyfriend.

"Hold on, Lizzie. Tell him I'm in the middle of something and I'll call him back."

"Shall do. Remember, find out when they plan to send a photographer. If I know in advance, I'll book an appointment at the beauty parlor."

And I'll book the next flight to JFK.

I was about to head to the bistro and have Fred or Emma fix me a breakfast panini when I got a text from Bradley: *Urgent matter in Manhattan. Flying out this afternoon. One of Marvin's clients and Marvin's got bronchitis. Will call when I check into the hotel.* Then heart and hug emojis.

I texted back, *Of all times for me to be here when I live there!! Call me. Crazy stuff going on.* More heart and hug emojis.

"What's the matter, Norrie?" Emma asked when I stepped into the bistro. Her long dark hair was in a tight ponytail and she looked as if she was still in junior high.

"Bradley has to handle a case in the city, the board voted to approve the high-rise, and everyone is on edge."

"By everyone, do you mean Zenora? She was particularly anxious the other night."

"She's always anxious. Anyway, I'll wolf down my sandwich and give the crew a hand in the tasting room."

Emma smiled. "Sounds good."

At that moment Herbert, one of the assistant winemakers, walked in. "Hey, Norrie! How's it going? I'm picking up some premade sandwiches for Franz and Alan. We're in the middle of racking and they couldn't take a break. I drew the short straw!"

"Some short straw! You're taller than any of us!"

Herbert laughed. With his athletic build, he looked the part of an NFL player and not a winemaker. Like Franz, he came from a long line of winemakers, only in Pretoria, South Africa, and not Germany.

"Comes in handy when someone needs something from a high shelf."

This time I laughed and it felt good. "I suppose you guys heard about the vote from the Benton Town Board."

"Oh, yeah. Franz has been grumbling about it all morning. He got a call from Paolo, the winemaker at Billsburrow. They were all set to add another vineyard for future traminette grapes and now that's on hold."

"Tell Franz that it's not over."

Emma handed Herbert the bag of sandwiches and he took off just as Fred arrived with my hot panini. Minutes later I was in the tasting room helping Roger and Glenda until Sam arrived in the afternoon.

I knew racking was a tedious process, and can happen a few times a year to finesse the quality of the wine. It's also absolutely necessary in the wine production business. When the liquid sits in one tank or barrel, sediment forms and that's pretty yucky. Not only that, but the wine will taste like yogurt. Ugh! Scientifically, at least according to Theo, "there are dead yeast cells left over from fermentation and they need to be removed." I always thought of it like skin exfoliation but not up close and personal. So, racking, or transferring the wine into a new tank or barrel, means the gross stuff stays in the original one and the new container starts over. Also, it provides oxygen to the wine, which is needed for maturation and for making sure stinky sulfur smells are gone. It's a laborious process for sure, so no wonder the guys weren't about to take an extended lunch break.

Fortunately, traminette is a German wine and it doesn't need to be processed in an oak barrel or enhanced with oak chips like other wines. One less step. Oak gives wine a toasty flavor and it wouldn't be consistent with this white grape. Heck, those guys have enough to do.

"I heard there was quite the brouhaha last night at the Benton Town Hall," Roger said as he walked past me to grab another bottle of our semi-dry Riesling.

"Oh, yeah. No one wants to see that high-rise. Well, no one except the greedy developer from Diamante."

"Heard there was a parking lot scuffle, too, and the sheriff's office had to be called."

"It must have happened after Theo and I left. How'd you hear?"

"Got a scanner. You know, if they had one of these during the French and Indian War, things would have gone differently."

I cringed. Not the French and Indian War! Roger, a retired educator, did his dissertation on that war and is still reliving it.

"Uh, yeah. For sure."

I immediately turned to the three customers who approached me and greeted them with so much enthusiasm they must have thought I was bonkers. Anything to avoid battle field strategies and descriptions of bodies piling up in the Ohio River Valley. Too bad I didn't know at the time we'd be looking at a body, too.

Chapter 6

Joel! I completely forgot I was supposed to return his call. About twenty minutes later, there was a lull in the tasting room and I asked Roger and Glenda to cover for me. I thought about texting Joel but the word *coward* cropped up in my head.

As I closed the door to my office, I wondered what the heck I was doing. Granted, having a reporter, especially one who worked for the *Finger Lakes Times*, could be invaluable if I needed information I couldn't get anywhere else, but I wasn't really sure that was my motive.

Ugh. Don was right. I needed to nix this idea ASAP. I grabbed my cell phone and tapped Joel's number.

His voice was chipper and upbeat. Why couldn't he sound miserable and morose?

"Hey, Norrie. Thanks for getting back to me."

Please tell me his call was about info and not an invitation.

"I wondered if you were available for coffee tomorrow. Tim Hortons, Starbucks, wherever you want. I found out something rather interesting about Diamante. Since you and your fellow winery owners had the rug pulled out from under you, so to speak, you might want to hear what I've learned."

Great. A two-edged sword.

"Uh, sure. Tim Hortons is fine. What time?"

"How about eight? I need to be in the office at nine thirty and that should give you plenty of time to get to your winery. I understand they all open at ten."

Hmm. The guy knows how to do his homework. Then again, he is a reporter.

"Besides," he continued, "no snowstorms are predicted so we'll both be okay."

"Fine. Eight at Tim Hortons. I'll see you then."

"Great. Looking forward to it."

And I'm looking forward to catching the first elevator down to purgatory for not telling Bradley.

For the rest of the day, I tried to convince myself this was strictly a business meeting. Lamentably, I wasn't very good at it. Even Theo and Don saw through me that night at dinner and I could have sworn Isolde gave me a narrowing look. Then again, it was hard to tell with her.

"Any luck googling?" Don asked as he spooned a large helping of the pot roast onto his plate.

"I only got as far as Avery and that wasn't far enough. He's in a number of social organizations but nothing that raises a red flag. I need to keep going. As for Michael, he's a fairly recent transplant from Syracuse so that might mean something. What about you?"

Don put his fork down and widened his eyes. "When I dig, I dig. Even went to the tax records. It's public knowledge. Seems Diane is behind on her county taxes. Only by six months but maybe she's in deeper debt and took a payoff if that's what Stanley offered for a yes vote."

"I really wish there was a way to find out more. You know, someone who has their ears to the ground all the time." And then, in that split instant it hit me—Marilyn Ansley, Rosalee's younger sister whose passion for gossip was unmatched.

"Marilyn!" I said. "Marilyn Ansley. You know, Rosalee's sister."

Theo and Don looked at each other in horror.

"I'd rather keep googling," Don said. "I ran into her at Wegmans not too long ago and she talked my ears off about her neighbor who underwent body sculpting to attract younger men. Is that a thing? I was too afraid to ask what they sculpted."

I laughed. "Anything and everything. Look, I think I can manage coffee or something with her. I'll try to set something up soon."

Theo grinned. "Good deal. Better you than us!"

We agreed to keep digging up dirt on the four yes votes and left it at that. That night, I went to bed wondering what it would take for someone to accept a payoff, even though it meant ignoring the very people who voted to put them in office. Finally, I fell asleep thinking about coffee, pastries, and Joel. Not necessarily in that order.

• • •

One of the things I loved about Tim Hortons was the amazing aromas whenever I opened the door, and Thursday morning did not disappoint me. I inhaled the pungent coffee and sweet-smelling pastries as I looked around for Joel. Sure enough, he was seated near the window and waved as soon as he saw me. He had a large cup of black coffee in front of him and used it to warm up his hands.

"It's bitter cold out there. No hat?" *Good question. And I'm scared to admit the answer.*

"Have you ever seen hat hair? It's not pretty. Besides, it was only a few steps to the entrance."

He smiled. "Let me get you a coffee. Just tell me what you want. Same for donuts or pastries."

I reached for my bag and he stopped me. "I'll write this off as business expense, okay? It's on me."

I nodded. "Thanks." *And I'll write this off as losing my mind.*

Joel returned with my chocolate croissant and a regular coffee and cream. Plus a frosted donut for himself.

"Okay," I said. I bit the tip off the croissant and let the buttery flavor remain in my mouth for a few seconds. "What's the story on Diamante?"

"First off, I have impeccable sources. Well, two friends from my journalism classes who now hold jobs for newspapers in Syracuse and Cazenovia. According to both of them, Diamante put up similar structures in Onondaga County on Owasco, Otisco, and Skaneateles lakes."

"Yeah, Stanley mentioned us not keeping up with Skaneateles."

"But what he didn't mention was that they used cheap construction, resulting in numerous problems and lawsuits. That's probably why he needs this project. To pay his legal fees."

"What kind of problems?"

"Let's see, regular Sheetrock in the showers instead of the more expensive waterproof kind for starters."

"Doesn't a building inspector check for those sorts of things?"

"They're supposed to, unless—"

"They're getting paid off?"

"Nothing that can be substantiated."

"What else?"

"Insufficient insulation, inferior pipes, low-quality paint . . . I could go on and on. The thing is, all the Benton Town Board received was a feasibility study."

"If Diamante skimped on the construction and complaints were registered, wouldn't they have been in the Onondaga papers? You know, an exposé."

"There were numerous letters to the papers but no articles were written. When my colleagues approached their editors about it, they were directed not to pursue it. Kind of makes you wonder, huh? That's why I thought you might be interested."

"Uncanny how that company targeted small towns with equally small-town boards. All it would take is a little convincing. Especially if a payoff was involved to sway the vote. Unfortunately, unless there's solid proof, all we have is an accusation that could be considered slander."

"Do you think Avery was bribed?" He bit into his donut and finished it off with a sip of coffee.

"Maybe. Hard to say."

"Look, how about if you keep your eyes and ears open and I'll do the same."

"Why are you sharing this with me? Not that I don't appreciate the inside information, but you hardly know me."

"I saw how determined those winery owners were about that high-rise proposal. Not to mention the homeowners and small businesses on your side of the lake. I'm from a small town, too, and I watched how developments like the one Diamante is proposing took away the community atmosphere and changed it into an impersonal cookie-cutter landscape."

Good. It has nothing to do with me.

I nodded and he continued. "When you asked me to text you about the vote, I knew that this was more than a business issue, it was personal."

"Yeah, I suppose."

"I also thought you were worth getting to know."

And here it comes. My free ticket to purgatory.

"Like I mentioned, I am seeing someone, but that doesn't exclude me from having friends." *What the heck am I implying?*

"Good. I hoped you'd say something like that. Anyway, I hate to rush out but I need to get to the office. Let's do this again when we're not in a rush."

"Thanks for the coffee and croissant."

"Anytime. And I meant what I said. Let's keep each other posted on this. I have a feeling something's about to unravel but I'm not sure what."

Who knew at the time that Joel Margolis would be more prophetic than Zenora?

I finished my coffee, then buttoned my fleece jacket and took off for Two Witches. Joel was right about no snowstorms but snowstorms always mean slightly warmer weather—at least in the thirties. Today felt like a single-digit number and I wasn't too far off. My car registered eleven degrees outside. Time for the heavy parka.

When I got back to the winery, I spied Alvin tossing his hay all around his pen. It was adjacent to the winery entrance so visitors could enjoy petting the goat. That's right, a goat. A Nigerian dwarf goat who was the size of a medium camel. Go figure. Francine and Jason thought Alvin would add something to the family-friendly atmosphere at the winery but all he added as far as I was concerned was more work for the vineyard guys who had to feed him and change his bedding.

From day one, Alvin made it clear he didn't like me. Showed it by spitting and continued to show it. The odd thing is, he loves children. Nuzzles them, lets them pet him and never once spat at anyone else except me. Good thing the dog likes me. Heck, Charlie adores me. I'm the one who lets him sleep in my bed and eat decent dog food, not that bland doggie health food Francine buys. Plus, I give him table scraps. A real no-no for my sister and brother-in-law.

• • •

"Hi, Norrie!" Lizzie said when I walked inside and unbuttoned my jacket. "You just missed Deputy Hickman by twenty minutes."

Thank you, Route 14, for slow traffic.

"Deputy Hickman? What did he want? Don't tell me they found a body somewhere?"

"No corpse, but it seems a gentleman by the name of Avery Pullman from the Town of Benton Board received a rather threatening letter taped to his front door this morning and the sheriff's office is investigating the wineries who were in attendance at that meeting."

"The wineries? Why just the wineries? We weren't the only ones objecting to that high-rise. Greg Baker was there from Port of Call, and some lady named Audrey Killion from a bakery down the lake, as well as a bunch of property owners who objected too. Loudly, I might add."

"He showed me a copy of the note and as soon as he left, I wrote down what I read. 'Shame on you for crushing the wine industry. Watch your step. You'll be the next victim. And this isn't sour grapes.' Deputy Hickman told me his office narrowed the threat down to us and our five neighboring wineries who were in attendance."

"Does that mean he'll be back later today?" Suddenly the croissant I ate turned to lead in my stomach.

"I would assume so, yes. He needs a word with you."
"I can think of a word but he won't like the four letters."

Chapter 7

I went into my office, hung my jacket on a wall peg and booted up the computer. At that moment my cell phone buzzed.

"Norrie, it's Madeline. Sorry to bother you on your cell but I didn't want to hold up the winery line. Did Deputy Hickman show up at your place?"

"Yep. Missed him by twenty minutes. Talk about good luck. But he'll be back. What do you know? Good old Avery got a death threat, but I can guarantee it's not from any of us."

"Too bad he doesn't see it that way. More than insinuated one of us had something to do with it."

"Stanley ruffled everyone's feathers at that meeting. And then to have a yes vote? With the board president at the helm? We were bulldozed. There's no other word for it. Well, none that I'd use in polite company."

"Yes, he certainly upset all of us. Too bad Audrey Killion is on our side because she's one person I wouldn't mind seeing upset."

"The lady from the bakery? Cute and petite? Doesn't look her age."

"Not when someone spends a fortune on facial fillers."

"How do you know?"

"She told me once. I used to do business with her. We sold lots of her pies and cakes here."

"Used to?"

"Until she stiffed me and told all her customers it was our fault. A few years before you arrived, I put in a huge order for a weekend event. She promised she'd have everything delivered on time."

"I take it she didn't."

"Oh, it got delivered, all right. But it was wrong. Grain breads and wheat breads. No one wants those on a holiday weekend. Worse than that, she claimed I never specified the order. When I asked if she could remedy it, at least for the second day, she said no. We had to purchase bakery goods from the local supermarkets to get through the weekend. And then, talk about rubbing salt in the wound, she charged us an exorbitant price for the breads."

"That's awful."

"What was awful was the fact she blackballed us by telling her customers we left her high and dry when she counted on our business. Can you imagine?"

Lately I can imagine anything.

"Yeah, I can. Did Deputy Hickman mention anything else?"

"Told me that if I learned of anyone in our 'close-knit winery group' who left that threat, I was to contact his office immediately. Naturally I told him he was barking up the wrong tree."

"And then?"

"He left."

"Listen, I found out something about Diamante developers and it's not pretty. Got it from a reliable source. It's all I can say. Diamante did similar developments on other Finger Lakes and used shoddy construction. Lots of issues."

"Any chance they'll be put out of business?"

"Here's where it gets sticky. My source, and don't ask who, believes Diamante bribed some of those town board members."

"Too bad we can't prove anything, but I'll mention this to my attorney."

When I got off the phone with Madeline, I sent a text to Theo to let him know what I found out from Joel. He texted back, *Good intel but don't fall into another net. You know what I mean.*

Oh, I knew, all right. That's why my relationships never got too far. I would have thought that in my twenties I would have outgrown being so fickle. It was a character trait that still needed more work. And right now, I was in a great relationship and really didn't want to mess it up. Besides, what harm was there in having coffee with someone?

I busied myself the rest of the morning by helping out in the tasting room and working on the winery's newsletter. Yes, newsletter. It was

Francine's brainchild and she left it with me to take her primitive MailChimp and turn it into something eye-catching and enticing. Not to mention, monthly.

Each month I featured a different wine and this time, I decided to focus on traminette since it seemed to be a hot topic, even though it wouldn't be on the market until the fall. I had just completed my description of the grape itself when Lizzie burst into the office.

She clenched her fingers and whispered, "Deputy Hickman is here to see you and he brought that other deputy. The one who looks like a cherub."

"Clarence Eustis. Send them in."

I stood and motioned for the men to come inside and grab a chair. "Hi! Can I get you anything? Coffee? Juice?"

Deputy Hickman answered without looking at Clarence. "Thank you, no, Miss Ellington. We're fine. I missed you this morning and need to have a word with you about a threatening note found on Mr. Avery Pullman's door. I'm sure you recognize that name. He's the president of the Benton Town Board and if I'm not mistaken, you, along with your neighboring wineries, attended that meeting to voice your displeasure about a building proposal."

"Oh, it wasn't displeasure. It was outrage."

I looked at the expression on Deputy Hickman's face and wondered if I should have stuck with displeasure.

"Outrage enough to threaten Mr. Pullman?"

"Of course not. Although my take is that some hanky-panky went on with that vote. Everyone in attendance was against that building proposal and yet it passed four to three. With Mr. Pullman voting yes."

"Those issues are best taken up with legal counsel."

"Oh, believe me, they will. I mean, they are. As far as leaving a threatening note, I certainly didn't and I can assure you none of the women in our group would do a thing like that. And Theo and Don from next door wouldn't stoop to such babyish behaviors."

"Threats are not babyish. They're taken seriously by this office and are investigated thoroughly. Winery chatter is abundant. If you hear anything about that note, contact my office immediately."

I nodded. "Shall do."

Both men left without another word, when I heard a familiar pang on my phone. This time it was a text was from Renee, my producer in Toronto. *"Where the roses wilt" goes into production in two weeks. No more British countryside. Scrap what you are doing and write a paranormal romance. Renee.*

I read it again to be sure I had gotten it right. First beach romance, then quaint English villages, now paranormal. I texted back, *As in ghosts in love or ghosts around people in love?*

Renee responded, *Ghosts who toy with people in love. Send me the first 10 pages in two weeks. Cheers.*

Yeah, cheers to you, Renee. I love the industry I'm in, but honestly, it's as fickle and unpredictable as the weather around here.

The remainder of the day was ho-hum at best and Friday started out the same way. Then, a little past noon everything changed when Franz called me from the lab.

"I need to go to Billsburrow Winery. I may be there a while. Alan and Herbert will continue the racking."

Franz rarely called me about wine production and I certainly didn't keep tabs on his daily whereabouts. Those guys were tethered to the place, like the vineyard workers.

"Is everything all right?"

"I'm not sure. Paolo Agosti, one of their winemakers, called. They need my opinion on something."

"Uh, sure. Whatever."

"I shall keep you informed."

The call ended and I shrugged. Guess Glenda and Zenora aren't the only weird ones lately. Now Franz.

An hour later, Herbert called.

"Hey, Norrie, Franz just phoned us from Billsburrow. Wants Alan or me to go there pronto. I said I would."

"What's going on?"

"Not sure. He wouldn't say over the phone. All I heard was Paolo ranting in Italian. Look, I'll give you a heads-up if Franz doesn't call first. Alan's got the racking under control and I shouldn't be too long. Thought you should know."

"Thanks."

I figured it was winemaking business and nothing that would concern me, because if it involved anything else, Madeline would be all over it.

The Friday afternoon crowd intensified and I found myself chatting with more customers than usual for this time of year. I attributed it to the fact that there were no snowstorms in sight and people seemed impervious to the frigid temperatures.

Shortly after three, Lizzie walked over to my tasting table and told me Herbert and Franz were back in the lab and that I should call over there when I got a free minute.

"Did it sound like everything was okay?"

Lizzie shrugged. "I spoke with Herbert and he wouldn't say but I could hear Franz in the background, shouting in German. Never a good sign."

Terrific. Italian and now German. And all I know are a few words in Spanish.

"Ugh. I better call as soon as this table clears out. Thanks."

By the time I walked into my office, I didn't need to call because Madeline stood a few feet behind me and I nearly jumped.

"Oh, Norrie, sorry to barge in but something horrible happened. It's going to cost us a fortune and I have a very good idea who the culprit is. Told Deputy Hickman as much but he called it speculation. I call it sabotage, plain and simple. Sabotage!"

"What? What sabotage? What's going on?"

"We have two stainless-steel barrels for our traminette. One is indoors and the other is on the concrete slab in back of the lab. Seems someone put oak chips in the outdoor barrel and ruined the entire batch. Ruined. Traminette may be a hearty grape, but it's a German grape and oak chips are never used in the fermentation process. It would alter the flavor completely! For the worse! This was a clear case of sabotage. Not simple vandalism or destruction of property. Well, that, too, but I guarantee it was a well-thought-out act meant to tell me to mind my own business as far as Diamante developers are concerned."

"You're saying you think Stanley is responsible?" I adjusted the cowl neck on my top and asked if she wanted a cup of coffee or anything.

"It certainly wasn't one of our winemakers. Paolo is practically hysterical and the assistants aren't far behind. Thanks for your offer though, but I came here to let you know none of us are safe. Especially Two Witches since you're the only other winery making traminette this year. Paolo had Franz come over to taste the wine and both of them agreed it was from the addition of oak chips. Then they took the ladder, opened the vat and saw it for themselves."

"They used a ladder?"

"It was a smaller barrel so no fork lift needed."

"What about security? Surveillance cameras?"

"We have them in the lab as well as the building itself and the exterior. Not the back. That's about to change but it's too late now. When I left, my husband was on the phone with the insurance company."

"What did Deputy Hickman say he'd do?"

"He sent a forensics team over to dust for prints, but face it, whoever was responsible had to have used gloves."

"What about the oak chips? Any way to make a determination where they came from?"

Madeline shook her head. "Even if they did, those companies sell them everywhere. Online, and in specialized stores. This is a nightmare. All Deputy Hickman told me was that they would investigate the matter thoroughly."

"Or add it to the list along with Avery's note."

"That's the other reason I drove here. I know you have a penchant for sleuthing. Will you—"

"Poke my nose where it doesn't belong?" Then I chuckled. "As a matter of fact, I was about to give Marilyn Ansley a call about those board members."

"Rosalee's sister? Mouthy Marilyn?"

"The very one."

"See, Norrie, you're one step ahead of the game already. Thanks."

Madeline dashed out the door before I could say another word. Maybe Zenora was right after all—a bad premonition. And it was just getting warmed up.

Chapter 8

"You did what?" Cammy widened her eyes and grimaced. "Offered to buy Marilyn breakfast at the Penn Yan diner tomorrow? She'll empty your bank account!"

"Believe me, I know. I've watched her eat before, but I need information and the way to get it is through her stomach."

It was a half hour before we closed and the first time I got to chat with Cammy. As we washed dishes in the kitchen, I told her about what happened at Billsburrow as well as the reason Deputy Hickman, aka Grizzly Gary, stopped by twice.

"Writing a threatening note is one thing, but whoever sabotaged Madeline's traminette is working with a whole new set of rules. What about us? Do we have enough surveillance?"

"According to John and Franz, we do. Still, John installed additional motion sensors as soon as he found out what had happened at Billsburrow. Plus, our traminette is in one of the inside vats. I'm not sure but I think the Cab-Franc is fermenting in our outdoor one."

"Any idea who might have done it?"

"Madeline is convinced Stanley Hurst is responsible. They had quite the spat in the parking lot after the meeting."

"Enough to toy with someone's livelihood?"

"From what I heard, the man has no scruples. Unfortunately, we have no evidence."

"Just be careful. Having breakfast with Marilyn is one thing, but watch where you snoop around."

"Don't worry. So far it's been strictly in cyberspace."

"Keep it that way."

The next morning, I fed Charlie early and took him for a short albeit brisk walk down the driveway/road. The snow-covered ground was crunchy and I hated the way it felt when my boots sunk into it so I avoided it at all costs. Once home, I took a hot shower and dressed for breakfast and another day at the winery. Then it was off to the Penn

Yan Diner.

Fried sausage and bacon hit my nostrils the second I opened the door. As the steamy air assaulted my face, I looked around for Marilyn. Sure enough, she was seated in a booth off to the left, perusing the menu even though she has breakfast there at least three times a week according to Rosalee.

I walked over to her booth and tossed my jacket onto the seat. "Good Morning, Marilyn. Thanks for meeting with me. Especially on such a cold morning."

"The food will make up for it. Nothing like starting the day with the Hungry Hunter's Breakfast. Eggs, bacon, ham, sausage, pancakes and toast! It's my favorite. Well, that and the cinnamon rolls."

Naturally.

I ordered two eggs over with bacon, toast and coffee. That was hungry enough for me. Then I got down to business before Marilyn decided to have a second breakfast. Something, according to Rosalee, that she was prone to do.

"I was hoping you might know something about the town board members in Benton who voted yes for that high-rise. With the community up in arms, it struck our winery group as incredulous that anyone would be in favor of it."

"I figured as much. My sister has been ranting about it for days."

"Do you know them? Or anyone who might know them?"

"I know Diane Oftspringer. She lives on the same road as my friend Nellie. Last week, Nellie got Diane's mail by accident and took it to her. According to Nellie, Diane's house was like a meat locker and Diane answered the door wearing three layers of clothing. You know what that means, don't you?"

Yeah. It's winter.

"Uh, it's cold."

"It means Diane can't afford to heat the place. Must be behind in her gas and electric bill. Can't say for sure. And she never goes out to eat with the chitchat ladies anymore. That's a sure sign."

"Do you think she'd be the kind of person who would take a bribe easily?"

At that moment, our waitress delivered our meals and Marilyn smothered her pancakes in syrup and tore into them. A mouthful or two later, she answered my question.

"When people are desperate, they'll do anything to survive. Now mind you, I don't know if Diane's desperate, but I don't think the words *cash flow* are in her vocabulary. It's quite possible."

"What about Michael Antonacci? Have you heard anything about him?"

"Tidbits here and there. He moved recently from Syracuse. Was in the paint business. I found out from Gus in the paint department at the hardware store. We got to talking last week because I needed to touch up my bathroom cabinets and couldn't remember if the paint was Swiss Coffee or Coffee Cream."

"Anything else?"

"It was Coffee Cream. Gus had the old records."

I did a mental eye roll and took a bite of my toast. "About Michael. Anything?"

"Gus thought he retired but if you ask me, why on earth would someone retire to Penn Yan? Florida or the Carolinas are more like it."

Hmm. I wondered if maybe he didn't retire after all and he was planted by Diamante to get on that board and pave the way for the high-rise. Money speaks and it speaks loudly.

I glanced at Marilyn's plate and the bacon was gone. In fact, so were the eggs. Only one small piece of sausage remained and it was now on her fork.

"That leaves Victor Dahl. Name sound familiar?" I asked.

"It should sound familiar to you, too."

"Huh?"

"Dahl Farms. They sell milk, eggs, and cheese. All the stores around here carry their dairy products."

"Red logo with a chicken on top of a cow?"

"That's the one."

"Yeah. Wegmans carries it. I never bothered to look at the name. Only the price. Is there any reason a local dairy would vote yes? They usually want farmland to remain farmland."

"It's lakefront. Vineyard land."

"Meaning?"

"It doesn't infringe on his land or his acreage. Listen, I don't know if anything's going on with Dahl Farms, but most of our local farms are in debt so bad for equipment that they'll never get out from under. If you really want to snoop around, start there. See who he owes. It might surprise you."

I finished my meal and thanked Marilyn again before she had a chance to catch the waitress's eye. I paid at the cash register and left a generous tip before driving back to the winery. The Hungry Hunter's Breakfast paid off. Two board members might have taken a bribe to alleviate their debt and the third might be a plant and not a board member in the actual sense of the word.

Before I got out of the car, I sent a group text to Theo, Don, and Madeline letting them know about my meeting with Marilyn. I ended it with, *Possible bribe, possible bigger bribe, possible mole in our midst.*

Then I raced inside to find Cammy and fill her in.

"I'm not sure how anyone can find out if Diane or Victor took a bribe," she said. She put a bottle of semi-sweet Riesling on her tasting table and motioned for a couple to take a seat.

"I know. I need to give this some thought."

I looked around and everything was under control. Our entire tasting room crew was working since it was a Saturday and thankfully, the flow went well. That meant I could get caught up on emails and anything else that landed on my desk. What I didn't expect was a centipede encased in plexiglass with a note that read, "Sorry about the pizza. I had to cover for Arvin Pincus. You remember him. The recent study on gnats. How about tonight? Unless you have plans with

Bradley. Call me. I was in the neighborhood. Sorry I missed you."
Godfrey

Nope. No plans with Bradley unless a miracle happened and Marvin sent a private plane to bring him back to the Finger Lakes. I grabbed my cell phone and called the entomology office, knowing full well Godfrey would be there.

"Hey, it's Norrie. Pizza sounds good but I'm picking the toppings, remember?"

Godfrey laughed. "Sure, but no anchovies. I draw the line at anchovies."

"Since when have I ever ordered anchovies? Sausage, pepperoni, mushrooms, green olives, garlic, meatballs, but no anchovies. And I get to pick the place, too. Uncle Joe's. How about seven thirty?"

"Sounds good. See you over there."

"By the way, thanks for the centipede. Always wanted one."

"My pleasure. It's not every day something like that comes along."
Thank the Lord.

Godfrey continued. "The Chilopoda myriapoda is a prime example of a predatory arthropod."

"I need to track down a predatory briber and prove it."

"I'm not sure I understand."

"I'll explain once I've had my first bite of a gooey cheese pizza with a zillion toppings."

"Oh no. Not one of your amateur investigations."

"More or less."

"At least this one doesn't involve a dead body."

And there it was—the jinx of all jinxes. And no amount of sage was going to save me.

Chapter 9

Sunday and Monday came and went and my pizza with Godfrey was like a distant memory. I toggled my time between working in the tasting room and googling anything and everything I could find on Diane, Michael, and Victor.

Dahl Farms had a Facebook page but mostly photos of cows and chickens. Nothing that would point to the need for a substantial loan, or a bribe in this case. Diane was on Pinterest with quilt patterns. Again, nothing that hit home. Then I got to Michael and he had a profile on LinkedIn, Facebook, and Instagram.

When Gus at the hardware store told Marilyn that Michael was in the paint business, it was an understatement. He *was* the paint business. He held a top managerial position for a well-known brand whose jingle has been sung for generations. On the surface, it didn't look like much so I took a new approach.

I had Lizzie delve into the business profile of that company and chart gains and losses from stocks, investments, you name it. By Tuesday morning, I added Michael's name to the possible bribe recipients. Seemed his former company reneged on the original pension distributions by fifty percent and the matter was now in the courts. Most likely it would remain there until the snow melted off of Mt. Everest.

No progress was made on the traminette tampering at Billsburrow Winery but that was soon to become Madeline's last concern. At a little past eleven that morning she called to let me know that Stanley placed a restraining order on her.

"What?" I choked on my chocolate chip cookie. "A restraining order? For that little scuffle in the parking lot after the Benton Town Board meeting?"

"No." Madeline's voice was gruff. "For the unfortunate Wegmans incident last night."

"What Wegmans incident? What did I miss?"

"We ran out of eggs and I promised my husband I'd bake some scones for breakfast. Not only that, but I needed to replace our old winery meat thermometer for special events. The new ones are far more accurate, even if they do require batteries. Anyway, I took a quick run to Wegmans and expected to be in and out. Ha! Wishful thinking. As I got into the open aisle by the dairy, I spied Audrey from that bakeshop and she spied me. Right in front of the cottage cheese and sour cream section. It was like escalating volcanic pressure the second our eyes met. Then, she said, 'I would have gotten Stanley a building permit myself if the only thing that high-rise interfered with was your view and not mine.' Then, that she-witch went on, 'And let me be the first to cry crocodile tears for your lost traminette.'

"I wanted to open the glass case and heave a large sour cream at her but I refrained and walked away. Believe me, it wasn't easy. Then, the worst happened."

"She threw something at you?"

"No. Although that would have been a better alternative. Heaven knows why, but Stanley was still in the area. Probably rounding up more unsuspecting small-town board members for his next development. Anyway, there he was, the lizard himself. He was reaching for a quart of milk when he saw me."

"And?"

"He shouted my name, I turned quickly and accidently dropped the carton of jumbo grade A eggs on his feet. You would have thought I stabbed him with a harpoon! Demanded restitution for his fancy-dancy shoes. I told him I'd spring for a roll of paper towels and he went ballistic. It was the second time that night I didn't respond and walked away. Must be my new medication."

"Good for you."

"Not really. Assistant Deputy Clarence Eustis appeared at my door at nine forty-five with a restraining order. Poor man kept apologizing. I told him it wasn't his fault he had to serve the restraining order."

"So now what?"

"Now I figure out a way to get even."

I wished Madeline had never said that. It was one of those comments made in anger that really didn't amount to anything. Unless of course it did.

I told her Theo, Don and I were finding out as much as we could about the yes votes but unless we could prove an actual bribe took place, we were stumbling in the dark.

"I'll let you know what my attorney tells us. Thanks for listening. Thought I'd keep you posted. We're still reeling over the traminette loss. Thank goodness the other barrel was indoors."

Bradley called and he was still stuck in the city but thought he'd be back by the weekend. Said he was so inundated with work that he couldn't even enjoy the four-star hotel his firm arranged.

And the highlight of my week was watching Marilyn devour the Hungry Hunter's Breakfast at the local diner.

At closing time Glenda rushed over and grabbed my arm. "Zenora had a horrible vision of a corpse lightly covered in snow. She just sent me a text."

I shrugged. "Zenora has horrible visions all the time."

"We're supposed to get a light dusting of snow tonight."

"Glenda, we get light dustings, heavy dustings, wet and heavy dustings . . . it's the Finger Lakes in January, for crying out loud!"

"This corpse was under a tarp between the vineyard and the patio where our outdoor wine barrel sits."

"Did Zenora see our logo in her vision?"

"Visions are nonspecific. That's why they're called visions."

"Unless Zenora gets an eyewitness account of a dead body near one of our stainless-steel barrels, I wouldn't put too much credence into it."

Glenda was always melodramatic and Zenora was, well, just plain nuts. Still, the thought bothered me. I called Franz, since John had already gone home for the day along with the vineyard workers, and asked him if the additional surveillance cameras were up on the back patio."

"Yes. John took care of it. He intends to speak with you about some fencing as well. Just around the patio."

"Probably a good idea."

"Lately people seem to have no boundaries."

"I know. It's getting scary."

I thanked him and helped Cammy lock up for the night.

"Think there's any validity to Zenora's trance or hallucination about a corpse?"

"Only to Zenora. I guarantee you'll get to the winery tomorrow and nothing will be near our wine vat except some light snow that got blown around."

Sure enough, Cammy was right. Only a dusting of snow the next day and no corpse. I actually called over there and had one of the winemakers check it out.

"What makes you think there'd be a body near the barrel?" Herbert asked.

"A bad dream."

"Drink tart cherry juice before bed. You'll sleep better."

"We're fine, everyone!" I shouted as I walked into the tasting room. We had a half hour until we'd open our doors and the staff scrambled to get everything set up. In the distance I heard sirens and wondered if there was a house fire somewhere on the lake. So many folks use wood-burning stoves and not everyone is careful.

The sirens continued and I began to think maybe it was a major car accident so I texted Theo. *Do you see any fire trucks?*

He texted back, *Only sheriff cars. No ambulance or fire truck. Escaped convict? LOL*

Actually, that wasn't so unusual. We'd had a few escaped convicts from the local jails as well as the state prison in Auburn. Not a settling thought. Still, with a manhunt out, *if* it was an escaped criminal, I doubted he or she would be stopping in here to taste wine.

All of us went about our business and at ten on the dot, we opened our doors. A handful of early morning wine tasters came in and a few early morning in-need-of-a-coffee-before-wine tasters headed straight to Emma and Fred at the bistro.

"Anyone know what's going on at Billsburrow Winery?" one of the men asked as he passed by me.

"What do you mean?" I put down the water pitcher I had in my hand and walked closer to him.

"There's a lineup of sheriff cars from the road to the driveway. Ontario and Yates counties."

"Any fire trucks?"

"Nope. And no sign of smoke. A robbery maybe?"

I thought about Zenora and a shiver went through me. *We should be so lucky.*

"Maybe. It could be anything." Or the one thing I didn't want to think about.

"Whatever it is, it's not good for business."

Understatement of the year.

"I'm sure they'll get it sorted out. Meanwhile, enjoy your coffee and eventually our wine."

He smiled. "I intend to."

I didn't waste a second. I pulled my cell phone from my pocket and texted Theo.

The cavalry is at Madeline's.

I didn't want to call her if she was embroiled in something so I shot off a text. *What's going on? News travels fast.*

No response. Not that I expected one right away. Heck, some people only check their text messages once or twice a day, unlike me. I'm totally OCD when it comes to that.

"All those sheriff cars are at Billsburrow," I told Cammy as she motioned for a few people to join her tasting table.

"Why? What's going on?"

"That's what I'd like to know. I sent Madeline a text but no answer. Do you think they had a break-in? If it was anything else, I think the fire department would be there."

Cammy shook her head and raised her shoulders. "No idea."

Resigned to the fact that it was one piece of news that would have to wait, I opened my own tasting table and welcomed customers. A few minutes later, Lizzie walked over. "Alan from the winery is on the phone. Sounded stressed."

"The winemakers always sound stressed. Tell him I'll call him right back as soon as I'm done here."

Alan was one of our assistant winemakers and the spitting image of his boss with one exception. He towered over Franz by at least four inches. When seated, however, it was nearly impossible to tell the difference with their untamed red hair and ruddy complexions.

It was an anomaly the other day when Franz called about the sabotage at Billsburrow and I wondered if the situation had escalated today. Then again, that kind of thing doesn't call for a nuclear response with a full force of sheriff cars.

When my last taster left, I retreated to my office and phoned Alan. "What's up? Is everything all right? None of our vats got sabotaged, did they?" I crossed my fingers and held my breath until he answered.

"No. Worse news."

"Someone opened the faucets? We lost our wine?" The pitch in my voice became loud and shrill.

"No, we're fine. Unfortunately, Billsburrow isn't. Paolo just called over here. Franz is off today and I took the call."

"What happened? Is this about all the sheriff cars?"

"I'm afraid so. Seems they found a dead body near their sabotaged traminette barrel."

Chapter 10

"Who? Whose dead body? A vagrant?" Then I caught myself. What kind of vagrant walks miles from the nearest town? Unless he or she froze to death. Ew!

Alan spoke as if he was relaying the stock report. "I don't have the details but I seriously doubt it was a vagrant. Paolo discovered the unfortunate deceased when he went outside to check on the other barrel. The one without the traminette. He saw a large dark lump by the hedge of their Chardonnay vineyard and went to check it out. You know as much as I do."

"Thanks, Alan. I'm glad we've got more surveillance on our property. Do me a favor and let Franz know?"

"Shall do. Thought you should know first. Have a good day."

Have a good day? Who can have a good day with a dead body near a sabotaged traminette barrel at a neighboring winery?

I wasted no time texting Theo. *Dead body at Billsburrow. Call me when u get a break.*

A few seconds later he returned the text. *Do u know who?*

I responded, *No, I don't. 2 soon 2 call Madeline.*

I figured someone from the Ontario County Sheriff's Office was most likely grilling Madeline, and besides, she'd be so off-kilter from this that she probably wouldn't make sense anyway. At least for a few hours until it sunk in. However, my crew needed to know, especially since it would hit the news and every cell phone app that went with it.

Starting with Cammy, I did the rounds and shared the unsettling news. Worse than a seventh-grader gossiping about who had a new boyfriend. When I was comfortably assured that none of us would be taken by surprise, I sent John a text and asked him to notify his vineyard workers. I also thanked him for the extra surveillance.

That's when Glenda caught a break at her table and rushed over to me. "If you want to know more about the body, we've got to get Zenora over there so she can conjure his soul before it moves on."

"Um, I think it already moved on." *Or froze on the way.* "Besides, they've got zillions of deputies over there. It's not as if we could breeze in." *Or even want to.*

"I'll let Zenora know, in case there's something else she can do."

I nodded and forced a smile. By noon, what had started out as a mere buzzing of information in our winery turned into a regular gossip fest and most of it came from our customers. Face it, a slew of deputy cars and yellow crime scene tape in front of a winery was not exactly conducive to business. And a dead body found on the premises was a surefire way to shut that business down, at least for the day.

What didn't shut down was our landline. Lizzie fielded calls as if she ran a switchboard. By one o'clock, not only did our entire WOW group know about it, but so did Godfrey. At a little before one, he called. "Hey, Norrie, I heard about the excitement at Billsburrow. Not the greatest way to start the new year. One of our entomologists was heading to another winery and saw the commotion. A two-county response. Since our entomologist helps Billsburrow out with vineyard pests, he was able to get through the barrier and speak with their vineyard manager."

"Which entomologist? Alex?"

"No, Arvin Pincus. Alex is busy with his cockroach study."

Ugh!

"What did Arvin find out? Does he know whose corpse it is?"

"Male. Forties or fifties maybe. The deputies aren't about to release any information until they find next of kin. You should know that by now."

"Yeah, but sometimes information leaks out."

"Only because you nag half those deputies to death. I have it on good sources that one of them is petrified of you."

"Who? Eugene from the forensics lab? Just because he requested a transfer to get away from me during a prior situation doesn't really mean anything."

Godfrey groaned and I kept talking. "Any chance Arvin knows

what caused the guy's death? Frostbite? Gunshot wound? Stabbed?"

"He didn't say. And neither did the news stations whose vans are up there, according to him. Look, if I hear anything, I'll let you know. A word of caution though, don't be poking around outside after dark until the sheriffs' offices get a handle on this. And by outside, I mean up at Madeline's place. Even if she calls you."

"No worries. It's below thirty. Don't need to freeze to death."

"Okay. And make sure someone at Two Witches keeps an eye on you from the parking lot as you walk back up the hill after work."

"You're scaring me. You're sounding like my mother."

"Good! Catch you later."

It was sweet that Godfrey cared, but talk about scared, I didn't want to read too much into it. It was just a kiss. And it was a while ago. My sister was right when she told me a year ago that I'd turn out to be one of those fickle women who don't marry until they're "well past the child-bearing age." Aargh!

I looked around and everyone had customers at their tables. A smooth, steady flow. Too bad the same couldn't be said for getting more information about the grim discovery at Billsburrow. Then it hit me. Joel! He must know something. Especially why two counties were involved. I shot off a text in record time and held my breath it would move from "Delivered" to "Read."

Then I got antsy and decided that waiting wasn't my strong suit. I tapped his number instead and was relieved it didn't go to voicemail.

"Joel? It's Norrie. Are you aware of a dead body at Billsburrow Winery? They found it this morning."

"Aware of it and standing with a slew of other reporters freezing to death."

"What can you tell me?"

"That my next job will be in Florida."

"Seriously. What have you found out?"

"Other than the fact it's a middle-aged man, not much. The deputies are hesitant to disclose anything but sometimes they'll give info like, 'appears to be a gunshot wound,' or something of the sort. We're waiting. The coroner left a while ago and the techs are looking for evidence. Maybe the light snow dusting on top of what's already here may give them a clue, but most likely someone dumped the body and that light snow covered all tracks."

"Please do me a favor and let me know what you find out? It's nerve-wracking to have something like this happen at a neighboring winery."

"Hey, I know it's none of my business, but be careful, will you? I've been chatting with the other reporters and newscasters. Like I said about the body being dumped, it doesn't take a genius to figure out this isn't death by natural causes. Face it, the deceased was found under a tarp. People don't have heart attacks and grab for the nearest tarp."

"Thanks for the comforting thought." And the second "Be careful out there."

"I'll call you when I hear something. Actually, I'll stop by later. You're right down the road."

Great. And now even more gossip.

"Uh, sure. Thanks."

As I ended the call, Cammy turned to me. "What's with the sheepish look on your face? And don't tell me it's about that dead body because I've seen *that* look before."

"It is and it isn't. I mean, I called Joel from the *Finger Lakes Times* for some info and he's stopping over here when he's done gathering info at Billsburrow."

"I take it he's a good-looking reporter or you wouldn't have that expression on your face."

"He's a source of information."

"And consideration?"

"You know me too well but I'm pretty secure in my relationship with Bradley. Except he's out of town when I'm in town."

"Just don't get in too deep. And I'm referring to the men in your life. Dead or alive."

I shrugged and went over to the bistro for a sandwich before returning to my office. I had a newsletter to finish—*Thank you, Francine*—and a ton of snail mail that needed attention. An hour later, Joel appeared at my door with Cammy right behind him.

She mouthed, "Watch it. He's cute," before walking away.

Joel flashed a smile and stepped inside my office. "Hey, hope I'm not interrupting but it sounded like you were anxious for information. Not sure I can give you much, but it may fill in some blanks."

"Grab a chair. Can I get you anything? Coffee? A muffin? Anything?"

"I'm fine. I had a big breakfast and so far, it's holding."

"Okay. Tell me what you know."

"The Ontario County Sheriff's Office had a delegate speak to the reporters so you'll hear this on the news. They're working with Yates County since that office has dealt with similar situations in the past. No sense reinventing the wheel."

I shifted in my chair and he continued.

"They found identification on the body but need to contact the family. They're classifying it as a 'suspicious death,' but we already figured that out. Duh."

"Anything else?" I tapped my foot under the table, thankful Joel didn't see how anxious I was.

"Yeah. The time of death was estimated to be around eight or nine last night, according to the deputy. When the coroner completes his or her preliminary postmortem, they'll share that information with the public."

"That's it?"

"No. The public is being asked to contact the Ontario County Sheriff's Office or the Yates County Sheriff's Office if they noticed anything suspicious."

"Unless someone was traipsing around Billsburrow Winery at all hours, who would notice anything?"

"I know, but they always say things like that."

I laughed. "You're right. When do you suppose we'll get more info?"

"As soon as my article is published. At least the online version will be up-to-date. Frankly, I don't expect to hear anything. It always takes a while to contact next of kin."

"When you do, will you please let me know?"

"Sure thing. Say, I enjoyed coffee the other day. Want to chat again this week? Maybe the day after tomorrow. Same time. Same place. By Friday, I should know something."

No such thing as "only coffee."

"Uh, sure. Text me."

When Joel left, my stomach got queasy and I knew it wasn't from anything I ate. I immediately turned my attention back to the newsletter and tried to think of what interesting articles I could write. Titles like "Dead Body Found in Local Vineyard" and "Corpse Found Amid Chardonnay Vines" sprung to mind. That's when I realized I had moved into sleuthing mode and once there, it would be impossible to extricate myself.

Chapter 11

And while it wasn't as if it was my neck on the chopping block, or Two Witches', for that matter, I knew how stressed and anxious Madeline would be. I also knew how slow and glacial the sheriffs' offices would be. Especially since they were working together.

Maybe another coffee with Joel wasn't such a bad idea after all. Especially since he seemed willing to share what info he had. I stared at the computer screen and forced myself to continue with the newsletter. Francine wanted timely and appropriate features about the seasonal nuances in the vineyard. *Seasonal my you-know-what!* All I could picture was a corpse strategically placed, or *dumped*, as the case may be, adjacent to the lovely Chardonnay vines in Madeline's vineyard. Then it hit me—I'd write a short mystery about death in the vineyard instead of some boring article about fermentation, or worse yet, the malolactic process.

Who knows? Maybe I'd even pen a screenplay and kill two birds with one stone. *Provided* it was a paranormal screenplay to appease Renee. With a sudden burst of energy, the creative part of my brain came alive for the next fifty-five minutes and before I knew it, closing time had approached.

I shut down the computer and helped clean the tasting room tables and set up for the next day.

"I doubt we'll hear anything new," Cammy said as she brushed past me, a water pitcher in each hand. "The news anchors will simply repeat what we already know. And until the sheriffs' offices release the name, we'll all be in the dark. Any word from Madeline?"

"Not a word exactly. About a half hour ago, she sent the WOW group an emoji that looked like a silent scream. I'll call her later tonight. Give her time to decompress."

I took Joel's advice and had Fred and Emma keep an eye on me as I trekked back to the house. This time Alvin didn't bother to run to the fence and spit at me. I attributed it to the cold weather and not that he had finally gotten used to me.

When I entered the house, Charlie immediately charged to his empty kibble bowl and stood there. I filled it before I even took off my jacket and changed his water as well. That's when I noticed the red light flashing on the landline.

"Looks like we got a message, Charlie." I glanced at the caller ID and it was from the entomology department. Not Godfrey's usual number but that didn't mean anything. Half the time he's in another lab or doing field work without his cell phone handy. I pushed the button and listened to his message.

"I know you'll find out eventually and then you'll be furious with me for not telling you." I paused the message and took three long breaths. Forget three months! Francine and Jason want to stay in some uncivilized hellhole for the next year. Biting my lower lip, I resumed the message. "This isn't for anyone else's ears. Understood? The Ontario County Sheriff's Office has requested a forensic entomologist for the body that was found at Billsburrow. Since Dr. D'Anri is still in Ecuador, I've been given the case. Just wanted to keep you apprised. And no, it doesn't mean you get special access to what I determine when my analysis is completed. Let's do pizza again, shall we? Or maybe Chinese? FYI—your cell phone was busy all day."

I all but jumped in the air when the message ended. Francine and Jason weren't going to be gone all year and I knew I could wheedle information out of Godfrey with the right amount of pleading.

"This calls for a celebration, Charlie! I'm defrosting those barbequed sausages and I'll even share them with you."

The dog lifted his head from the kibble and went back to chomping on the dry morsels. That was my cue to change into comfy warm sweats and turn up the heat. A short while later, I nuked the sausages and drowned them in baked beans. Francine would have been horrified. Organic soy curls topped with twigs and sticks would have been more her veggie organic diet style.

At a little past eight, I finally heard from Bradley. At the sound of his voice, all thoughts of Joel vanished but I wondered how I could flip-flop on this so easily.

"Hey, Hon, I'm missing you like crazy. Any news on the person found at Billsburrow? Got your text as well as one from my mother in Cazenovia who caught the news and wondered how close I was to that winery."

"Miss you, too. The only thing I know is what everyone does. Male. Forties or fifties. Wrapped in a tarp at the end of their Chardonnay vineyard. Classified as a suspicious death. Gee, you think?"

Bradley chuckled. "Yeah, until there's a preliminary postmortem and a tox screening, that's the best designation they can give. Guess we'll all find out the person's identification when it gets released. That's *if* he had ID on him. If not, it'll take longer. What did Madeline tell you?"

"Does an emoji count? Because otherwise, nothing. I'm going to call her in a bit."

"Good news! I'll be back on Saturday. Let's do dinner at Port of Call. They should still be serving their butternut squash soup and four-cheese souffle."

"My mouth's watering already."

For the next ten minutes we talked about Bradley's complicated case and another one waiting for him in Syracuse. Then the usual words of endearment before we said our good nights. I wanted to tell him about eking out information from a *Finger Lakes Times* reporter but I decided to let it ride.

"Well, Charlie," I said when Bradley's call ended, "I suppose I'd better call Madeline. By now she should have her wits about her." The dog looked up from the floor as I tapped her number.

Madeline answered on the first ring. "I'm glad it's you and not one of my relatives. They've been calling all day."

"It's me, all right. How are you doing?"

"Horrible. I took an antianxiety pill, left over from a year and a half ago when my sister-in-law came for an extended visit. I hope it still works."

"Probably. I don't think it's like food that can spoil after the expiration date. I think they put the date there to sell more stock."

"I hope so. What a nightmare! When Paolo phoned the winery about his discovery, we couldn't believe it. Then those dreadful deputies from two counties. But that's not the worst of it."

"What do you mean?"

"They asked our vineyard crew and our winemakers if they could identify the body. The tasting crew hadn't arrived yet but when they did, they were shown a photo."

"And?"

"No one recognized the man, but I sure did! That's what makes it so awful. So absolutely awful."

"Oh no. Was it someone you and your family were close with?"

"Oh hell no! And I'm not supposed to breathe a word of it, but what the heck! Just don't repeat it, okay?"

"Okay."

"It was Stanley Hurst."

I gasped and Madeline continued. "And that's not the worst. Remember when I told you about the Wegmans incident? Well, seems someone with more time on their hands than brains posted it to Facebook and it's gone viral—'Woman Smashes Eggs on Man's Feet!' Can you imagine? You know how it looks, don't you? I expect to be a person of interest if it turns out he was murdered. And of course, he was murdered! He didn't shroud himself in a tarp and drop dead in my vineyard!"

"Maybe you should—"

"My husband called our attorney. It's a waiting game at this point. At least the county didn't shut us down for their investigation. Bad enough we lost business today. And if I don't sound remorseful about Stanley's death, that's too bad. The man was a tyrant. A deceitful, conniving tyrant."

"Um, you may want to keep those thoughts to yourself. Act shocked and saddened when the deputies question you." *Been there. Done that.*

"Norrie, like I said, you can't breathe a word of this to anyone. Not until his name is released publicly."

"Do you have any idea when that will be?"

"Your guess is as good as mine. The coroner carted him off, tarp and all, to the Ontario County lab. The lead sheriff from Ontario County said they'd be sending some deputies over tomorrow to meet with the tasting room staff. They already spoke with our vineyard workers and winemakers."

"Sounds about right. Did the deputies give you any indication when Stanley's name would be released to the public?"

"No. Your guess is as good as mine. My identification isn't considered official. Apparently, they have other steps to take as well. I guess I can understand that. People do make mistakes when they're distraught. And I was certainly all of that. But still, I could have picked Stanley out of a cemetery full of corpses. And if this antianxiety pill doesn't start kicking in soon, I'm going to have horrible nightmares."

Apparently Zenora wasn't the only one who could prophesy future events. Because Madeline was about to have the nightmare of the century, only she didn't know it at the time, and neither did I.

Chapter 12

The next day droned on and on with no updates on the "suspicious death of a middle-aged man found at a local winery." I darted back and forth between the tasting room and the newsletter, aka murder mystery, with hopes of completing and mailing it to subscribers by the end of the day. If nothing else, it would get their attention.

At a little before noon, Bradley took me completely by surprise with a phone call. I had just finished up with a few customers and was headed to the bistro to grab a sandwich. "Norrie, can you speak privately without anyone around? If not, I'll wait and call right back."

"I'll hustle to my office. Sounds ominous. Are you okay?"

"I'm fine. But you need to keep what I tell you to yourself."

I raced past everyone, got to my office and closed the door. "I'm back in my office. What's going on?"

"Well, the least of it is that I won't make it this weekend. Seems the dead body in Madeline's winery was the husband of one of our very high-profile clients—Lila Stratington-Hurst. She phoned Marvin at daybreak to tell him he no longer had to proceed with the divorce because her 'rat of a husband' was found dead."

"Stanley Hurst, right? From Diamante Developers in Syracuse."

"You know? His identity hasn't been released to the public."

"Madeline had to ID the body and she released the info to me." I could almost see Bradley rolling his eyes but he continued without commentary.

"According to Lila, who was 'interrogated like a common criminal' by the Ontario and Onondaga sheriffs' offices, she thinks they may charge her with murder."

"Why? What evidence do they have?"

"A contentious divorce for one thing. And a tricky prenup agreement. Easier to knock the guy off than go through a staggering court case."

"Any physical evidence?"

"No word yet. Listen, I feel really badly about the weekend but Marvin has me flying back to Syracuse on Saturday to meet with him and Lila at her place. I'll be swamped all weekend. Then back here. Aargh!"

"I understand." Terrific. Even dead, Stanley managed to make my life miserable.

"I'll keep you posted. If I can sneak away, I will. Miss you like crazy."

"Me too."

"Remember, not a word. Even if Madeline told you."

"No worries. Take care."

At that moment, someone knocked on my door and we ended the call. I quicky jotted down the name Lila Stratington-Hurst and called out, "Come in!"

Cammy stepped inside and closed the door behind her. "This is only for your ears because Melissa Gillotte will have my head if she knew I told anyone."

"Melissa? Madeline's tasting room manager? *That* Melissa?"

"How many Melissas do you know? Never mind. She and I go way back to North Street Elementary School in Geneva. Sweet girl but so klutzy. The other day she rammed her finger into a door and went nuts trying to find a Band-Aid. Said she must have opened every drawer in the place looking for one. Anyway, Melissa may be shorthanded this week without Madeline and wondered if we could give her the names of our temporary college student employees. Just in case."

"Sure. We're all set—Wait a sec. Why isn't Madeline working?"

"Uh, yeah. That's the hush-hush part."

I widened my eyes and focused them directly on Cammy.

"Madeline is now an official person of interest but may be arrested for murder by the end of the day."

"What? Because of a verbal altercation at Wegmans?"

"Partly, yes. According to Melissa, who spoke with Madeline, the Ontario County forensic crew found fingerprints on one of Stanley's polished shoes. Since she had a public altercation with Stanley that resulted in her getting a restraining order, their sheriff's office brought her in for further questioning. They also took her fingerprints to compare them."

"Oh no! Don't tell me it was a match!"

"A pretty close to perfect one, yeah."

"Wait a minute! The egg thing! Madeline dropped a carton of eggs on his feet. Maybe she bent down to remove the shells or whatever. In fact, Madeline told me it was all over Facebook. All she needs to do is pull up that post and show it to the sheriff's office."

Cammy shook her head. "One step ahead of you. She already did. On the advice of her lawyer. Unfortunately, the video showed the escalation of the incident but cut off. It doesn't show Madeline trying to wipe off shoes or anything that would exonerate her."

"What about video footage from Wegmans? What did that show? Did Melissa know?"

"It didn't show that part of the dairy section."

"Rats. Poor Madeline. She must be a basket case. Hey, you don't think they can really charge her, do you? I mean, it's circumstantial evidence. More or less."

Cammy sighed. "I wouldn't know. Look, if I hear anything else, I'll let you know. Remember, this is on the q.t."

I nodded. "I'll follow you out. I'm headed to the bistro for a sandwich. Then I'll work the tasting room so folks can take their breaks."

"Sounds good."

My normal instinct would have been to call Theo since there wasn't much we didn't share when it came to winery business and amateur investigations. However, I had it drilled into me by my mother that if I shared a secret with just one person, they'd share it with another and before I knew it, it would no longer be a secret and I'd be the one to blame.

I took a deep breath and walked through the tasting room to the bistro. Without Stanley's identity being released to the public, I was at a standstill. Unless Godfrey knew more than he was willing to say. Then again, he'd be studying insects, insect droppings, and insect larva from that tarp, not dealing with suspects.

"You look deep in thought, Norrie," Emma said as I approached the glass food case and gazed at the pastries.

"Yeah. My mind is all over the place with that dead body at Madeline's. Not to mention their traminette sabotage and that awful yes vote for the high-rise. Which, by the way, was most likely bought off by unscrupulous bribes. Too bad I can't prove a thing. Well, not yet anyway."

"What do you mean?"

"In a broad sense, I'm picking up rocks and looking to see what's underneath."

"Huh?"

"I'm looking deeper into the yes votes. Or voters, as the case may be."

"Oh."

"But right now, I'm starving. Can I grab a ham and Swiss sandwich on sourdough?"

"Absolutely. Hang on."

A few seconds later, Emma handed me a plate with a thick sandwich and some veggie chips.

"Thanks. I'll keep you posted."

"As long as you keep yourself out of trouble."

"It's only a paper chase."

She laughed. "That's how they all start."

When I finished my sandwich and washed it down with coffee, I rotated around the tasting room giving everyone a twenty-minute break. Too bad no one gave me one. It was question after question.

"Have you heard anything?"

"Any news on the body?"

"Do you think this has anything to do with the traminette sabotage?"

"Do we have enough surveillance here?"

And from Glenda, "Don't you think you should be cleansing the winery with sage and lavender? This isn't a time to take chances."

No, but it's certainly a time to get off my duff and start a deep dive into Diane, Michael, and Victor. And this one may not be on the computer.

And while I couldn't say a word to Theo about finding out it was Stanley under that tarp, I had no problem suggesting we do a bit of on-site surveillance on one of our three yes voters.

"Have you completely lost your mind?" His voice was midway between panic and disbelief.

"Let me explain first. You'll see it makes perfect sense."

"Sure. If you want a criminal record hanging over you."

"All we need to do is find out if one or more of our three yeses received monies from Diamante to sway the vote. At first, I thought only Avery, but it could have been any or all of them."

"And how *exactly* did you plan on doing this? And for the record, I am *not* on board."

"Think of the greater good. Think of saving Seneca Lake as we know it."

"Thank you, Upton Sinclair. Just go on."

"Fine. The answer is in their bank accounts. If they were bribed, the money went somewhere and I seriously doubt it was handed to them in a back alley. Most likely an online deposit to their checking or savings. But we have no way to determine that."

"Good. For a minute I thought you were about to suggest computer hacking."

"Nope, more like finding a way to see if any of them made any big purchases lately. Or took any extended trips."

"And how exactly do you plan to find that out? You already tapped into Marilyn Ansley."

"But not her chitchat group."

"You really are a glutton for punishment."

"Not me. Both of us. The chitchat group meets for breakfast at the Penn Yan Diner every Friday morning. And on days when 'the gossip is ripe,' according to Marilyn."

"Yeesh!"

"They meet at seven a.m. The perfect time for you and me to enjoy their winter pancake special with bananas and caramel syrup."

"Covered with a dollop of fresh rumormongering."

"For all we know, Marilyn could be the amateur in that group. It may turn out to be a veritable gold mine as far as information goes. I say we give it a shot."

"The pancakes are tempting. I'll give you that much."

"Good. I'll drive down and pick you up at six thirty tomorrow. Think Don would want to join us?"

"Only if hell froze over. I'll get his order to go."

Chapter 13

"I can't believe I was swayed so easily by bananas Foster on top of a huge stack of pancakes," Theo said. He slid into the passenger seat of my car and buckled up. "How long before the heat's going to come on in your car? And why aren't you driving Francine's loaded Subaru?"

"Her car is at the garage getting an oil change and some other stuff. The siren feature on her fob went berserk and the sound is at least a zillion decibels over what it should be. Plus it doesn't shut off easily. They may have to send for a new one. Anyway, we're stuck with my old reliable Toyota."

"*Old* is the keyword and it better be reliable. Had I known, I would have offered to drive. I think it's colder in your car than outside. I hate when these temperatures hover around zero."

"At least it means we won't get snow. Well, usually."

"I take it you didn't listen to the forecast. They're predicting a whooper of a storm sometime next week. Only thing good about it is that some folks stock up on wine before groceries."

"I know. It's that cabin fever thing."

A few minutes later I pulled up to the Penn Yan Diner and found a decent parking spot near the front. "Must be not all the chitchat ladies arrived."

Theo turned his head and laughed. "Look in your rearview mirror. Five women are getting out of a van that's a few yards back. Has to be them."

"Let's wait till they walk in and then follow. We can seat ourselves near them. Of course, once Marilyn spots us, she'll probably invite us over."

"As long as I don't have to sit next to her. Don once saw her help herself to someone's French fries at the Wagner."

"Oh, brother. It doesn't surprise me."

The steam from the diner made my eyes water as I stepped inside.

Sure enough, the chitchat ladies were at the large booth in back. All eight of them, including Marilyn. There was a smaller booth adjacent to theirs and we grabbed it.

"Norrie," Marilyn waved. "And Theo. Winery business?"

Theo kicked my ankle as I got into the booth. "Nope. Banana pancake business."

One of the women sat upright in her seat and leaned toward us. "Have you heard the latest about the body they found at Billsburrow Winery? My sources tell me it was that developer from Syracuse. No one is supposed to know but my source is very close to the investigation."

And probably close to losing his or her job.

Another woman nudged her. "Not Gladys Pipp from the sheriff's office? That poor secretary."

The first woman shook her head. "No, not Gladys. She's got Deputy Hickman breathing down her neck all the time. Besides, *my* source works at the Ontario County Sheriff's Office. I should have mentioned that first. Sorry, ladies." Then she looked at Theo. "And gentleman."

"I'm sure it will be on the news pretty soon," I said, turning my head toward them. "Right now, Theo and I are concerned about those yes votes for that high-rise. We still can't wrap our heads around how something like that could have happened."

A tall woman with Raggedy Ann red hair leaned an elbow on her placemat and then gave the table a bang. "I'll tell you what I think. Someone must have blackmailed them."

Blackmail. I never considered that. Bribery, yes, but not blackmail. I shot Theo a look and then spoke. "What would make you think that?"

The woman wasted no time with her response. "I happen to know for a fact that Dahl Farms didn't candle all of its eggs. Its electronic candling machine broke and they did not stop production."

"How do you know that?" Theo removed his jacket but kept it on his shoulders.

"I found out about it after the fact from my nephew who used to work there."

"Are you insinuating someone from Diamante Developers found out and blackmailed him?" Theo wasn't about to let anything slip by.

"Oh, I'm not insinuating. I'm putting two and two together."

"Huh?" This time we both responded.

"That developer was notorious for sneaky, underhanded stuff. In Cicero, where my sister lives, something similar happened but with a paper company. Good luck proving it, though."

"Blackmail?" I asked.

"Uh-huh. If you want my take, Diamante found their weak spot and knew one of their higher-ups was also on the Skaneateles Town Board. Next thing you know, they've got a major development going."

"So you think they found out about Dahl Farms skipping a vital health step in its egg production and blackmailed Victor Dahl for a yes vote?" Theo narrowed his eyes at the same time our waitress appeared.

"Sorry, everyone! I'll get carafes of coffee, regular and decaf, on your tables in a jiff."

She took off and the red-haired woman continued. "Oh, they found out, all right. My nephew saw the Diamante Developers truck at Dahl Farms on more than one occasion. Trust me, gals, it had nothing to do with the dairy business."

When the waitress said "in a jiff," she meant it. Coffees were on our tables and our orders taken in record time. Marilyn introduced Theo and me to her band of merry gossipers but there was no way I could have kept track of their names.

The chitchat continued and it was a hodgepodge of "who knew what," "what was going on," and "who was seen with whom." While everyone dove into their food, Theo and I included, he whispered, "Two down, two to go. Ask about Diane or Avery."

I swallowed a mouthful of hash browns and took a quick sip of coffee. "But what about Diane? I understand she used to be in your group. You don't suppose she was blackmailed by Diamante?"

"Wouldn't put it past them," a woman with frosted hair and dark black glasses said. "Especially since Diane was charged with shoplifting a few years ago but it was dismissed as a misunderstanding. Misunderstanding my patootie! I wager Diamante had something on her and forced a yes vote."

Yeesh. These women need to be writing crime fiction instead of inventing it.

"Or they took Avery's lead and voted yes in that closed session," the red-haired woman added. "Everyone knows how persuasive he can be. Especially if it meant his own hide."

"I'm not sure I understand," Theo said.

This time another woman spoke, a tall, pencil-thin woman with wispy blond hair. "Avery's been covering his own derrière for years by making the right social connections. The Elks, the Order of the Moose, you name the animal lodge and he's in it. I don't believe he was blackmailed, but I do believe he could have been bought off for the right amount of money."

"Was he in debt?" Theo asked.

"No, not as far as I know. But his father had to be moved to assisted living and didn't have long-term insurance. He was diagnosed with MS years ago and didn't qualify for financial aid. Avery and his wife have to pay. And if you ask how I know, Colleen attends my church."

"Those costs can be staggering." I remembered hearing my parents discuss it once.

"Staggering is mild. They can wipe out a bank account and leave you living on the street," she said. "If Diamante made Avery an attractive offer, he'd take it. Scruples go out the window when poverty comes in the door."

Not exactly the gospel I was taught.

"That's been most enlightening, ladies. Thanks for sharing."

We hurried through the rest of our breakfast and wished everyone a wonderful day. Once on the street, Theo grabbed me by the wrist, doubled over, and started laughing.

"Whoa! Did you take all of that in?"

"How couldn't I? They give rumor and speculation a whole new meaning. But the good news is that we walked away with more info than before. It really *is* possible Dahl Farms was blackmailed. And Avery was bribed in order to foot those bills for his father. As for Diane, your guess is as good as mine. And Michael was a complete wash. Still, we know more than when we started out this morning."

"And we had a better breakfast than the usual. Don will appreciate his take-out pancakes with all the fixings. Say, what did you make about that woman insisting the body was Stanley Hurst's?"

I tried not to look Theo in the eye. "It's anyone's guess, really." *And I wish I could tell you the truth.* So now what? It was like I was in a holding pattern. Until the sheriffs' offices released the name, that is. Then I could talk openly with everyone and see if the vote, the sabotage, and the murder were connected.

"I don't think it will be much longer," I said. "Maybe another day or so."

"Surprising Madeline didn't say anything. I mean, it *is* her winery, and wouldn't she have been asked to look at the body and identify it if she could?"

"True, but maybe she was told to keep quiet." *I am such a terrible liar.*

"Since when does Madeline keep quiet?"

"Always a first time."

I dropped Theo off and headed home. I hated not sharing what I knew with him but I couldn't afford to leak out the information Madeline gave me. I supposed another day or so wouldn't make that much of a difference.

It was still too early for the winery so I decided to use the extra hour to work on my paranormal screenplay. Either that, or dig out the corkboard and start a murder map. It was a toss-up either way.

In the end, the murder map won. Mainly because I could write the screenplay on my laptop while in bed, but I needed a large space to pull all the suspects together. What I didn't count on was that I'd need more than one corkboard because the suspects started piling up like the snow that was about to grace us next week.

Chapter 14

"They always predict major snowstorms," Cammy said when I walked into the winery a few hours later. "Half the time it's all hype so people will keep their TVs tuned to the news stations."

"Theo listened to the farm report and they said we're going to have one whopper of a snowstorm followed by a possible ice storm a few days later."

"Who were the sponsors? Probably the local grocery stores."

"If it winds up on the Weather Channel, I'll be stocking up at Wegmans."

Cammy laughed. "You and half the county!"

"By the way, he and I had breakfast at the Penn Yan Diner to see if we could get any dirt on those yes votes."

"Don't tell me. You snooped on the chitchat ladies?"

"Didn't have to snoop. They spread the gossip like fertilizer on a field."

"And?"

"Other than Michael, the other yes votes may have been bribed or blackmailed for their votes. Not to say Michael *wasn't,* but the chitchat ladies didn't have anything on him."

"Yet. Give it time." Cammy chuckled. She headed off to the kitchen and I retreated to my office to catch up on emails and the pile of papers that was literally falling off my desk.

Like the usual Fridays, business picked up from the weekdays. Not the nonstop craziness during the fall and early winter holiday season, but enough to keep our crew busy. In addition, we used the lull time to check inventory for merchandise and to discount items for the clearance weekend.

Talk about the murder continued as customers asked if any of us knew who the victim was. It was tough for me to keep tight-lipped but I had no choice. I kept praying Stanley's name would be all over the news so I could confer with Theo and try to get Madeline as far away from the hook as possible.

Sadly, only one of my prayers was answered and it came at daybreak the next morning. Not the best way to begin a Saturday. Theo called and I was barely coherent.

"Hey, Norrie. Hope I didn't wake you."

"Huh? Who?"

"Oh. Guess I did. Sorry. It's Theo. Well, now that you're awake, I can tell you whose body was found at Billsburrow—Stanley Hurst. Stanley! From Diamante Developers. Holy moly! It was on the breaking news right before the farm report. Don't you listen to the farm report?"

"That's why we have a vineyard manager. So he can get up at an ungodly hour to find out about cash crops, commodities, weather patterns and more boring stuff that barely crosses my mind. But forget the farm report, tell me what they said about Stanley."

Even though I got it up close and personal from Madeline.

"Only that the sheriff's office in Ontario County was able to make a positive identification and notify next of kin."

"What next of kin? Did they say who?"

"No. But they did say to expect a full report on their news roundup at five."

"The TV stations will have already covered it on their noon report. At least I'll be awake for that. Did they mention cause of death?"

"Nope. Only that the preliminary autopsy confirmed the death to be a homicide and that a full toxicology screening will take at least a week or two."

Madeline hadn't mentioned seeing anything gory, but that didn't mean a thing. For all anyone knew, Stanley's bloody intestines could have leaked all over him, but with that tarp wrapped around his corpse, it would have been impossible to tell.

"This isn't going to look good for Madeline," I said. "That verbal fencing match at the end of the town meeting was hard to miss." *Not to mention the Wegmans incident.* "Everyone at that town meeting was ready to hang him at the gallows. The winery owners, the business owners, the restaurant owners, the homeowners . . . And what about his own family? Maybe there was bad blood."

"Bad blood isn't a motive. Exactly. But the threat of losing business coupled with a rather noticeable exchange of words sure is. Especially if the body just so happened to land on the property of one of the combatants."

Suddenly I became aware of a tightness in my stomach and I doubted it had much to do with being hungry. "Let's give the news time to settle in. I'll call Madeline in a few hours and see what's going on."

"Better you than me. I saw her get hysterical once when a bat got into her patio during a luncheon. Finding out she might be a suspect will make that experience feel like a walk in the park. Let me know how it goes. Got to get ready for work. Will talk later."

"Thanks for the news, Theo. Say hi to Don."

When I finally made it to Two Witches at a little before ten, one thing became stunningly clear—everyone listens to the farm report around here.

Lizzie was the first to catch my attention before the front door had even closed.

"It was Stanley Hurst. That developer from Syracuse. His was the body they found at Billsburrow. Oh. Good morning, Norrie. I should have greeted you first, but ever since I heard the news, it was all I could think of. You don't suppose anyone at Billsburrow was responsible, do you?" She took off her glasses and wiped them on the bottom of her cardigan. "It would be too sloppy. Having the body right there where anyone could find it. Especially during this time of year with the racking. Those winemakers are moving product from one vat to another. Bound to notice a body, wouldn't you say?"

"Uh-huh."

I started for my office but Glenda swooped in like a pelican hovering over the waters for a fish. "Zenora woke from one of her nautilus dreams at three o'clock this morning and phoned me."

"She couldn't wait till the farm report like everyone else? And what's a nautilus dream?"

"It's part of her premonitions. Some occur in the dream cycle."

Of course. Why do I even ask?

Glenda brushed a wisp of hair from her brow and sighed. "You know what a nautilus is, right?"

I nodded.

"Well, in the dream, Zenora is winding around and around as she passes through the tightening chambers until there's no place else to go and she's trapped. The compartment closes in and it's all over."

"What is? The dream?"

"The outcome. It's too late for whatever she needed to accomplish. Only the dream wasn't intended for her. It's a warning. A premonition. For you."

"Okay. I'll steer clear of oceans. Thank Zenora for me."

"You can't afford to be flippant about it, Norrie. Your life may be in danger."

"Why my life? That shell could have been anyone."

"Because Zenora saw you when she wound her way through it."

Wonderful. Just what I need.

"What was I doing?"

"Running."

"And that's it?"

"What else do you need? Burn those sage sticks around your house. That tightening chamber in the nautilus can only mean one thing. Two Witches may be next. *You* may be next."

"Glenda, the body they found at Billsburrow belonged to that developer from Syracuse and he didn't have an issue with me. Well, a general one, in terms of preserving our community, but not a business or personal one like Madeline did. She had an offer in on that property."

"Not Stanley Hurst. Something else."

"What? What else?"

"She wasn't sure. Dreams and visions aren't specific."

"Well, until Zenora hands me a detailed outline of who, what, where, when, and how, I'll just have to muddle through."

"What do we have to muddle through?" Cammy approached and caught the last few words of my conversation with Glenda.

"Just a vision of Zenora's," I said.

Glenda shook her head. "More like a premonition."

"Oh. Okay." Cammy rolled her eyes at me when Glenda turned away for a second. "Guess everyone's heard the news about the victim by now," she said. "Wow. Never expected it to be that developer. From what I heard, there's no shortage of suspects. I only caught a bit of the breaking news before the farm report came on."

What is it with these people and the farm report?

"Yeah, well, right now the only suspect I'm worried about is Madeline. In fact, I was planning to call her this morning."

Cammy winced and bit her lower lip. "Uh, about that, you may want to put it off."

"Why?"

"Melissa just sent me a text a few minutes ago. I was about to tell you. She was taken into custody by the Ontario County Sheriff's Office and charged with murder. Not exactly a great way for Billsburrow Winery to start their day."

Or Madeline.

"With what evidence?"

"They found what they believe to be the murder weapon in her possession."

Chapter 15

"The murder weapon? They know what the murder weapon was? What about the stupid toxicology report that everyone has to wait for?" By now, I was ranting like an adolescent. "What was it? A knife? A rope? Not a gun. Other than hunting rifles, no one I know in the wineries carries around guns."

"Melissa didn't say. Only that they had a search warrant for the winery kitchen and walked off with something in an evidence bag. And it gets worse. They informed the staff that a forensic entomologist would be by later to look for evidence of pantry pests. Beats me why. Not as if a weevil killed the guy."

Godfrey! The evidence on the tarp. Maybe I can get one step ahead of the game.

I shrugged. "I suppose I'd better let Theo know and we can call the WOW ladies."

Glenda widened her eyes. "Tell them if any of them wish to cleanse their wineries, Zenora and I would be more than glad to leave some sage sticks and lavender here for them."

"That's very generous. I'll be sure to spread the word."

With that, Glenda trotted off to her tasting table and Cammy rubbed her chin. "It'll take more than sage sticks to deal with this mess. You know what it means, don't you?"

I shook my head.

"While Madeline's in the lockup, someone else will have to take over that Winery of the West group. Good luck with that."

Suddenly, getting Madeline off the hook became a secondary concern. My first was to keep myself from getting snared on this one. Last thing I needed was being asked to run that show. It had been Madeline's baby all along and none of us had the enthusiasm or desire to take over. Rosalee would claim she was too old and tired. Stephanie would bring up her twins and all the work that involved, Catherine would say her nerves couldn't handle the stress and the guys from the

Grey Egret would simply say "No way, José." That left me. The screenwriter who everyone perceived had lots and lots of time on her hands.

I glanced at the wall clock and knew that Gladys Pipp was going to take her coffee break in ten minutes. Not to mention she only worked half days on Saturdays, so I had to get a move on if I ever expected to find out what was really going on. Since it was a shared jurisdiction, she would know all. And she would readily share it if I arrived at the Yates County Sheriff's Office with Francine's blueberry-lemon jam.

"Time for me to have a conversation with Gladys at the sheriff's office."

Cammy burst out laughing. "The thought of running those WOW meetings scared you, huh?"

"Worse than a horror movie. Besides, none of us want to see Madeline charged with a crime she didn't commit. Even if the evidence points her way. Those deputies are always in a hurry to wrap up a case, no matter what."

"She's lucky she has you to pry into it. That's all I can say. But be careful. Those amateur investigations of yours have a tendency to spin out of control."

"I don't think this one will. Even if Zenora has a bushel of premonitions."

Worst words ever spoken, but how was I supposed to know?

Cammy had plenty of coverage in the tasting room so I headed home, added more kibble to Charlie's dish, grabbed a large jar of Francine's blueberry-lemon jam, and started up my Toyota. The roads were clear and that might not be the case in a few days. It was now or later. And later might be too late.

• • •

The parking lot in front of the Yates County Sheriff's Office and County Jail was practically empty. Not bursting at the seams like it's a weekday. No trials. No county meetings, just the usual business.

I reached across the passenger seat for the jam and walked directly to the entrance. A quick stop at the registration booth and I was off to Deputy Hickman's office, where Gladys was posted like a sentry. The good news, according to the deputy on duty, was that Gladys was in and Grizzly Gary was out and not expected back until noon. Hallelujah!

"Good morning, Norrie!" Gladys looked up from her computer screen and ushered me over. "You don't have to say a word. It's about Madeline Martinez's arrest, right?"

I handed her the jam and sat in the chair next to her desk. "She's innocent, you know. Those Ontario County deputies are making a huge mistake and the real killer is running around out there."

Gladys shifted in her chair and moved closer to me. "You and I may feel that way but they go by the evidence and unfortunately, it doesn't look good."

"Yeah. That's why I'm here. I was hoping you might be able to clue me in to what they confiscated from her winery kitchen."

She gazed at the jar of jam and looked around. "I'm not supposed to say anything so keep it to yourself." Then she chucked. "Fine. Tell Theo Buchman. The two of you are becoming quite the sleuthing team."

"Don't worry. Theo knows how to be discreet."

Gladys spoke in a whisper, darting her eyes to the door every few seconds. "Mr. Hurst succumbed to a fatal stab wound in his chest. The puncture indicated a narrow instrument about five to seven inches long. Definitely not a knife or dagger."

"So what did they take?"

"A meat thermometer."

"Seriously? They think *that* could have killed him?"

"The old ones certainly could. They were made to withstand everything. I imagine the new ones could as well."

"You wouldn't happen to know if the one they found was old or new, would you?"

She shook her head. "Sorry, no. But I forwarded an email to Deputy Hickman that came in from the Ontario County lab. They found traces of blood on the thermometer."

"That could have been anything! Like chicken blood. Those chicken breasts always have bloody spots on them. And what about raw meat? That stuff's as bloody as a third-grader's nose after recess."

"The lab will make a further determination but, in the meantime, the evidence points to your friend. *That*, in addition to firsthand evidence. She was seen getting into two verbal altercations with the victim. *And*, she had a solid motive for doing away with him. Sorry, Norrie, but it's not looking good."

"Will you let me know if you find out anything else? You can send me a short text and I'll take it from there."

"I'll try my best. Remember, not a word. And by the way, thank you for this marvelous jam. I've missed Francine's wonderful recipes. You really should have her show you how she does it when she gets back from . . . hmm, where are they?"

"Still in the Philippines. That country is laden with insects. A regular treasure trove for her and her husband."

Gladys laughed and I thanked her again before leaving. Once in the car, I phoned Theo.

"No one is supposed to know this," I said.

"Then how come you do?"

"Outright bribery with blueberry-lemon jam."

"Gladys?"

"Who else? Listen, the Ontario County Sheriff's Office confiscated something from Madeline's winery kitchen. I found out from Cammy, whose friend is the tasting room manager over there. Anyway, according to Gladys, Stanley was murdered with some sort of small, narrow skewer or pin. An *impaler*, only I don't think there's such a word. You know what I mean, don't you?"

"I get the idea."

"That's not the worst. Madeline's being charged with the guy's murder. You know what that means, don't you?"

"Uh-huh. They've got the wrong person and will stop looking."

"Worse. One of us will have to run the WOW group."

"That's not funny, Norrie."

"Theo, we really need to dig around and find out who really killed Stanley. Heck, everyone at that town meeting had a darn good motive and I imagine most of them own narrow little kitchen impalers for something or other."

"Did you have a plan in mind or do you propose we do what we always do?"

"Kind of wing it and pray for the best?"

"Yeah. That. Don will be really pleased when I tell him."

"Wow, I can hear the sarcasm over the phone."

"Good."

"So that means you'll do it? You'll help me figure out who knocked off Stanley?"

"When have I ever turned you down?"

"Great? Let's get together after work. I'll order pizzas for you and Don and we can actually devise a plan."

"That'll be a first. What time?"

"Seven thirty, okay?"

"Sure. We like pepperoni, sausage, mushroom, olives—"

"I know. Everything except anchovies. See you then. Call me if you hear anything else."

"Shall do. I don't know what's more terrifying—a friend being charged with a homicide or having to run the WOW meetings."

Chapter 16

Charlie darted out the door to his yard when he heard Theo's truck in the driveway. The pizzas were on their way and the timing couldn't have been better.

"Come on in, guys," I said and motioned from the front door. "Pizza's going to be here any minute. I've got soda, juice, and O'Doul's."

"What? No wine?" Don laughed as he came inside and removed his jacket. "Only kidding. I'll actually take an O'Doul's. That stuff goes great with Italian food."

I looked at Theo and he nodded just as Charlie returned from the yard. "Same thing. Can't beat O'Doul's."

"I've got the heat cranked up so we can grab seats in the living room and enjoy our pizzas there. I ordered one special and one pepperoni."

"A woman after my own heart," Don said. While I went to get the drinks, I caught a glimpse of him patting Charlie on the head and Charlie eating up every moment.

"Might as well cut to the chase," Theo said as he took an end seat on the couch. "What nefarious plan do you have in mind?"

"I left a voicemail for Godfrey since I found out part of the evidence at Madeline's was pantry pests and he's the acting forensic entomologist since the other guy is in Ecuador. Remind me not to go to South America. Too many insects." I handed the guys their drinks and plopped down next to Theo.

"Wait a sec." Don drew his shoulder blades together and stretched his legs from the wingback chair that had been in my family's possession since the discovery of dirt. "I don't understand this pantry pest thing. Backtrack for me, will you?"

"Stanley's body was found wrapped in a tarp. Godfrey was called in because there were yucky insects on the tarp and they were pantry pests. So, that means—"

Don held up a hand. "I get it. Source of origination. Only most wineries and food establishments have to contend with pantry pests from time to time. Goes with the territory."

Just then, there was a knock on the door and Charlie raced over. "Yay! Pizza's here!"

Theo got up to give me a hand with the two pizzas and we put them on the coffee table next to the paper plates and napkins I had taken out.

For the next ten minutes, we gobbled up pizza and guzzled O'Doul's and didn't utter a word about Madeline, the pantry pests, or the impaler thing. Finally, when only three slices remained, Theo said, "I suppose you already have a murder map. Where is it this time? Not the bathroom mirror again?"

"No, I used construction paper and rolled it up. You two can clear the coffee table and I'll go get it."

The map was as primitive as they come. Artistic talent certainly didn't run in my genes but no one could miss the stick figure of Stanley with webbing spokes indicating possible suspects. I all but had to cram them in.

"Uh, hate to say this, but Madeline seems to have the points stacked up against her," Don said as he perused the map.

I squinted and took another look at my map. "That's because no one has looked into the other players."

Theo put his hand on my shoulder and looked directly at me. "Before we go hog wild chasing down everyone with a possible motive, why don't we narrow it down to the first three people who might have had a compelling reason to knock Stanley out of the picture? If that doesn't work, we move to the next three. Orderly and sequential. Unlike our usual runaround with our fingers crossed."

"Fine. As long as we get a move on! So, who's first?" I pointed to the construction paper that was weighted down on the coffee table with salt and pepper shakers, a creamer, and a paperweight.

Don leaned over and rubbed his chin before slipping Charlie a piece of pizza. "I wasn't at the meeting but Audrey from the bakery would have a lot to lose if that high-rise was built. I know she was planning on expanding her porch and half the patrons come for the view as well as the scones."

"What else do you know about her?" I asked.

"Not her. But her older son. He's part owner of a winery in Chester, Virginia. He apprenticed at Bully Hill in Watkins Glen a number of years ago. According to the mother, he's positively brilliant. Not to mention handsome."

Theo narrowed his brow. "How do you know all of that?"

"Last year I had to wait for a grape pie to come out of the oven and Audrey pretty much gave me her eldest son's life story."

I laughed. "She and Catherine Trobert should get together. They can compare notes. Catherine uses every opportunity to tell me what a gift to mankind Steven is. Some gift. He practically ignored me all during high school. Mankind can have him. And from the sound of it, they can have Audrey's son, too."

"Okay," Theo said. "Let's put Audrey's name down. Who else?"

"Did any of the no votes have anything to lose?" I asked. "We really didn't delve into them."

Don looked at Theo, then me. "Tell you what. You two keep working on your top three suspects and I'll take a gander at the no votes. See what I can dig up. If anything."

"Sounds good. Okay, who gets the number-two spot?"

"The wife," Theo and Don said at once.

"The guy was married," Theo announced. "I saw the wedding ring."

"I wasn't that observant." *But I know a whole lot more about Lila Stratington-Hurst, but I need to keep mum or I'll lose a boyfriend.* "It's a good idea, though. The spouse is always a top suspect. I'll see what I can find."

"That leaves our lucky third-spot runner-up." Don grinned.

"I don't have a *who* as much as an idea. What if there was a competing developer? Someone that Stanley beat out with his dirty shenanigans, just like he did with Madeline. I can always check with her realtor. They all speak with each other."

Theo and Don exchanged glances before Theo spoke. "That's the first real possibility, providing there *was* a competing developer. Okay, fine. We'll give it a shot. Two real people and one wishful thinking may-not-exist person. Sounds like we're ready to go. Now what?"

I took the last gulp of my O'Doul's and put the bottle on the coffee table. Then I turned and faced Theo. "How about if you pay a visit to Audrey and see what you can find out. Pointed questions and all. And see if you can spot anything in her bakeshop that might have been used to kill Stanley."

"Great idea!" Don chimed in. "And while you're at it, see if she has the winter babka with the chocolate. Get a loaf. And her raspberry, dark chocolate chip banana bread, too, while you're there."

"I'm supposed to be gathering information."

"You can gather baked goods, too, buddy."

My eyes darted back and forth as I listened to the two of them. "I'll see what I can find out about the wife and I'll get the name of Madeline's realtor. I'll also see if I can visit Madeline in the Ontario County Jail. Rats! That's all the way in Canandaigua. I suppose I should do that soon before the weather makes it impossible."

"When *is* that snowstorm expected?" Don asked.

"Middle of the week from what I heard. From the Weather Channel. I'm not getting up for the farm report."

Theo started clearing the paper plates and napkins. "What do you say we keep each other posted via email? Text messages get erased by accident all the time. Email can always be retrieved."

"I'm good with that," I said. "But let's still text, too."

"Hate to eat and run, Norrie, but some of us have to get up early," Don said and chuckled.

"As long as it's not me."

I walked the guys to the door and thanked them for helping me out.

"Hey, no one wants to get stuck running the WOW meetings," Theo joked. "But seriously, this is really bad news for Madeline."

How bad, none of us knew, but bad was bad, especially since one of our suspects may not have existed at all, and the other two might as well have been shots in the dark. Still, none of us were willing to sit around and watch justice take a wrong turn. We just needed to move fast because once one snowstorm moves in, the other one won't be far behind. And it's always the second one that's a doozy.

I wasted no time phoning Bradley even though I knew he'd call me before ten. And while the issue of ethics regarding their client was a top priority, the issue of saving Madeline and the rest of us from running WOW wasn't far behind.

• • •

"Norrie?" Bradley's voice sounded concerned. "Everything okay?"

"Not exactly. Madeline's been charged with murder and the investigation will stop in its tracks unless the real killer can be uncovered. They found her fingerprint on Stanley's shoe, even though she explained about the egg incident and trying to wipe it off. Then of course, the verbal altercation at the town meeting and the one at Wegmans. The sheriff's office is convinced she had a motive for killing him."

"Sounds like a weak motive, but it's all they've got apparently."

"What about Lila? The spouse is always a suspect. Is there any way to track her whereabouts around the time of the murder? Skaneateles isn't that far away. Less than one and a half hours from there to Penn Yan. Shorter to Geneva."

"That would be up to the sheriff's office, but I'll give her a call under the pretense of eliminating any accusations and have her give me her detailed itinerary from those days. And I'll check it out, Norrie. I can't have you involved directly."

"I understand. Oh my gosh! Thank you *so* much!"

"Hey, I'm on the side of justice. And if one of our clients is responsible for a murder, then I can't ignore it."

"I knew there was a reason I fell for you."

"Good. Keep it that way."

When I got off the phone, the fog that loomed over my head lifted slightly. Now I could concentrate on the possibility of a competing developer and a bakery owner who had a heck of a lot to lose.

It was a game of Clue, all right, but without the cards.

Chapter 17

When I went to bed, I had full intentions of waking up to begin my sleuthing. Too bad it would have nothing to do with perceived developers or obnoxious bakery owners. John called me at four thirty and my first instinct was to ask him who died. Or, due to past experience, where the body was.

"Sorry to wake you, Norrie, but when the guys and I got here a few minutes ago, we noticed someone had been monkeying around with one of our outdoor vats. That's where the Cab-Franc is fermenting. We're supposed to rack it today. Herbert is pulling up the surveillance video as we speak. In light of Billsburrow's situation, I phoned the sheriff's office and a deputy is on his way. Thought you should know ASAP."

"Did they do any damage to the wine?"

"We don't know yet, but we will. I also phoned Franz. He muttered something in German and said he was on his way. If they added chips thinking it was the traminette and not Cab-Franc, it would do damage but not ruin the wine entirely. Just give it a darker, headier oak taste. Plus, with the racking, we'd be able to remove most of the wood chips. The vandalism was recent."

"How did you know the vat was vandalized?"

"A lever was moved slightly, and whoever it was, wasn't too careful. Tire tracks in the snow leading up to the patio, plus they must have brought their own ladder because there were idents in the snow and some sort of substance on the barrel going up in a straight line. Whoever it was must have had some sort of ink or something on his or her gloves. Anyway, I'm sure a forensics crew will dust for prints."

"I can be down there in fifteen minutes."

"No need. When I told dispatch about it, they were very specific. The lab technician is a guy named Eugene and he left instructions that you were to keep away. Anything I should know?"

"Eugene gets rattled easily. He needs to chill."

John laughed. "I'll phone you back once Herbert reviews the footage and Franz tastes the wine."

"Sounds good. I'll let the tasting room crew know what's going on."

"Our vandal may have thought it was a traminette vat since Billsburrow's was outside. I'm going to give a heads-up to Lakeside Vineyards near Dresden. They're producing a small quantity of traminette as well."

"Sounds good. Let me know if anything else happens."

"I hope to heck not! Have a good morning."

"Have a good morning." Not again! Especially since Two Witches is now on the traminette hit list.

It was now a little before five and I was too wired to go back to sleep. And, since it was way too early to call Madeline's realtor, I did what I was paid to do—work on my paranormal cozy mystery in a quaint setting. Or at least I thought that was what Renee wanted. I raced to my desk to check my notes and then began to write in earnest.

Charlie nudged me at a little after six and I fed him and let him out. Still no call from John. I resisted the impulse to race down there for fear Eugene would pack up and leave. This time for a lab in Seneca Falls like he threatened to do numerous times before.

According to most of the deputies, my "abrasive, demanding decorum" scared the daylights out of him. Unbelievable!

For the first time in months, I got to the winery and unlocked the entrance before the tasting room crew arrived. Then, I booted up my computer and headed over to the bistro for a large coffee.

"Norrie!" Fred exclaimed. "Is everything all right? Nothing happened to anyone, did it?"

"No, only some minor vandalism to one of our vats." I went on to explain what happened while Fred poured me a large coffee and added vanilla.

"You think it might be the same person who sabotaged Billsburrow's traminette?"

I shrugged. "Seems likely."

"We heard about Madeline. That's horrible. I can't imagine anyone thinking she could have murdered someone."

"Me neither. It's all circumstantial, but until a really viable suspect is uncovered, she's going to be the fall guy. Or gal, in this case."

"Listen, Emma and I hear all sorts of chatter in here. If something points to someone knowing anything at all, we'll give a shout-out."

"Thanks, Fred. Good coffee!"

I returned to my office, coffee in hand, and perused my emails. Nothing spectacular, only a reminder note from Henry Speltmore, the president of the Seneca Lake Wine Trail, about making sure our walkways and parking lots remained clear for our winter guests. At least it wasn't one of his never-ending epistles about some nuance or other in the wine industry. No wonder his son Eli was such a miscreant. Having a Boy Scout for a dad must be a challenge.

• • •

I deleted the email and contemplated phoning Godfrey. True, it was early, but he gets to that lab by seven, so it wasn't as if I'd be waking him. I only hoped he hadn't turned his cell phone off.

"It's five thirty-nine! Is everything all right?" Godfrey's voice was louder than usual.

"Not exactly. Glad you're up."

"I'm always up early. You're the one who confuses noon with dawn. So what's going on?"

"Someone tampered with one of our stainless-steel barrels that was on the patio. Cab-Franc fermenting. They might have thought it was traminette."

"Lots of damage?"

"Not to the vat, but we won't know about the product until later. The sheriff's office is sending a deputy and Eugene."

"Steer clear of Eugene if you expect him to get any analysis done."

"Aarugh. You're like the third person who told me that. Listen, word gets around. I found out from someone at Billsburrow that your lab is looking into pantry pests and they confiscated something from their winery kitchen. Is that what was found on the tarp? Come on, you can tell me. Everyone else seems to know."

"It's going to be disclosed to the public today or tomorrow. I submitted the first part of my report yesterday. And yes, Lasioderma serricorne, or drugstore beetles, often found in grain-based products, and Tribolium confusum and T. castaneum, more commonly known as flour beetles."

"And the second part of your report?"

"Comparing the insects found in Madeline's kitchen to what I identified on the tarp."

"Aren't they all the same?"

Godfrey gasped and I knew the noose was tightening on Madeline's neck. "No, they have distinguishing features. Their antennae for one thing. And the coloring for another. It's not definitive, but if they are indeed the same beetle, then it's a possibility they may have emanated from Billsburrow Winery."

"Every winery deals with those things at one time or another."

"Like I said, it's not definitive, but it may add to a preponderance of evidence."

"I see. Hmm, you said grain and flour beetles, right?"

"Uh-huh. Why?"

"Because restaurants have them too. And there are lots of restaurants on this lake whose views would be destroyed by that high-rise."

"But no restaurant owners were seen having verbal altercations like Madeline."

Or that fingerprint evidence on Stanley's shoe. No need to remind me.

"If you find out anything, good, bad, or indifferent, let me know, will you?"

"Do I have a choice? And keep me posted on that barrel tampering. One occurrence is concerning, two smacks of a pattern."

"Yeah. The same thought crossed my mind. Say, how about we grab coffee later this week? We can catch up. I'll even treat."

"You've got a deal. I'll give you a buzz or text."

"Great. And glad I didn't wake you."

Godfrey laughed and I ended the call.

By now it was a little past six. I'd never been to the winery so early or so wide awake. I went into the kitchen and took the clean racks of wineglasses from the dishwasher and set them on the table to be moved to the tasting room. Then I checked the mini-fridges to make sure they had ample wine, and set out the bowls for crackers before returning to my office. At least Cammy would have less to do when she got here.

I was about to return to the bistro to grab a breakfast sandwich or toast when my phone buzzed—John! Maybe they had some answers regarding possible product tampering or worse.

"Hey, John, what's up? Did you find out anything yet?"

"Franz and Alan sampled the vat. It was tampered with, all right. Abundance of oaky taste. They're racking it right now. Worse-case scenario, the wine will have to be used for a blend. Actually, that's not the worst-case scenario. Eugene and other gentlemen from the forensic team will be checking for toxins."

"Toxins? Seriously?"

"Between you and me, it's highly doubtful. The wood chips were obvious. I think the intent was to ruin the wine, not poison anyone. Still, it's unsettling. But there's something else. We may have lucked out."

"How so?"

"A crumbled piece of paper was found underneath the barrel. It must have blown in there. The top part was ripped off but it looks like it was written on the back of a receipt or order pad from Dahl Farms. It was hard to determine."

"What did it say?"

"It was a short list of wineries with one name crossed off—

Billsburrow. Two Witches was next on the list followed by Lakeside Vineyards. I was right. Someone may be targeting the wineries who started producing traminette."

All of sudden, my head began to swim. Dahl Farms. I knew they had a motive for axing Stanley, but why on earth would they mess with the traminette? Then again, if it was a receipt and not an order pad, anyone could have one.

"I take it the lab will check for prints?"

"Prints, substances, you name it. Listen, that's not all."

"Oh no. Now what?"

"The piece of paper also had an asterisk next to our name. Not sure what it means. Anyway, don't go snooping around and make sure you don't leave the winery alone in the dark."

"You sound like my mother. And Bradley. And Godfrey. And Theo and Don."

"Fine. I'm in good company."

"Thanks, John. I'll be okay. Keep me posted and give my regards to Eugene."

Chapter 18

I had to admit, it was rather unsettling to have our winery singled out, but that asterisk could have meant we were next in line for a hit. Anyway, it was something I figured Eugene and his lab cronies would be able to discern. I proceeded to the bistro, shared that info with Emma and Fred, and devoured an egg frittata with ham. Then it was back to my office and Renee's screenplay. Then I waited until eight thirty, which I deemed a reasonable time to call Madeline's realtor.

Joyce MacKenna from Seneca View Realty answered my call after two rings. I was thankful I didn't have to deal with voicemail.

"Hi! I'm Norrie Ellington from Two Witches Winery in Penn Yan and I'm hoping you can help me out."

"I'll try. I've heard about your winery and will have to stop over there sometime. Preferably when it's not so cold."

"I don't blame you. It's more fun sampling wine when your fingers aren't frostbitten. Anyway, I'm calling about a friend of mine, Madeline Martinez. She—"

"I know. I heard the news but I can't believe it. What were those deputies thinking?"

"They weren't. That's why I'm calling you. I believe the real killer is literally getting away with murder and Madeline is being railroaded."

"How can I help?"

"Stanley Hurst outbid her in a sneaky backhanded way and she lost out on that property across the lake. I think Madeline may not have been the only person making an offer. That property is prime real estate, and if Stanley was interested, I'd bet dollars to donuts so were other developers. Maybe ruthless ones like Stanley who could have very well done him in so that the property would come up again for sale."

"Hmm, that's a viable premise, but even if there were other interested parties, it would be hard to prove they were culpable in anything."

"Nevertheless, it's worth looking into and the sheriffs' offices aren't about to do that. I was hoping you might be able to find out for me and let me know."

"It's not that easy, Norrie. There's client confidentiality involved, but I can tell you that Madeline was my only interested party. Stanley had another realtor. A competitor."

I sighed and didn't say a word because I wasn't sure where to go with this. Then, Joyce continued speaking. "Listen, I have a county real estate agents' brunch tomorrow morning at Belhurst Castle. The best I can do is ask around. Give me your number and I'll call you tomorrow or text you if I find out anything. Maybe the rules can be bent considering the circumstances."

"Oh my gosh. Thank you so much! It's kind of a last-ditch effort but it may lead to something."

"I understand."

When I got off the phone, I felt confident Joyce would have a name for me. Maybe even more than one. Those developers can be ruthless when it comes to finding property that meets their project needs. And as far as murder is concerned, it's that old adage—People have killed for less.

It was a little before nine and I knew the public safety building in Canandaigua would be open by the time I got there. I shot off a quick text to Cammy telling her I'd done some of the setup and I'd be in once I saw Madeline.

She replied with a thumbs-up.

I was glad I wore a heavy sweatshirt and a fleece jacket. The cold was that damp miserable kind that gets under your skin and makes you question why on earth you're still living in upstate New York. As I exited the winery, I locked the door and glanced over at Alvin's pen. He was still in his little hut and it looked as if the vineyard guys gave him enough hay to eat and frolic around with. Thankful he didn't race over to the fence to spit at me, I walked back to the house and started up the Toyota.

Thirty-five minutes later, I pulled into the Ontario County Jail, located on County Complex Drive, off County Road 46 and a stone's throw from the Humane Society. I had used a link before I left the winery to book a visit with Madeline, thankful visiting hours ran on Sundays as well as the other six days. Last thing I needed was to be turned away.

Like the Yates County Jail, this one was all business. A rectangular brick building with a number of glass panels shielded by bars. The parking lot was ample and I had no problem finding a spot near the entrance. I took a breath, grabbed my bag and walked straight to the main entrance.

I'd been through jail visitations before and this one was no different. Not far from a TSA check-in but without the plane flight. I provided the guard with Madeline's name, and since I was already on the list, I was asked to sit in a reception area until a deputy could escort me to the visitation area.

Thoughts of Madeline behind a glass panel with a phone receiver sprang to mind, but that wasn't the case. I was taken to a small room with a two-way window, a metal table, and two metal chairs. A minute or so later, Madeline was escorted in and both of us were told we'd have thirty minutes and not a second more.

She wore the orange county uniform, which did little to promote her slender figure. At least her hair was done and she had makeup on.

"Norrie! When I was told you'd be here, I was ecstatic. With the exception of my husband and my lawyer, no one has been here. Catherine called as well as Stephanie but I was unable to speak with them. The guard delivered their messages. Mostly expressions of concern."

"Yeah. All of us in WOW are concerned." *Mainly because we don't want to take over.* "Theo, Don, and I are looking into other suspects. And your realtor, Joyce, may be able to find out if any other developers put in an offer, because that would give them a motive to knock off Stanley."

"That's hopeful news, I suppose, but it's not looking good for me. Two much circumstantial evidence." She laced her fingers and put them on the table. I could see some of the burgundy polish had been chipped and I wondered if she had bitten them.

"I'm also trying to get information on Stanley's wife. I can't say more, except that she's a suspect in my book. You know, the spouse thing."

"Don't do anything that would put you or the Grey Egret guys in jeopardy."

"No worries. So far, our prying has only been on paper and on the computer." *But not for long.* "Tell me, what did your lawyer say?"

"He's trying to get me released since the evidence isn't concrete and I'm not a risk to the general community. He's optimistic that he'll succeed but I'll need to wear an ankle monitor and not be able to leave our property. Hey, anything to get out of here. Although, I must admit, the food's been pretty good. It's a minimum-security lockup so most of the guests are first time petty offenders. Forged checks, minor theft, that sort of thing."

"Any news on your traminette tampering?"

"None yet. What a loss for us. And we were just getting started with this new variety."

I told her about our incident and the evidence found, including the note. She swallowed and widened her eyes. "So it wasn't a one-shot deal. I mean, we weren't singled out and targeted. But still, from what you said, it was a short list."

"Do you think the traminette incidents and Stanley's murder could somehow be connected?"

Madeline shook her head. "I don't see how. He wasn't in the wine business, but then again, I have no idea what kind of business the wife was in. Or who his connections were. Especially if we're talking payoffs and favors. He was also a rather disagreeable man. Who knows who he managed to tick off."

"Madeline, you're in the perfect position to eke out information.

Canandaigua, Geneva, and Penn Yan are small-town places. Gossip hubs. And everyone is related to everyone else. Follow the conversations in your pod. It *is* a pod, right? I once saw a special on county jails."

"Yes, that's what they call it. There are eight of us. Nice ladies. Okay, maybe thieves and swindlers, but nice personalities."

"Well, see what you can glean from them. We may have to widen the net if our original suspects don't pan out. Whatever you do, don't take a plea deal. You're innocent."

"Oh, believe me, I have no intention of pleading to anything."

"Good. Try to be positive."

"I am being positive. I'm being framed!"

When I left the jail, exactly twenty-nine minutes later, thoughts of Madeline being set up kept me on edge the entire way home. I mean, if that kind of thing could happen to her, it could happen to any of us. I took a deep breath and resolved to do whatever it would take to vindicate her.

• • •

"Hey, Norrie," Cammy called out when I stepped inside the winery. She was on her way to the kitchen with a rack of used wineglasses. "How'd your visit with Madeline go?"

I followed her to the sink. "About as good as could be expected, I suppose. Her lawyer will get her out on bail but the target points to her back. One good thing—she'll be able to pick up any street gossip from her fellow roommates."

"You mean inmates."

"I wanted to use softer wording."

"Oh, brother. Those women aren't sharing a dorm. They're sharing a cell block."

"They call it a pod."

"I think that's worse. You know, 'like peas in a pod.'"

106

"If she can get some answers, I'll take them. No matter what they call the place."

"I guess."

At that moment, Lizzie walked in. "Norrie, Godfrey Klein is on the phone for you."

"This could be important. He may know something. He's the leading bug guy for the tarp evidence." I rushed out of the kitchen and into my office, where I picked up the landline. "You compared the evidence and it's a different beetle, isn't it? You can get Madeline off the hook!"

"Whoa. Slow down. I'm still running the comparisons. That's not why I called."

"Oh."

"I forgot to ask you something. Three weeks from Friday, the entomology department is holding a symposium on the Order Blattodea, or roach. From seminars on the developmental changes in the oothecae, or egg case, to nuances in the exoskeleton. Not to mention the specific workshops on the varieties—the Periplaneta americana, or American cockroach, the Blattella germanica, or German cockroach, the Supella longipalpa, or brown-banded cockroach, and the filthiest of all—the Blatta orientalis, or Oriental cockroach, with its shiny black body. Alex Bollinger will be conducting the one on the brown-banded roach."

"Good for Alex. Good for the roach. Sounds horrible. Is that what you called to tell me?"

"No, I called to invite you to the dinner after the workshop. Oh, and that's not all. A number of esteemed speakers will be dazzling participants with updates on their own related insect studies."

That's even worse.

"Roaches aren't on the menu, are they?"

"Don't be ridiculous. It's being catered by Spinelli's out of Rochester. Hold on, here are the choices: prime rib, chicken marsala, marinated salmon, and some vegetarian ones. Eggplant and zucchini parmesan, vegetable lasagna, and cauliflower couscous with assorted mushrooms."

"Spinelli's, huh? They're supposed to be amazing."

"So, you'll come as my plus one?"

"If I don't have to attend any of the roach lectures or be forced to look at slides during the dinner."

"You might find those lectures interesting. We've got panels, discussion groups, and numerous presentations."

"Do they have one on selecting the best kind of insect spray?"

"Actually, a representative from Orkin will be conducting a program on how to eradicate them with a solid treatment plan."

"Oh my gosh. I wasn't being serious."

"Pest removal is serious business. Lots of entomologists go into that line of research. Anyway, I thought you might enjoy the dinner."

"Actually, it does sound good. What time and where?"

"At the Scandling Campus Center. Banquet area. Seven p.m."

"I'll meet you there. Put me down for the eggplant and zucchini. And thanks. But maybe we can talk about something other than roaches."

"I should have more information on the pantry pests. That should make for some very interesting conversation."

And maybe the evidence we need to spring Madeline from jail or house arrest.

"By the way, Norrie, did you remember to refrigerate the roach DNA?"

"It's in the small dormitory fridge in our basement, tucked behind an old couch. I didn't want it near any of my food in case it leaked."

"It's got a special seal. It won't leak. Trust me. That stuff's more valuable than gold."

Great. Maybe I can start an IRA with it.

"Really?"

"And how. It's being used in the labs for the purpose of isolating potential lifespan altering."

"Seriously? Roaches?"

"They're impervious to most anything and their DNA is highly sought after. Not an easy process to extricate it. Most research labs would give their eyeteeth to get their hands on it. You're sitting on the treasure of the Sierra Madre."

Complete with the disgusting factor.

"Uh, yeah. A gift to be truly treasured."

"For sure. Anyway, glad you'll be joining me at the dinner."

"Me too. Thanks for asking."

Chapter 19

Mondays are notoriously slow and today was no exception. The frigid air had reached its misery level as far as I was concerned, and I knew it signaled a snowstorm would be on its way.

According to the news, Wednesday would be the lucky day. Then again, they've been known to get it wrong before. Worse than the impending weather was the wait. Wait to hear from the lab about any prints on our Cab-Franc barrel or the note. Wait until Godfrey's pantry pest comparison was done. Wait to hear from Joyce about a possible new player. Wait to hear from Theo to see what he found out about Audrey, and finally, wait to hear from Renee to see if the screenplay I started was what she wanted. Ugh. I felt as if I was on the deli line at Wegmans on a Saturday morning.

Thankfully there was one thing I didn't have to wait for—the surveillance footage. Herbert phoned me shortly after my call with Godfrey ended the night before. It was good news and downright frightening news, all rolled into a ball.

"Got the footage results, Norrie," Herbert said. "Thought you'd want to know. You could also pop down here if you want to see for yourself."

"What did it show?"

"A medium-height figure with a dark hoodie. Also dark pants. Maybe jeans. Hard to say. Impossible to see the face or determine if it was a man or woman. But whoever it was, they were in good physical shape. They had one of those fold-up ladders and used it to get on top of the tank. Couldn't really see them adding the chips but the evidence is indisputable. Unfortunately, the car they drove wasn't in range. At least not at that time."

"What do you mean?"

"This is the part you're not going to like."

"I don't like any of this. Go on."

"We ran the outside video to the road and a car went uphill past the winery to your house. Had to be his. Or hers."

"And you couldn't get a license?"

"Snow-covered and blurry. The guys at the sheriff's office will see if they can pull anything up."

"Did the surveillance tape give you the time?"

"Sure. Three fifteen in the morning."

"Close call. John gets there around four."

"Someone may have known that. It's the usual starting time for vineyard workers. Listen, you may want to have a look-see around your place. If you notice anything out of the ordinary, call the sheriff's office. We'll also run that tape a bit longer to see if anything else appears."

"Thanks, Herbert."

I thought back to yesterday morning but nothing out of the ordinary sprang to mind. Then again, I wasn't looking for tire tracks or anything else. Besides, with a light snow falling, any tracks would have been covered. But what if the saboteur snuck around the windows? Ew! That was an image I didn't need. Then again, they may have dropped something that would help to identify them.

"I need to go back to the house for a few minutes," I told Lizzie as I grabbed the doorknob and braced myself for the cold, damp air.

"Everything all right?"

"I hope so. Just checking on something."

"I'll let Cammy know."

"Thanks. I'll be back in a jiff."

I wasn't exactly sure what I'd be looking for but I figured the window ledges on the first floor would be a good start as well as the front porch and rear door.

Charlie charged out to his fenced-in yard the second he heard me pull up. Odd, but if someone *did* drive a car up here, wouldn't he have barked? Even if he was inside. Dogs' hearing is very acute.

"Hey, Charlie! I'll be inside in a minute. Good boy."

I walked the perimeter of the house and nothing was out of place or unusual. At first glance, none of the windows had been tampered with and the entrances seemed fine. Still, it was unsettling as all heck. Reaching for my key to the front door, I remembered a time when we never locked the house. Not even when we were gone for the entire day. But that was years ago and things changed. Even in small communities like ours.

As I turned the key, I glanced at the narrow glass panel that framed the left-hand side of the door and froze. The icy image of someone's face clung to the glass like an abstract painting, and two seconds later I was on the phone with one of the Yates County deputies.

"That's right. Someone peeked into my house. Send a forensics team. Can you use facial identification on glass prints? I've seen something like that on *FBI International*. I know for a fact this happened within minutes of our wine barrel getting tampered with."

"Slow down, Miss Ellington. I can't take notes if you talk nonstop."

Then take a course in shorthand. (If they still teach it.)

I inhaled and counted to five. No way could I make it to ten. Then, I explained everything Herbert told me.

The deputy's voice was calm and soft. "Fine. We'll send someone by. Don't touch anything, understood?"

"Yes. No problem. Thanks."

"And one more thing. We're the Yates County Sheriff's Office, not *FBI International*."

You think?

Once inside, I phoned the winery and let Lizzie know what was going on. Then I made myself a cup of coffee, refilled Charlie's food and hunted down my laptop. No sense wasting time when I could be in the paranormal mystery world making Renee happy.

Twenty-five minutes later, a forensics van pulled up along with a deputy car. There was only one deputy and it was Clarence, the only one in that office, other than Gladys, who didn't have a perpetual scowl on his or her face.

Then I looked to see who got out of the van and gasped. It was Eugene and he didn't appear to be overjoyed.

I rushed to the door and threw it open. "It's right here!" I pointed to the glass panel. "Look closely. I can see the outline."

"Our lab tech will take it from here." Clarence smiled. "Mind if I step inside to get a statement? It's miserable out here."

I motioned him inside and took a step toward Eugene. "You might want to take a photo of it first. It's pretty clear, isn't it? If I were you, I'd also dust for prints. They might be on the frame."

Eugene looked up and I swore he shuddered. "Please don't tell me you're going to lean over my shoulder and direct me like you've done before."

"That was only once and I thought I'd be a help."

"You weren't."

"Fine." I started to follow Clarence into the house, then turned to Eugene. "Um, would you like a cup of coffee or maybe hot chocolate?"

"Thank you, no. I want to complete my job as soon as possible and get back to the lab."

"Yes. A much better idea. And if you don't mind, I'd like to leave you with two words—facial recognition."

"Miss Ellington, we're dealing with an icy imprint on glass. Not a three-dimensional image from a living person. No matter what the movies or TV show."

"That's a bummer. You guys really need to work on the technology."

"I'll be sure to put that in my notes. Now, if you don't mind, I'd like to get started."

"Absolutely." I walked past him to where Clarence stood in the foyer. Like Eugene, he declined a hot drink as well. I gave him my statement and once he wrote it, he repeated it to be sure it was accurate. Then he headed back to the sheriff's office, leaving Eugene to contend with the icy image on the glass panel.

There was no reason for me to hang around, so I told Eugene I was going back to the winery. I think it was the first time I saw him smile.

"Someone snooped around your house Sunday night?" Theo asked when I called him a few minutes later from my office. The tasting room was running smoothly so no need for me to step in.

"That's right. Eugene is dusting for prints or whatever it is he's doing. It's really creepy."

"I'll say. Make sure your doors and windows are locked. And keep your cell phone within reach."

"My cell phone is practically glued to me. It's a generational thing."

Theo laughed. "Hey, wanted to let you know Audrey's bakery is closed on Mondays but I plan on going over there first thing tomorrow morning. I'll poke and pry around. Then I'll let you know if I turn up anything."

"Thanks. I'm on hold with everything else and that means one thing. I should have mentioned it the other night. We really should take a closer look at Dahl Farms."

"By 'closer look,' you don't mean a little after-hours BE, do you?"

"Well, not when you put it *that* way. Besides, it's not really breaking and entering if the place isn't locked tight. More like visiting when no one's around."

"I'd love to hear you explain that to a judge."

"I'm serious. The Diamante truck was at Dahl Farms on more than one occasion. And we know for a fact they didn't candle their eggs. What we need to find out is if Stanley blackmailed them and Victor had no choice but to kill him."

"And how do you propose to do that?"

"Everyone has a paper trail. Even if it's on a computer. We need to get into their office and track it down. You know as well as I do that the sheriffs' offices aren't going near this."

"That's because they don't have any evidence."

"Well, we do. And word of mouth speaks louder than circumstantial hoo-ha."

"Remind me to have that silk-screened onto a T-shirt."

"Very funny. So, are you in?"

"We'll see."

"Oh no! Not the 'we'll see.' My parents always said that. It's synonymous with *no*!"

"Fine. I'll give it some thought."

"Much better. Oh, and one last thing."

"Aargh. What?"

"Actually, who. It's Avery Pullman. We're not done with him."

"One thing at a time, Norrie. You're making my head spin."

"Take a breath. I'm just getting started."

Chapter 20

We had a steady stream of customers for the rest of the day so the time went fast and it was five fifteen before I knew it.

"Expect a larger crowd tomorrow," Cammy said as she wiped down a table. "Whenever a storm is forecast, people stock up on wine like nobody's business. If you ask me, it's because they're anticipating a horrible day at home with the kids."

"My mother always put us to work. Dusting. Vacuuming. Or worse yet, cleaning pantry shelves."

"It's the twenty-first century. The best they can hope for is that the Wi-Fi doesn't go down."

"Heck, that's the best I can hope for."

Sure enough, Cammy was right. The next day started off busy and remained that way. The storm was supposed to make an entrance the following morning with heavy bands of lake effect snow coupled with wind and the accompanying white-out driving conditions. Even the schools got one step ahead of the game and canceled classes for Wednesday. If Theo and I had any chance of snooping around Dahl Farms, it would have to be now.

"What?" He shrieked over the phone when I called him at noon. "I'm still pulling myself together from this morning's foray over to the bakery. Too busy here to phone you and I didn't think you'd appreciate a shocked emoji on a text."

"What did you find out? Any obvious impaler-like instruments laying around?"

"None that I could see. But I did have a rather interesting conversation with Audrey. Boy, she really does have it in for Madeline."

"What else is new?"

"She also had it in for Avery. Made no bones about it. Said he was a self-serving snit who'd sell out his own mother."

"Yeesh. What about Stanley? Any mention of Stanley?"

"Said she didn't want to speak ill of the dead, then went right ahead and did exactly that."

"Any chance she despised him enough to do him in?"

"Even if she did, I don't know how she'd pull it off. She's a wiry wisp of a woman. Oh, and one more thing. I don't think the pantry pests came from her bakery. She's got rosemary and lavender all over the place. I was pretty clever about how I got her to talk about it. I told her that with winter here, it's a concern for the wineries. Then she went on to tell me what she does and how well it works. Hasn't seen a weevil or flour bug anywhere."

"Okay, guess we can scratch her off the list. Time to pay Dahl Farms a visit and tonight's our best shot. Well, our only shot. We're working tomorrow and that storm is moving in."

"I'm not liking this, Norrie."

"Think of Madeline. No. Wait. Think of WOW. You're not going to like that either."

"Ugh. What time?"

"How about seven thirty. That will give us enough time to have a bite to eat."

"Forget the bite to eat. I need enough time to figure out a way to break it to Don so he doesn't go bat-poop crazy!"

• • •

At precisely seven thirty, I pulled up in front of Theo and Don's house, adjacent to their winery. Theo must have been at the window because seconds later, he burst through the door and over to the car. It was a moonless night, and if it wasn't for their porch light, I wouldn't have seen him.

"You look like you've been exiled to Siberia," I said as he fastened the seat belt.

"Yeah. I ditched the jacket and sweatshirt for my parka. In case we get stuck on the road or something."

"The storm isn't coming until tomorrow."

"I'm not taking any chances. Those jail cells can be quite cold."

"Thank you, Mr. Optimism. We're not going to get caught. I have a plan. Sort of."

"Do tell."

"Emma and Fred have been to Dahl Farms for their eggs and they're familiar with the layout. All I told them was that I was curious. Anyway, the office is connected to one of the barns. The cows, I think, but Emma wasn't too specific. Barn doors are rarely locked. All we need to do is get into the barn and make our way over to the office. Easy peasy."

"Unless we trip an alarm."

"We won't. Those cows move around and they'd be setting off alarms all the time."

"What about the owners? Won't they see us from their house?"

"Emma said they live behind the barn on the hill. About a quarter mile away. We should be fine."

"I hope you're right."

I hope so, too.

Dahl Farms was a large operation, located on County House Road, above Keuka Lake, in Penn Yan. If they were in Manhattan, their five-barn operation would have taken up an entire city block.

There were a few farmhouses on the road but spaced far apart so it wasn't as if anyone would see us pulling into the driveway on the south side of the road. The nearest house, other than the owners', had to be at least three-quarters of a mile away and no other houses were in sight. I was thankful Emma and Fred knew the area.

"You may be right, Norrie. Looks like clear sailing."

"Aaargh! Don't say that. You'll jinx it."

Oh my gosh. I sound like Glenda.

I killed the headlights as I pulled into the driveway and parked adjacent to a large pine tree. "Okay, it's showtime. We tiptoe over to the barn and try the door. It's got to be a glider and I doubt it's locked. I can see some dim lights through the barn slats."

"Yeah, well, that's all I can see."

"It's all we need. Come on."

Theo and I walked quietly to the barn, even though there was no one around. When we got to the sliding door he poked my elbow. "Take a look. One out of two isn't bad. Slider, yes. Unlocked, no."

"Rats. We need to look closely." I pulled out my cell phone and turned on the flashlight. "Drat. It's a combination lock. Who uses combination locks other than high school students?"

"Dahl Farms, apparently. Now what?"

I thought back to high school and remembered helping one of my girlfriends break into her ex-boyfriend's locker. All we did was move the knob and listen for a slight click. Then move it in the opposite direction and back.

"I think I can do this," I said. "We have nothing to lose."

"Tell that to Don."

I handed Theo my phone and told him to focus the light on the lock. Then I leaned in and listened. Sure enough, the clicks. I held my breath and told myself that if it worked before in high school, it would work again. Those locks haven't changed.

One click. One backtrack. Another click. And release!

"I really didn't expect that to happen." Theo handed me my phone and I removed the lock. He slid the door open and we stepped inside. Dim lighting but plenty of it. And cows, all right. Lots of them. Each in their own small pen with sand or sawdust on the floor. Some were moving about but the others were lying on the ground, oblivious to us. The only thing we weren't oblivious to was the smell. Even with an overhead air system going, it still stunk to high heaven.

Theo gave me a nudge and whispered, "Don't do anything to upset the cows like you do to Alvin."

"The goat hates me. That's all there is to it. These cows don't know me."

"Give them time. Come on, we need to find the office and get this over with."

As we looked around, one thing became clear—the barn was enormous and we had no idea which narrow path between the pens was the one that led to the office. We'd start down one row only to find it led to another and we found ourselves in what could best be described as a corn maze but without the fun.

"I think we went down this row before," I said. "That brown cow looks familiar."

"They're either brown or black and white. They all look familiar."

"We can't keep walking around in circles. Think!"

"Okay, let's try to get to the perimeter. There's got to be a door on the perimeter." Theo walked to one of the pens and hoisted himself on one of the wooden rungs. "Hey, I see it. A door! It's on the left but I don't see how we can find the row to get there."

"Can we get there if we climb through the pens and keep going?" I looked at the cows and wondered if there had ever been a cow attack.

"I suppose. We don't have much choice." He flung himself over the barrier and held out his hand for me to follow. "Act calm and focused. Hopefully the cows will go about their business. The good news is that there's only one in each pen so they won't stampede us."

"Stampede us? Do cows do that?"

"Bulls do. And cows are female bulls."

I looked at the large animals half asleep in their pens and prayed they'd remain that way. Then, I took a breath and hoisted myself over the barrier too. First one barrier, then three more. So far, so good. None of the cows appeared to be interested in us.

Theo was a few feet ahead of me and I could see a narrow sliver of light coming from the office door. "It's open. And that's a night-light if you were wondering. Hurry up."

I hurled myself over the last barrier and followed Theo inside the office, careful not to bump into anything in case the place was rigged.

"Okay, now what, Miss Marple?"

The office was small, consisting of a straight-back wooden chair, an office chair, two desks, both with computers, and two four-drawer file cabinets. Other than a large calendar on the wall featuring scenes of the dairy industry, the place was as plain and uninviting as could be. It was hard to tell what color the walls were but my guess was beige or a horrid shade of green.

There was one double-hung window with Venetian blinds pulled down and closed.

"There's enough light in here from the night-lights on the floor so let's leave it that way," I said. "No sense calling attention to the place."

"Where do you want to begin? And what is it we're looking for? I have a nebulous idea that it's some sort of correspondence implicating Stanley."

"Yeah. We've got to find something that shows Victor Dahl was being blackmailed or bribed. An ironclad motive for murder. I'll take the desk with the office chair and you can have the other one. Root around. If it's a bust, we go to step two."

"Which is?"

"Seeing if we can get into one of the computers."

"If you ask me, that's the first thing we should do, providing they're not password-protected. Everything is on the computer these days."

"Not everything," I said. "Not when it comes to extortion. Perpetrators don't want to leave a cyber trail."

"I don't think they'd want to leave a paper trail either. Okay, fine. Let's root first."

The next five minutes were spent in silence as Theo and I opened desk drawers and pried into Dahl Farms' workspace. Together we uncovered paper clips, broken pens, hard gum, a magnifying glass, lots of scrap paper, wadded up tissues, a ruler, an old calculator, a stapler and reams of plain paper. Not exactly what one would deem a treasure trove.

Some of the scrap paper had phone numbers written on them but no names.

"Ready to play cyber sleuth?" Theo booted up one of the computers and waited for it to start. "Yep. Needs a password. Now what?"

"Hmm, try Dahl."

"Nope. Next?"

"Try Dahl Farms."

"Nope. One more or we'll be locked out for thirty minutes. Don't know about you, but I can smell those cows and it's not pretty."

I looked at the calendar on the wall and crossed my fingers. "Try County House Cows."

"Holy Canaveral! It worked! We're in. Where'd you get *that* from?"

"There's a pile of mail on this desk and the top envelope is addressed to County House Cows. It's from a grain vendor."

"Maybe we'll be in luck after all."

Too bad those words were spoken way too soon because luck was the last thing we had. Unfortunately, we didn't know it at the time.

Chapter 21

"Want to try the other computer as well?" I asked Theo.

"Let's stick to this one and see how far we get. The home screen has a lovely pasture background and a zillion icons. I'm heading straight over to their Word file."

The good thing about Word files is that they're easily accessible. Not like spreadsheets that require some serious interpretation. The bad thing is that file names don't always tell the viewer what the file really is.

"See if you can find anything under Diamante, Stanley, or Hurst."

Theo's response was quick. "Zilch. There's a template for contracts but nothing specific and maybe—wait a sec—we're in the wrong place. It wouldn't be in a Word document, it would be in email. A whole new animal. Pray there's an icon for it because we have no idea if it's Roadrunner, Hotmail, Yahoo, Gmail, or any other kind of mail."

I leaned over and perused the screen. Theo was right. More icons than most computers, but sure enough, the Microsoft mail icon stood out and Theo clicked it.

"What do you see? What do you see?" I was literally chomping at the bit.

"I see the standard blue line to the left with mail, folders, and all that stuff, plus the incoming mail. What I *feel* is your breath on my neck."

"Oops. Sorry. I'll back up a bit. Now what do you see?"

"The same stuff I saw before. Hold on, Norrie. I'll move to the left and then we can both see the screen."

"Looks like a list of orders to me. Click one."

I took a breath as Theo clicked the Penn Yan Market and we saw an order for thirty dozen large eggs and twenty dozen medium ones. "No surprise there. I think we can cross out the vendors we recognize. Does anything else stand out?"

"Yeah. Dahl Farms doesn't let their email pile up like I do. The incoming list is relatively short. Jump for a sec to trash and see what's there."

"Nothing. Same with spam and junk. Hang on, I'll see if the Sent list is long."

I pulled my scarf tighter around my neck. Apparently Dahl Farms didn't bother to heat their office at night. Only the bare minimum to keep the pipes from freezing.

Theo shook his head. "Only three Sent messages and they're all correspondence back to vendors."

"Okay, go back to incoming and we'll scrutinize it."

I furrowed my brow to get a closer look and for a moment, both of us were as quiet as could be. Finally Theo spoke. "Some utility companies and a few names but none of them say Diamante, Stanley, or Hurst."

"If you were blackmailing or bribing someone, you wouldn't use your real name either. If I'm counting correctly, there are only eight of them. Quick. Open each one for a look-see."

"Sure. Got nothing else to do." He gave me a kick in the ankle and I laughed.

"Hold on a minute. I'll be darned. Open up the one from Rantsshut at gmail dot com. I think it's an anagram for Stanley Hurst."

"There's no *l e y* in it."

"But there's a Stan. Open it."

The message was clear, succinct and bone-chilling. "Slip slop. We know what you've done. Better watch your cows or your milk will run dry."

"Oh my gosh." I shook Theo's shoulder. "If that's not a downright threat, I don't know what is."

"Norrie, we don't know what this is about. It could be anything. And it might not even come from the late Stanley Hurst."

"Check the date."

"Written two days before he met his maker."

"It was Stanley, all right," I said. "No doubt he had that egg thing hanging over Victor's head so Victor sent him packing. For good."

"Speculation."

"Evidence."

"Whatever. Can you print it out? Looks like there's a shared printer in here."

"It better not get stuck. That's all we need."

"Well, we can't forward it. They'd know."

"Cross your fingers the machine works. And by the way, you can't show this to Grizzly Gary or we'll be the ones under lock and key."

"I know that. But it's a start."

The printer started up with a grinding sound and in that second, I knew we'd be in for trouble, but the trouble we were about to have had nothing to do with printing an email. That was the easy part. Theo tucked it in his pocket and nodded at me. "Done. Let's get out of here."

"We can't go out the same way we went in because we were lost in a maze. What makes you think we'll be any better at it this time in the dark? And worse luck, we'll wind up stepping in cow dung. As it is, my clothes smell just from the fumes."

"The only option is the front door. We can unlock it from the inside. Then skirt around and relock the barn." Theo flashed his cell phone at the door. "Two locks and one is a dead bolt. We'll only be able to lock the regular one and hope that whoever unlocks it thinks someone forgot to lock the dead bolt."

"It's a plan. Let's hurry."

Our exit strategy went well. Until it didn't. As the door closed shut behind us, someone's headlights were visible on a small driveway we hadn't noticed on the other side of the building.

Theo stopped one step shy of opening the door. "Oh no! Did you hear that? Their car door slammed. That means whoever it is must be headed to the office. Where else would they go?"

"Nowhere but here. Hurry! We've got no choice but to go back into the cow barn."

"Crap."

It was one word but it sure was prophetic. Theo and I closed the door behind us and climbed the first barrier into one of the pens. Thankfully our eyes were still accustomed to the low-level lighting because we never turned the lights on in the office while we were there.

Seconds later we heard a man's voice. "Can't believe I left my cell phone here."

"I don't think there's anyone else," I whispered. "No other voices."

The man continued. "What the—Now I remember. I set it down in the milking room and forgot about it."

Next thing I knew, he turned on the lights in the barn and Theo and I ducked into a pile of wet muck and didn't budge. The stench was overwhelming, but short of giving ourselves up, we had no choice. Unfortunately, the minute the guy flipped on the lights, one of the cows mooed. Then another.

I kept my voice as low as possible. "Those cows think it's feeding time."

"No kidding."

"We've got to make a move out of here before they either go berserk or the guy feeds them. Right now he's in the milking room. Hurry!"

"How fast can you jump that barrier?"

"Like the speed of light."

We stood and made a run back to the office with Theo in the lead. Out the door and across the lawn toward the main driveway. It wasn't until we got into my car when we realized just how putrid that manure was.

"Ew! I'll never be able to wash this out of my hair," I said.

"Your hair? I'll never be able to explain this to Don."

"Forget Don. Think of my car. It's going to reek. Especially when I turn on the heat."

"Don't turn on anything. We need to wait until whoever it was drives out of here. Shouldn't be too long."

"Too long? Look! His car lights came on and he's halfway down the other drive. Talk about a close call! My pulse is still racing."

"Need I remind you that this was your idea?"

"Yeah, but now we have some evidence that Victor might indeed be our killer."

"Um, it was a threat, all right, but not exactly an admission of murder."

"It's a start. Can you take a photo of the email and send it to me? That way both of us will have a copy."

"On it right now." I glanced over and Theo held his phone over the printed sheet of paper that rested on one knee.

"Now what do you propose? It's a really nebulous email but yeah, it does have threatening overtones."

"I suppose we should have another look-see at the other yes-vote suspects. If nothing else we should rule them out. Then we can focus on Victor Dahl and come up with a plan."

"I dread the thought of what *that* may be. So, who's next on your merry list?"

"The chitchat ladies confirmed that Diane had all sorts of money problems. Makes her a good candidate for taking a bribe, but I don't know what motive she'd have for killing Stanley. Same deal with Michael. His company reneged on his pension so taking a bribe might not have been too far off."

"Hmm, Diamante is big business. Big money. But after the vote was taken, Stanley could have reneged. And face it, there'd be no way for Michael to get his money, since he broke the law as well."

"What about Avery?" I asked. "Anyone could have written that threatening note. Even Avery himself. It wouldn't be the first time someone did something like that to take all suspicion off of them."

"That note was written before Stanley's dead body showed up."

"All the more reason if the murder was premeditated."

"That's chilling. All right, on the spin-the-dial to see who's next, my vote goes to Avery. Let's take a deep dive on this and see where it gets us."

"At least it won't land us in manure," I said and laughed.

What we didn't know was that it would land us in hot water. And hot water can be scalding.

Chapter 22

The next morning was so bone-numbing that I thought my fingers would get frostbitten, even with gloves on. It seemed pointless to start up my car for less than a quarter mile down to the winery but halfway through my walk, I had second thoughts.

At a little before ten, I walked inside and was immediately greeted by Lizzie. "Morning, Norrie. You just missed Deputy Hickman's phone call. He's on his way over. Didn't sound too happy."

"He's never happy. Did he mention what it was about?"

"Nope. Only that he needed to speak with you."

"It could be good news. Maybe the lab found out who peered into my window the night our wine barrel was tampered with."

"Let's hope so."

I breezed into my office, booted up the computer, and then went to the bistro for a large coffee. My fingers hadn't yet thawed and I really needed to warm up and wake up. I'd spent most of the night trying to get the manure residue out of my car before showering and washing my clothes. One good thing—at least my parents decided to become vintners rather than dairy farmers.

A few minutes later, having greeted everyone, I started for my office when Grizzly Gary made his appearance. Lizzie was right. He looked even more craggy than usual. That heavy furrow line between his brows seemed to have gotten deeper and I could have sworn his eyelids drooped more than usual. Maybe he didn't get much sleep either.

"May I have a word with you, Miss Ellington?"

"Uh, sure. Let's go into my office. Do you want coffee or anything?"

"Thank you, no. I'm fine. This should only take a minute or so."

I offered him a chair and pulled mine next to it. "Is this news about the peeping Tom?"

He chuckled. "In a manner of speaking, yes. But not the one at your place."

Uh-oh. This isn't going to be good.

The deputy leaned back in his chair and looked directly at me. "I got a phone call this morning from Victor Dahl at Dahl Farms shortly after the farm report."

Really not good. And again with that farm report. "Uh-huh."

"He has a surveillance camera aimed at the driveways and checks it every morning."

I nodded and didn't say a word.

"Tell me, why was your car parked midway down his driveway at precisely seven forty-nine p.m.? And yes, I checked the license plate myself. Good thing New York State requires front and back licenses."

"I plead the Fifth."

"You're not on trial, Miss Ellington. *Yet.* Let's keep it that way, shall we?"

"All right. Theo and I drove over there to see if Stanley blackmailed or bribed him. We figured there would be some sort of evidence in the office. Like a letter, or email. If it was blackmail, then Victor would have had a motive for murder."

"So, essentially, breaking and entering."

"More like entering. We didn't break anything to get inside the barn door where the cows were. The barn led to the office."

Grizzly Gary ran his fingers through his hair. "Miss Ellington, that *is* considered breaking and entering. Look, I know how fanatical you can get when you think someone has been wronged. In this case, your friend Mrs. Martinez. However, taking chances like that can be dangerous, let alone against the law."

I nodded again and let him continue.

"You did *not* hear this from me. Understood?"

"Yes." My voice was barely a whisper.

"The evidence is strong enough against your friend to charge her with murder, however, in my experience, when that happens, it's almost too easy."

"So you're saying you think she's innocent?"

"I'm *saying* that I am open to further investigation. This puts me in a rather precarious situation with Mr. Dahl, as I will need to explain what on earth you were doing in his driveway. Do you have reason to believe he was the one responsible for Stanley Hurst's demise?"

"He could be. And Theo and I found a threatening note in Victor's email."

"Computer tampering as well?? You don't make this easy, Miss Ellington. Do go on."

I told him every single detail, including how Theo and I found ourselves face-down in manure. It was the only time I detected a slight grin.

"I'm sure that email is in your possession. I'll need a copy. Although, without implicating you, which, by the way, I should do, I'll need to have my own conversation with Mr. Dahl."

"Does this mean we're working together on the case?"

He recoiled faster than a snake at the sound of footsteps. "Absolutely not! It means that I don't have the time to deal with all the complications involved regarding your soiree into the Dahl Farms' barn. If Madeline isn't the responsible party, then we have a clever murderer who could strike again."

"I understand."

"I shall certainly hope so. Let this be a warning. Leave the investigation to the sheriffs' offices. Next time I might not be so accommodating."

"Understood. Thank you. Really."

He stood and walked toward the door, before turning around one last time. "That storm is supposed to blow in pretty quick tonight. Maybe sooner. I'd keep an eye on the forecast if I were you. You wouldn't want your crew or customers stuck here."

"Thanks. Shall do."

My mind was so centered on what happened last night and what Theo and I discovered that I completely forgot about the winter storm. If what he said was true, Two Witches would have to consider closing early. I turned the computer to the Weather Channel and held my breath.

Yep, closing early for sure. I stood and left the office in search of Cammy. Unfortunately, I ran into Glenda first.

"An ill wind blows this way. Zenora sensed it last night. She sensed the putrid wasteland of muck seeping into your boots."

Holy cow! Not the manure. She's not that psychic, is she?

"Um, was Zenora a bit more specific?"

Glenda shook her head. "She has visions. Prophetic visions. She predicted the Cornell campus will be closed tomorrow."

"So did the Weather Channel. Cornell, Ithaca College, Hobart & William Smith, all area schools . . . that's why I need to find Cammy. We've got to close early and put it on our website as well as notify the local news."

"She's in the storeroom checking on the cases of our winter blends. Very popular during storms."

"Thanks." I trotted off to the storeroom, adjacent to the bistro, and called out to Cammy.

"Over here, behind the cases of Chardonnay. What's up?"

I asked if she'd please notify the local news about closing early as well as putting it on our website, but not before telling her about last night's visit to Dahl Farms.

"You can't be serious? You and Theo climbed over pen fences and still wound up in manure?"

"Not like we had much choice. Worst of all was that my car was caught on their surveillance and as a result, Deputy Hickman paid me a visit. He left a few minutes ago."

"Too bad Bradley's still out of town. Sounds like you might need a lawyer."

"Actually, Grizzly Gary and I have an agreement. Sort of. But I can't push my luck. Not right away anyhow. That means I'll need to take a different route to get the info I want."

"And what route is that?"

"Joel Margolis, from the *Finger Lakes Times.* He must have found out something by now."

"When did you say Bradley was coming back?"

"It was supposed to be early this week but Marvin had more work for him. He finally finished this morning but missed the last flight to Syracuse. Tried Rochester but no luck. The planes have been grounded until the storm is over. He sent me a text an hour or so ago."

"Sure there's nothing going on with you and Joel?"

"Information gathering. That's all."

"Hmm, so that's what they're calling it these days."

"Not funny." *But tempting for sure.*

I hated to admit it, but my conversation with Deputy Hickman left me rattled. One more step over the line and I doubted he would look the other way, even if I had indisputable evidence of the real murderer. I sent Theo a text explaining we'd need to hold off for a bit where Avery and Diane were concerned. Then I let him know about closing early.

He texted back that they'd do the same and maybe it was a good idea to lay low. Besides, with that storm coming, we weren't about to take unnecessary chances.

That meant one thing—Joel. I rushed back to my office and phoned him.

"Norrie! Hi! I meant to call you but things have been frenetic around here. One of our reporters came down with the flu and the other one went into early labor. I've been juggling everything."

"Does that include Stanley's murder?"

"And then some. I know that storm is supposed to hit late this afternoon so it's best if we stay where we are. Otherwise, I'd want to meet and share notes."

"Does that mean you've uncovered something?"

"I might have. Listen, this isn't a great place for me to talk. How about I call you tonight after seven?"

"Sure. I'll be home riding out the storm like everyone else. Thank goodness we have cell phones because past experience has shown me that our landline is the first to go down."

"What's the second?"

"The electricity, followed by the furnace. At least we have a woodstove and lots of logs."

"Hope it doesn't come to that. They're predicting three feet of the heavy stuff."

"At least the snowplows can shovel it. I don't even want to think about part two of this nightmare."

"Maybe it will fizzle out. That's been known to happen."

Not in my lifetime.

"One can always hope. Talk to you later. And thanks."

"Absolutely."

When I ended the call, I phoned John to make sure the vineyard guys would be all set for plowing our driveway and taking care of Alvin. He reassured me not to worry and that the backup generator for the lab was set to go.

"And don't worry if the county roads get closed," he said. "Travis and I both have snowmobiles. In fact, that might be more fun."

His words were upbeat but even John had no idea that the three feet of snow was just the beginning as far as a killer was concerned.

Chapter 23

Because we knew we'd be closed the next day, Emma and Fred made the tasting crew care packages with sandwiches, pastries, and whatever salads couldn't be served two days later.

We closed at four, just as the heavy flakes started making their way to the ground.

"First it's those lovely big snowflakes," Lizzie said. She headed out the door first, then turned to continue talking to the rest of us. "Then they get smaller and smaller. Then faster and faster. Then the wind picks up and next thing you know, you're in a whiteout."

Glenda looked up for a second before dusting some of the flakes off of her coat. "Don't know about anyone else, but Zenora and I have a mystic moon watch planned for tonight. Of course, it may get clouded over, but we'll still perform the chant."

A series of mumbles followed and I thought I should say something. "Um, sounds wonderful." *Whatever the heck it is.*

Minutes later, everyone peeled out of the driveway and onto Route 14. I headed up the hill for a quiet night working on my paranormal cozy screenplay. *Thank you, Renee.* No sooner did I unlock my door when I felt the vibration of my cell phone in my jeans pocket. I put Emma and Fred's care package on the kitchen table and tapped my phone.

"Norrie? It's Herbert. Meant to phone you sooner but it's been hectic around here. Wanted to get a few things done since it's doubtful any of us will make it into the lab tomorrow morning. Listen, remember when I told you our surveillance tape spied a car going up your driveway after the traminette incident?"

"Uh-huh."

"Well, we backed up the tape and caught something interesting. There were two cars, not one. We were able to get a wider angle and saw one car heading down the driveway from our patio area, and another coming up. The car that went to your house wasn't the one that the perpetrator of the vandalism drove."

"That's even creepier. I need to let Deputy Hickman know in case there's a peeping Tom in the area."

"Look, I don't want to scare you, but most peeping Toms, not that I'm an expert, mind you, would be more inclined to go on foot. Like a city block. Not drive miles out of town to find an isolated farmhouse. Only—"

He caught himself just as I gasped. "Only serial killers and maniacs?"

"I wasn't going to put it that way. Only nefarious individuals with other intentions."

"Serial killers and maniacs. I'm calling the sheriff's office right now and I'll demand to know how fast Eugene is coming along with his investigation."

"Uh, you may not want to do that. It may have the opposite effect. Lock your doors. Lock your windows. And keep your cell phone in close proximity. Besides, with a storm like this blowing in, no one in their right mind will be out driving."

"In their right mind. And if not? I'll lock up. Trust me, everyone has given me that same message. I'll be safe. See you on Friday."

"Sure thing. I'm out the door now and I'm the last one here."

As soon as I ended the call, Charlie bumped me and walked to his empty food dish. I immediately refilled it with kibble and changed his water. Then, after double-checking the front door, I went to every room on the first floor to make sure all the windows were locked. Next, I retrieved the emergency "power out" kit that had been a staple in our family. Candles, battery-operated flashlights, battery-powered flickering candles, and lots of bandages for some odd reason. I put it on the kitchen table and suddenly realized I had left Emma and Fred's food there.

Thankfully I had the foresight to pile up enough logs for the woodburning fireplace if the heat went out.

"At least we've got dinner for tonight, Charlie," I called out as I grabbed the bag. "Tomorrow it will most likely be dry cereal and nachos."

I opened the fridge, expecting to toss the bag on top of one of the shelves, when I took a step back to catch my breath. I'm not the neatest person when it comes to stashing food in the refrigerator, but one look and it was obvious—someone had been rooting around in there and it wasn't me.

Jars of open jam were on their sides, the milk had been moved to one of the shelves, and my leftover plate of mac and cheese was toppled over. Packages of cheese were opened along with plastic containers of butter and Noosa yogurt. Rats! And just when I found a yogurt I actually liked.

When I opened the lower drawers, it was no different. Produce all pushed to one side, and grapes scattered about. Sweat emanated from my palms and I debated whether or not to call the sheriff's office. Nothing else had been disturbed. I would have noticed when I went from room to room checking the windows.

With the storm already on its way, and no imminent danger, I took photos of the fridge and texted them to the sheriff's office. Then I called them to report the incident.

The deputy on duty, whose name I forgot the second he took the call, wrote down the information. "Is it possible, Miss Ellington, for you not to touch anything in your refrigerator? Or maybe use plastic gloves. We can send a tech to dust for prints but it won't be until tomorrow. Not with the storm and the emergencies that are bound to go along with it."

"No problem. Got lots of food handler gloves. Like I said, I don't see any sign of a break-in but this is really creepy."

"Lock your doors, your windows, and keep your phone close."

Those words were fast becoming the slogan of the month. "I did. All set."

"Tell me, did you notice anything out of the ordinary when you went inside? Tire tracks? Anything?"

"No. Whoever did it must have come before the snow started. But how they got in is anyone's guess. The dead bolt was locked when I got home."

"Did you give a copy of your key to anyone?"

"Only my neighbors at the Grey Egret."

"Okay. Keep us posted and call immediately if you see or hear anything unusual."

The minute he said the word *unusual*, all I could picture was Glenda and Zenora doing their moon mantra or whatever they called it.

"I wouldn't be too worried, Miss Ellington," the deputy went on. "Chances are it was kids making good on a dare. Last year, the junior lacrosse team had a scavenger hunt to procure someone's underwear. Don't ask. The coach wound up benching most of them."

"Thanks. Very reassuring. I'll be sure to lock up my under-garments."

He laughed and we ended the call.

"Kids, huh?" I said to Charlie. "Only one kid I know would do something like that."

I speed dialed Eli Speltmore's house and held my breath that Delia, his mother, would answer the phone, and not his dad, Henry. Last thing I needed was to discuss the wine trail with its president.

Eli had a penchant for mischief and that was the understatement of the year. Now, halfway into his first year at middle school, he would give the word *miscreant* a whole new meaning.

"Norrie?" Delia asked when she took the call. "Your name popped up on the caller ID. Is everything all right? I mean, other than the terrible things that are already going on."

"Um, actually, that's why I called. This may sound strange, but it appears as if someone had been rooting through my refrigerator. No damage, just food moved around."

"Hmm, it sounds exactly like something Eli and his friend Stuart would do, but fortunately for both of them, they're on a school field trip to New York City with their science class. They left on Tuesday and aren't coming back until Sunday. The storm should be well over by then. Between you and me, it's the most peace I've had in months. Now, of course, I'm worried they might do something awful in the Museum of Natural History. Wouldn't put it past them."

"I'm sure they'll be fine. Those trips have lots of chaperones. I know. I've been on many of them."

"You may want to contact the sheriff's office and have them send someone out."

"Already on it. Thanks, Delia, and enjoy your mini-vacation."

"Oh, I certainly will. Believe me, it's a blessing."

"I'm never having children," I shouted to Charlie, who was now curled up on the living room rug. Glancing outside, it looked as if I was trapped in a snow globe. Fast flakes, all right, and lots of them. Then, it dawned on me. If the power did go out, the last thing I wanted to do was to go downstairs to the basement to get jams and jellies with only a flashlight.

"Better do it now," I mumbled to the dog and took off downstairs, cell phone in my pocket.

I flipped the light switch and listened as the wooden steps creaked under my shoes. Francine's jellies, jams, and assorted pickled items were neatly stacked on two old bookshelves to my left. I grabbed a jar of grape and another of raspberry when I noticed something peculiar. The old wooden barrels that had blocked off the original entrance to the basement were tipped over.

In that instant, I froze. I knew immediately how the refrigerator raider had gotten in here and was terrified he or she hadn't yet left. I placed one of the jars on top of the bookshelf and held the other one as if it was a softball ready to be thrown. Then I turned on the flashlight from my cell phone and swept the area in a series of lighted arcs. No sign of anyone.

Wasting no time, I retrieved the other jar and darted up the stairs, making sure to lock the door behind me. Too bad I hadn't been doing that all along. And while the basement didn't harbor any intruders, thanks to an open basement door into the house, I couldn't say the same for the upstairs. My only choice was to find out for myself.

Chapter 24

I started for the stairs, then turned and snatched the fireplace poker. Two stairs up and I returned to the kitchen for a can of Raid.

"You can never be too sure," I whispered to the dog, who looked up for a brief second.

Yep. A Plott hound. Not a Rottweiler, German shepherd, or Doberman. A happy, laidback Plott hound.

"Just as well you stay here and be safe," I said, this time taking the stairs two by two. When I got to the landing, I stood and listened. Not a sound from the house, only the wind outside, and it began to pick up, rattling the siding and the shutters.

My room was the first one on the left and I approached it as if I was about to diffuse a bomb. With the Raid tucked under one arm and the poker in the other, I used the Raid arm to aim my flashlight. Nothing. I crept inside, flung open the closet door and used the poker to move the clothes on the racks. Again, nothing.

Great. Now on to the scary monster's place under the bed.

I figured I could push the spray knob if indeed someone lurked there, but fortunately, the only things lurking were dust bunnies. I made a mental note to buy a Swiffer.

Francine and Jason's room was next and like mine, there were no uninvited inhabitants. Same deal with the upstairs bathroom. Only one room left and it was a guest room/computer room/catchall room that had more boxes in it than Allied Van Lines.

Thoughts of a killer crouched behind a large cardboard box made my mouth go dry and I kept moistening my lips. A nervous reaction for sure but I needed to get control of the situation. I tightened my grip on the poker and charged inside as if I was holding a bayonet.

"The sheriff's office sent two deputies to this address. They texted me ten minutes ago," I said, "so you might as well show yourself."

Nothing. Only the wind. This time rattling the soffits. Fairly certain I was in the clear, I stormed around the room checking every single spot from the bed to the closet. Again, empty. I supposed I should have been relieved but part of me wanted to catch the culprit. If nothing else but to allow me a decent night's sleep.

One thing was crystal clear—no one had ventured upstairs. Everything was as it had been, not as much as a throw pillow out of place. I let the poker swing back and forth while I maneuvered the cell phone so it would slip into my pocket. Then I returned downstairs. Whoever entered the house through the basement door was there for one purpose only—a meal. Too bad he or she didn't go to Don and Theo's. Much better pickings.

Most unsettling was how they got in. No one had used that old wooden outside basement door. Too much of a pain to lift both sides and walk down those creepy four or five steps. As a kid I remembered always seeing disgusting bugs, or worse yet, garter snakes in there. Still, there was a lock on it and someone managed to open it. I laughed thinking back to the combination lock at Dahl Farms, but ours was keyed.

"I hate to do this, Charlie," I said, "but I'm putting on my winter coat, hat, and gloves so I can get a good look at the outside basement door. This time with the heavy-duty flashlight." The dog scratched behind his ear before resuming his nap.

It had only been a short while but the snow had piled up enough to obscure the walkway and the driveway. Impossible to find footprints. Even my own. They were covered the second my feet moved a few inches ahead.

You're right, Lizzie. Faster and faster flakes.

If the perpetrator left any clues, they were certainly obscured by the snow. I skirted around the house and walked directly to the outside basement door. The lock was still in one piece, but upon close inspection, the wood had gotten so old and brittle that a quick jab with a hammer or such resulted in a small pile of wood chips and an easily accessible entrance.

It didn't take a genius to figure out that old farmhouses like ours all came equipped with those old-fashioned cellar doors. If I had any thoughts of relocking it, they vanished the second I spied the wood chips. That meant a second trek to the basement with a makeshift plan to secure it. True, the storm was probably the best security I had, but still, a locked entrance would provide some peace of mind.

And while we had extra Kwikset locks in the pantry, it meant I'd have to dig around and find one of those latch things to secure it. Aargh. Last thing I felt like doing. Then again, it beat having a sleepless night.

An hour later, I had uttered more expletives than I'd heard in my lifetime. I'd also screwed a latch on to the interior door as well as the rounded other piece, for lack of a better word to describe the thing. A carpenter I wasn't.

Then, I opened a new lock, secured it, and for good measure took an old chair from the basement and propped it against the door.

"You're not getting in again, buddy," I shouted, but it didn't matter. The only noise was the wind and it wasn't letting up.

I took full advantage of Emma and Fred's turkey sandwich before starting up the woodburning stove. No sense waiting for a power outage to deal with the cold. Charlie must have liked the idea as well because he moved closer to it and curled up on the nearest throw rug.

I had just settled in on the couch with the remote when Bradley called.

"Hey, Norrie! Was going to call later but just saw those weather reports. Hope you're safe and warm in your house."

"Warm yes, safe is questionable."

I then proceeded to tell him what had happened, and once he got over the initial shock that someone might have been in the house, he had the same thought I did—either pranking kids or some drifter who was hungry. Still, why pick such an out-of-the-way place?

"Good thinking about installing that extra lock. Um, you may want to go one step further and have those cellar doors replaced."

"Already on it. Googled primed steel cellar doors at Home Depot in Geneva and will call them in the morning. Francine and Jason can pick up the tab for this one. Any chance you'll be back the end of the week?"

"For sure. Will let you know when. Meanwhile all flights to the Finger Lakes are canceled. At least I should be there next week when the second part of that storm is supposed to roll in. This time ice."

I winced. Ice storms are horrific for vineyards. The damage they can do to vines is incomprehensible and the havoc they cause on roads and structures is equally bad. Not to mention power outages, fallen trees, collapsed utility poles, and a plethora of accidents.

It's worse when they follow a major snowstorm because it's impossible to shovel or plow the stuff once freezing rain turns to ice. At least John and his crew would have time for a head start.

"Listen," he said. "I wanted to let you in on my conversation with Lila this past Saturday. I held off because of the confidentiality issue but your safety overrules any of that."

"Uh-oh. This isn't sounding good."

"Lila's pretty certain whoever knocked off her husband will try to cast suspicion on one of the winery owners who objected to the high-rise. She said it wasn't the first time something like this happened but refused to go into detail."

"Cast suspicion *how*?"

"Planting evidence, for one thing. All I can think of is a facsimile of the murder weapon and a silent witness."

"But how would they know what the murder weapon was? I found out from an inside source."

"Give it a day or so. It'll be on the news. Meanwhile, tell your staff to be extra vigilant when Two Witches opens up on Friday. And you probably should call Don, Theo, and the WOW ladies."

"Oh, brother, just what we need. Did Lila say anything else?"

"Said Stanley was a 'rough player' and always managed to stay one step ahead covering his tracks."

"Yeah, until he didn't."

"She's not out of the woods yet. Forensics have been all over her place and she's still considered a secondary person of interest."

"Small consolation for Madeline."

"Anyway, make sure your house is locked up and sleep with your cell phone."

"Boy, is that ever romantic." I laughed.

"We'll put it on mute when I get back in town."

Other than the usual exchange of virtual hugs and kisses, I told Bradley about the roach dinner with Godfrey.

"Do you have to watch any presentations?"

"Only if they want me to lose my appetite."

We both laughed and said we'd text or talk tomorrow.

When the call ended, I became even more aware of the wind. It had gotten stronger and whooshed against the house as if it was a precursor to a tornado. The snow globe that I saw earlier was now a sea of white dust with no ending in sight.

I double-checked the windows and the doors, even though I'd done it before. Then I made myself a cup of hot chocolate and turned on the TV, only to find the cable was out. Yep, the storm made its first move and it wasn't looking pretty.

"Might as well snuggle up and read in bed," I said to Charlie. "At least while we still have electricity."

The dog followed me upstairs and for the first time since I'd been staying here, I locked my bedroom door and wedged a chair against it.

Chapter 25

Not only did I sleep with my cell phone, but I got up at least four times to check email, Facebook, Apple News, and the weather. Not that I needed an icon for the weather. The wind never stopped and whatever sleep I got wasn't exactly restful.

I awoke to total darkness at 7:34 and my first thought was that the power was out, but I could hear the furnace fan and see that the digital clock on my nightstand was lit. At least I hadn't lost power.

"I'm going back to sleep," I announced to Charlie, who was sprawled out at the foot of the bed, his head resting on my feet. "Not much to do today except work an interfering ghost into a love story for Renee. Oh, and solve a murder so Madeline can be set free."

The dog yawned as I yanked the covers over me and closed my eyes. It was 9:53 when I finally opened my eyes to the swirling white stuff outside my window. I had an amazing view of Seneca Lake but all I could see were whirling white flakes. The storm hadn't died down the way everyone thought it would. In fact, it seemed as if the wind had intensified.

"Time for coffee and kibble," I mumbled as I threw my old terry-cloth robe over my T-shirt and sweat pants before washing up and heading to the kitchen. A few minutes later, Charlie had returned from a quick jaunt out the doggie door and shook snow all over the kitchen floor.

I poured his kibble, changed his water, and popped a dark roast into the Keurig. No sooner did the flashing blue light from the coffee maker come on when a call came in. This time from Godfrey.

"Morning, Norrie! Figured you'd be up by now. Just checking in. Everything okay?"

"You mean other than being snowed in? Because snowed in is the least of it."

"What do you mean? Don't tell me you're totally flipping out because the cable is off in Yates and Ontario counties."

"No, someone broke in here before I got home yesterday and rooted through my refrigerator. Nothing else was disturbed but I discovered how they got in and then I had to put a new lock on our basement door. The one on the outside of the house. I didn't bother calling anyone except the sheriff's office and they couldn't come because the roads were closed."

"I'm surprised you slept last night."

"Trust me, it wasn't easy."

"If the storm stops and they clear the roads, I'd be happy to camp out on your couch tonight."

"I'm fine, but thanks. That was a sweet gesture."

"Did the sheriff's office have any idea why someone would do that?"

"The usual—kids or a vagrant."

"Kids, maybe. But a vagrant? Over ten miles from the nearest populated area? Doubtful. Maybe a nutcase."

"Thanks. That was very comforting. So, what are you up to today?"

"Research at home. The lab, like the rest of Cornell's Experiment Station, is closed until Friday. Campus security figures everything will be cleaned up by then. The storm's supposed to dwindle down after two or three today."

"I'll give you a buzz later, but if anything crops up, call me."

"Shall do. And stay safe. You know what I mean."

I gulped my coffee, made myself cold cereal and topped it off with a sleeve of Chips Ahoy. I wasn't in the mood for anything healthy, or even close to it. Then I phoned John to see where we stood with the plowing.

He picked up on the second ring but the connection was spotty. "Hey, Norrie. Travis and I are at the barn. We came in on snowmobiles like I thought we would. Got the lower portion of our property plowed and are heading uphill toward the winery and your place. The snow's supposed to stop early this afternoon and believe it or not, the sun's supposed to come out. That should ice things up a bit. Want to get done before then."

I thought about telling him what happened last night but held off. He had enough to deal with and there was nothing he could do.

"Everything should be back to normal tomorrow," he went on. "Well, *normal* in a figurative sense."

"I know what you mean."

"We should be hearing from the sheriff's office on the traminette evidence pretty soon. Hang in there."

"You, too!"

As I stood to rinse off my bowl, the landline rang and I could see it was Cammy.

"Hey, girl, how are you doing? Your cell line has been busy, busy." Her voice was as bouncy as ever. "My aunts want me to walk over to their place and help them make cannoli because, and I quote, 'the TV is out, the restaurant is closed, and we'll be at each other's throats if we don't do something.' Geneva's a mess. You can't tell the sidewalks from the street. I told them I'd be over once the city crews come out. What's happening on Two Witches Hill?"

"Still snowing like crazy, TV out too, and some nutcase broke into my house yesterday while we were at work."

"What??" Cammy's voice was loud and all but took my eardrums out. I then told her what I told Bradley and Godfrey. Like Godfrey, she offered to camp out here "until the lunatic is caught," but I reassured her I'd be fine and that I'd see her tomorrow morning.

"Well, Charlie," I said, "all that's missing now is a call from Theo and Don." And in that split second, as if they heard me, my cell phone tone went off. Once again, I had to explain about last night and once again, the guys offered to have Charlie and me stay at their place.

It was nice to know I had friends who were protective of me, but honestly, I wasn't that worried. Not until later in the day when Eugene from the sheriff's lab showed up with another forensic tech guy. I was in the middle of some tricky dialogue with my screenplay, having gotten bleary-eyed with the murder map, when I heard a car engine and looked out the window to see the Yates County Forensic Lab vehicle pull up.

It was around two and like John said it would, the snow stopped and the sun came out. Roads were cleared and salted but residents were told to watch out for black ice, since road surfaces were wet and the low temps would contribute to it.

"Finally!" I shouted to Charlie. "They can dust for prints and I won't have to use food handler gloves every time I open the fridge." Seconds later, there was a knock on the door and I opened it to see Eugene and another guy I sort of recognized. Tall, thin, short brown hair and clean -shaven. Late thirties or early forties.

"Good, you're here! Come on in. Bring whatever you need. Oh, and I found out how the perpetrator got in. From the basement door. Might want to check that. What do you want to do first?"

Eugene shuddered and looked me straight in the face. "Transfer to Seneca Falls but that's not an option. Miss Ellington, we would kindly request that you direct us first to the refrigerator and we will check the basement door on our way out. No need for you to stand over us like you normally do."

"Fine. I'll sit quietly at the kitchen table and watch."

"Good. The gentleman with me is Dawson and he's been to your winery before."

Dawson smiled and waved a hand at me. It looked as if he might burst out laughing so I quickly turned away and focused on Eugene.

"Um, I'm not standing over you," I said, once Eugene put on purple gloves and took out a fingerprint dusting brush from a small bag, "but I am suggesting you also dust on the inside of the fridge door, in addition to the shelves. People have a tendency to brush up against it with their hands."

Dawson choked back a laugh, but it was obvious Eugene didn't share his sense of humor. He sighed and straightened his shoulders. "Miss Ellington, rest assured I *am* a trained professional, and yes, I most certainly will dust on the insides of the refrigerator door." He emphasized the word *insides* and this time I had to hold back a laugh. I retreated to the table and busied myself with my cell phone while he worked and Dawson took notes.

I was engrossed with a funny Facebook post when Eugene asked, "Do you wear black nail polish?"

"Huh? I don't wear any nail polish. I buff my nails. Too much work with nail polish and it always chips. Besides, where am I going to find a decent manicurist out here in the boonies? Now, if I were still in Manhattan, I might consider—"

"That's all I need to know."

"Why?" I asked. "Why do you need to know that?"

"Because there seems to be part of a chipped nail wedged between the door and the third shelf down, and it's black."

I paused for a second and thought about my crew at Two Witches. Cammy didn't wear polish and neither did Emma, who was way too earthy. Same deal as Francine. Glenda did but it was always green, purple or some silvery stuff. Definitely not black. Something about black being an anger color. Or was it a death color? And Lizzie has always worn a clear coat since she "never had to worry about it matching her clothes."

"Are you saying whoever got into my refrigerator was a woman who had black nails?"

"No, I'm not saying that. I'm *saying* I have uncovered a possible piece of evidence. *Possible.*"

"Well, maybe you can uncover something else. I'll leave you alone."

"Thank you."

Eugene worked in silence for the next half hour, and while I pretended to be entranced with my phone, I peered at him every few seconds to see what he and Dawson were up to. I might as well have been watching a silent movie because neither of them spoke until they were finished. Then Eugene stood and walked toward me.

"I was able to secure a few partial prints but most likely they're yours or your guests'. Still, we'll see if anything matches up in our system."

"And the chipped nail? What about the nail?"

"We will do our best to discern its origin."

I did a mental eye roll. "Good. Get that DNA or nail fungus. Or whatever you find."

Eugene shuddered. "Now, if you don't mind, would you please direct us to your basement door?"

"Absolutely."

I grabbed my heavy fleece jacket and put a woolen hat on while he and Dawson grabbed their jackets from the chairs by the door. Then I slipped into my heavy boots.

"Come on," I said. "It's on the other side of the house." I looked at Eugene. "You might remember that from last time but then again, we didn't have three or more feet of snow."

"Don't remind me."

With that, the three of us walked outside and I pointed to the door. It was covered with snow but before I could say anything, Dawson asked if I had a shovel or perhaps a broom.

"Both. Hang on."

A minute or so later, I returned with both objects and handed the shovel to Dawson. In a matter of seconds, he had removed the snow and I was able to use the broom to dust off the remaining layer.

"The wood looks rotted out," Eugene said. "You should consider having the doors replaced."

"I know. I already called Home Depot. Got it scheduled."

"Good idea."

I took a few steps back while he and Dawson perused the door. This time with high-powered flashlights.

"It's impossible to get prints with the snow," Dawson said, "but take a closer look. I think whoever was here left us some better evidence."

"What? What? I don't see anything." My voice sounded whiney.

"Look under the lock." Eugene snapped a photo with his phone while I squinted to see what they were talking about.

"Wow! Is that a diamond stud earring? Not mine. And Francine only wore teeny tiny gold studs. Something about being ostentatious otherwise."

Eugene put the earring in a plastic evidence bag and turned to me. "We don't know if it's a diamond, a zircon, or another stone. Our lab will need to make that determination. What we do know is that we have secured another piece of evidence."

"Yep," I said. "Most likely from the same woman who rooted around my refrigerator and used a hammer or whatever to break in."

"We don't know that yet, Miss Ellington. Do not let your screenwriting imagination take you to places where you shouldn't go."

Can I tell that to Renee?

"Don't worry. I'm very circumspect."

I could have sworn Eugene choked when he heard the last word, but it might have been Dawson.

Chapter 26

By early nightfall, I had either texted, phoned, or emailed everyone in my circle to let them know what had ensued. Roads had been plowed, the cable was back on, and I had completed the first few scenes of my screenplay.

As far as the murder investigation went, I was at a standstill. It was bad enough when I juggled that situation along with the traminette tampering, but now, with the uneasy thought that someone had been in my house, I found myself creating all sorts of scenarios that belonged in a Stephen King novel.

Then, out of the blue, Joyce McKenna called and took me completely by surprise.

"I meant to call you sooner, Norrie," she said, "but with the storm and everything else that had piled up on my desk, I'm just now getting around to it."

"That's fine. I appreciate you taking the time to see if anyone else had a major stake in that soon-to-be high-rise property."

"Seems you were on the right path. A gentleman by the name of Norwood Peltz, from Peltz and Peltz Developers in Ithaca, had more than his eye on that property. In fact, his realtor from there had put in his offer about the same time as Stanley. Clearly, Madeline's offer came first, but we know how that went."

"Can you tell me anything else about Norwood?"

"Similar to Diamante. Lots of lakeside construction but on Cayuga Lake. Seems they want to branch west to our area. Oh, and one more thing. According to his realtor, he attended that Benton Town Hall meeting demanding to know about water usage and utilities. He told the realtor that Stanley had a reputation in the industry for fudging those things. Norwood hoped the board would nix the project so he could zoom in. Not a high-rise but lots of garden apartment condos."

"Hmm, I seem to remember someone complaining about that, but there was so much ruckus going on that it was hard to tell who spoke."

"Well, I hope I've been helpful but please don't share your source with anyone."

"No problem. And thanks, Joyce. Stop by Two Witches sometime for a free tasting and a complimentary bottle of wine."

"Thank you. I may indeed take you up on the offer."

The minute our call ended, I phoned Theo for the second time and could hardly slow down. "We were right. There's a possible third player in the 'who killed Stanley' plot. A developer from Ithaca. Norwood Peltz. He was at the Benton Town Hall meeting. Complained about utilities and water usage but only because he wanted the board to vote no. He had an offer in on the property as well. Tiny condos."

"Holy cow! I've actually heard of Peltz Developers. They had a number of projects near Ithaca College on South Hill. Again, wow! That's like a dark horse entering the race. I really didn't give it much credence, but now I'm having second thoughts. I mean, that's a darn good motive for murder."

"No kidding."

"So now what? And please do not tell me you have another snooping-on-the-property plan."

"No. Well, not immediately."

All I heard was Theo's grumbling sound so I kept talking.

"While I'm at the winery today, I'll google what I can on the guy and let you know. Hey, this dark horse may turn out to be the killer and Madeline will be home free."

"I love your optimism, Norrie, but let's take it one step at a time. Meanwhile, I'm still not done with Audrey. Don thinks maybe her son, who works for that other winery, may be involved in the traminette tampering at Madeline's and the Cab-Franc one at your place, thinking it was traminette. We've still got to pursue that. Our businesses are at stake."

"I know. And the sooner the better. Yesterday's storm was bad enough, but what they're predicting with the ice storm on the way is bound to slow us down."

And while Glenda and Zenora made prophetic statements all the time, the one that came out of my mouth was right on the nose. And lamentably, so was the chaos that followed.

• • •

I was at the winery a few minutes before opening time the next day, much to everyone's surprise. As I helped set up, I told them about "the refrigerator incident" and my interaction with Eugene.

"You scare the daylights out of him," Lizzie said. "His mother goes to my church and asked if I needed to take antianxiety medication in order to work with you."

"Good grief! Now I've heard it all."

I retreated to my office as I pondered her statement. Did I really unnerve the guy? Yeesh. Anyway, I had a winery to run and really needed to focus on that. Funny how the days leading up to a snowstorm and the day immediately after it are always busy with shoppers. Not necessarily tasters out on a wine tour, but dedicated wine drinkers who know their Finger Lakes' wines and want to stock up. Most likely out of fear for future winter storms.

I spent more time helping Cammy take wine out of storage and set it up on shelves for purchase while Glenda and Roger handled the tasting room. Sam had college classes but would be in over the weekend or if a class got canceled.

Shortly after lunch, it was as if someone tossed me a crumb as far as my would-be investigations went. Herbert called to let me know the sheriff's office had contacted them with a follow-up to their investigation of the barrel tampering. The deputy said he left me a voicemail as well. *I really need to check my cell phone more often.*

"What was it? Did he say?"

"Very odd, to be sure. The black substance they found on the outside of the barrel was elderberry residue."

"Elderberry? As in wine?"

"Uh-huh."

"I don't know of any wineries around here that produce elderberry wine. It's more of a hobby wine."

"I know. Listen, we'll keep our eyes and ears open for sure."

"Thanks, Herbert. Appreciate it."

The instant the call ended, I made another one and could already sense my stomach tightening up.

"Hello? Marilyn? It's Norrie. Hope you're all shoveled out."

"Shoveled, salted, everything. Never lost power but really missed the Thursday 'Buzz about town' breakfast."

"You mean there's another chitchat group?" *Like one isn't enough to last a century?*

"It's a monthly group that includes Dresden, Himrod, and Branchport. You wouldn't think it, but there's a lot going on in those little hamlets."

I can only imagine.

"I'm sure. Listen, I won't keep you a moment but I wondered if you knew of anyone producing homemade wines, like elderberry."

"Elderberry? No. But quite a few people made elderberry pies for Thanksgiving and Christmas. They were for sale at most of the church bazaars. Must be an acquired taste. I never cared for it. If you've got a taste for it, I'm afraid you'll have to wait until next fall."

"Thanks, Marilyn. I appreciate it. Have a good day."

I got off the phone before she launched into something else and hoped I wasn't too curt.

"There are so many strange clues floating around for all of these things that happened," I said to Cammy. I told her about Herbert's call and Marilyn's take on elderberry wine. Cammy had just finished up with a group of four women and proceeded to wipe down her table.

"Everything seems weird, Norrie. And you're jumping all over the place. Maybe pick one thing and focus on it."

"That's the trouble. The clues keep coming out of nowhere and I'm flittering around like a moth."

Cammy laughed. "You've been hanging around Godfrey too long."

"Not long enough. I've got that roach dinner coming up soon."

"Well, that should prove to be as boring as anything. Better you than me. Hey, if you want to work on your investigation or screenplay, we've got the tasting room covered for the next hour or so."

"I'm taking you up on it. A new suspect crossed our paths and I need to scope him out."

"Genuine suspect or your imagination gone wild?"

"A little bit of both, I suppose. Give me an hour and I'll let you know."

Cammy winked and I raced back to my office. My fingers were literally itching to enter Norwood Peltz's name in Google and see what it brought up. Less than five minutes later, I had my answer and texted Theo at lightning speed. *Peltz construction is in Ithaca, but Norwood lives in Skaneateles.*

He texted back immediately with a *so what?* emoji.

I responded, *So does Lila Stratington-Hurst.*

Chapter 27

Twenty minutes later, Theo phoned. "Pull the reins in, Norrie. Just because they live in the same town doesn't mean they're in cahoots. This isn't one of your screenplays. They probably don't even know each other."

"I'm sure they've crossed paths. Look at how many vintners, winemakers, and vineyard managers we know. Why? Because we're in the same business. Same deal for Stanley and Norwood. Somewhere along the line they were bound to cross paths. And Lila might have been standing in the proverbial crosswalk, so to speak."

"One word for you—*far-fetched.*" Then he paused. "However, I wouldn't eliminate him as a suspect, just the Lila part of it."

"Fine. I'll keep digging but it may require some ground work."

"Dairy cows at Dahl Farms wasn't enough? We're lucky no charges were pressed."

"Skaneateles isn't in Yates County and neither is Ithaca."

"Worse yet. Grumpy as he may be, Detective Hickman may have a soft spot for you. That won't be the case with other sheriffs' offices. Tell me, what are you suggesting?"

"The weather is going to be pretty decent for the next few days until the ice storm makes its way here. I scoped out Lila on Facebook and found out she frequents the Krebs on Genesee Street in Skaneateles."

"The Krebs? I couldn't afford a glass of water. And I mean tap water!"

"We'll eat light. If it's a place she frequents, someone is bound to know something. And that advice came from Marilyn."

"Oh, brother."

"Besides, it's not breaking and entering, it's not snooping on private property. It's just two friends dining out."

"You mean maxing out as far as our credit cards are concerned. Does she frequent any place we can afford?"

"Photos on Facebook show her at a coffee shop in town. That may be a start."

"Good. It won't bankrupt me. I'm still not sure this is the best way to proceed."

"Okay. Then I'll give you one word—WOW."

"Ugh. Don't remind me." Then silence. "You win. But only the coffee shop. When and what time?"

"How about I pick you up at eight tomorrow? Tasting room business has been light. Our wineries should manage."

"Don will be overjoyed. And yes, that *was* an acerbic statement."

"I know. Tell him we'll bring him back a muffin or something. And thank him for me. See you tomorrow."

• • •

"I can't believe this has been dragging on so long," I said to Theo when we were less than five miles from Skaneateles the next day. "I expected some progress on the lab report for my door window, not to mention the lab report for Madeline's traminette disaster."

"I don't think anyone is in a hurry. They have a suspect and now they can take their dear old time. Tell me, what exactly do you expect to accomplish this morning?"

"Scuttlebutt gathering. Then, with all of our players in place, we devise a two-tiered trap whereby we ferret out Stanley's killer as well as the person who sabotaged Madeline's wine and tampered with ours."

"Two-tiered, huh? We can't even narrow this down to one person and one tier!"

"Hey, I could have gone for three tiers if I added the nutcase who rooted around my fridge. But honestly, other than bothering with our wine barrel, who would want to break in to my place?"

"Good point. Nutcase it is! Hey, it's right here on East Genesee Street, Green Mountain Coffee Shop. Wow—terrific lake view from here."

"That's because Stanley and friends didn't get to muck up this part of the village. Hang on, I'm going to pull into that parking spot a few feet ahead. Yay! Doris Day parking!"

"What the heck is Doris Day parking?"

"Something my mother would always say. In all the old Doris Day movies, there was always an available parking spot for her wherever she went. Convertible and all!"

"Good. Maybe we'll be lucky with the rest of this adventure."

No sooner did Theo say that when a woman walked in front of my car and straight into the coffee shop.

"Oh my gosh!" I grabbed Theo's arm and shook it. "That's her! Lila! Forget Doris Day parking! We got Marilyn Monroe seating!!!"

"That's a thing, too?"

"No! I'm kidding. But hurry up. This could be the break we needed. Plus, we're already experienced at this."

"Huh? What?"

"From sitting near Marilyn's chit-chatters. Lila's bound to have a conversation with someone, and if not, we'll introduce ourselves and start digging."

"Hope you brought along a good shovel."

We all but charged into the coffee shop so we could position ourselves near her, only we forgot one thing—customers order first at the counter and then take a seat.

"Plan B," I whispered to Theo. "Start talking to her."

"She'll think I'm coming on to her. You start talking to her." He stepped aside and gave me a playful shoulder shove. Only it wasn't exactly playful and I cascaded into her.

"I'm so sorry. My friend got a little zealous for his coffee. Didn't mean to run into you."

She turned and I realized she was even better-looking than her photos on Facebook. Frankly, if she and Stephanie teamed up, it would mean curtains for the male population.

"No problem. Seems to be the kind of month I've been having."

160

Oh my gosh. It's an opener. An opener!

I gripped my fingers and widened my eyes. "That bad, huh?"

She nodded and I continued. "I can beat that with my past year. I'm a screenwriter stuck managing my family's winery, where everything's been topsy-turvy."

"Hmm." Lila brushed her light bronze hair from her eyes. "Got you beat by a yard. My miserable ex-husband turned up dead and I'm an official person of interest." Then she looked at the barista who headed our way. "No worries. Everyone here knows. It's a small town."

"Stanley Hurst?"

"See, you know too. Are you from around here?"

"Penn Yan, but we're doing the touristy thing today. Fall and summers are too hectic." I turned to Theo. "This is Theo from the Grey Egret on Seneca Lake, and I'm Norrie from Two Witches. Oh, and I'm not one of them."

She laughed as she reached to shake Theo's hand. "Lila Stratington-Hurst. Nice to meet you."

At that second, the barista approached Lila. "Your usual? Large mocha latte with almond milk and no whip?"

"You've got it," she answered, handing him a ten-dollar bill.

Then she faced back to us. "I wouldn't mind some company. I know very little about the wineries although I do enjoy drinking wine when I have formal dinners."

"Sounds good. We'll join you after we put in our orders."

Lila walked to a quasi-table-bench for four and seated herself on the bench against the wall. I nudged Theo's ankle. "This is unbelievable, but I don't know how to start prying."

"That never stopped you before. Improvise."

I ordered the same thing Lila did but with real milk and plenty of whipped cream. I figured the twenties weren't going to last forever and once I turned thirty, I'd pay more attention to healthy eating.

Theo opted for a large coffee and cinnamon bun. Seconds later, we were face-to-face with Lila and I could feel a slight pulsing throughout my body. Nerves for sure. Last thing I wanted to do was botch up the first opportunity I had to find out who really killed Stanley.

Lila's demeanor was so unassuming that I secretly prayed it wouldn't be her. Then again, I'd been wrong so many times before that I didn't take anything for granted.

We initially chatted about the wine industry in general, my screenwriting, the Seneca Lake Wine Trail, and Don's amazing recipes. Then, I attempted to "go for the jugular." Once again, I gripped my hands, this time under the table. My feet seemed to tap on their own, until Theo gave my ankle a kick.

"Unfortunately," I said, "your ex-husband's body wound up near a sabotaged traminette barrel at my neighbor's winery and the authorities think she's the one who did him in."

"Was she having an affair with him?" Lila was dead serious.

I thought Theo was going to spit out his coffee but he turned away and grabbed a napkin.

"No!" Theo and I said in unison before I kept my mouth shut and let him continue. "Madeline Martinez, whose winery it was, is the quintessential mothering type. Happily married, grandkids, and a business to run. She's also in her sixties. Not likely carousing around."

"Good to know." Lila took a sip of her drink. "Too bad the same couldn't be said for my late husband's other female acquaintances."

I leaned into the table. "Do you think any of them would be angry or vengeful enough to do him in?"

Lila shook her head. "He seemed to simply move on without any excess baggage, except of course for me. Believe me, I would have known if someone was out to get him."

Theo glanced my way and shrugged.

Lila continued and I held my breath she'd reveal more. "Frankly, I was always concerned we'd run into one of his bimbos during a meal out or a jaunt somewhere. Thankfully that never happened. However, he did manage to irk people wherever we went. When you mentioned the Seneca Lake Wine Trail, I remembered going there with him a year or so ago and believe it or not, he got into a squabble with a woman who owned a small bakery."

I locked eyes with Theo and didn't say a word as Lila went on. "The man was so full of himself. Just *had* to share what he was up to. Regular braggart. Wish I'd known sooner. Anyway, he told the lady who owned the bakery about his plan to build a giant high-rise on the lake and she was aghast. Told him it would mean loss of customers for the small businesses and wineries around the lake because it would mar the view. But did he care? Not one iota."

I shifted in my seat and reached for my drink. "Um, yeah. We kind of know. We heard him at a town hall meeting in Benton. Still, his project passed."

"That's what my attorney told me. I would have thought the folks who owned businesses would be the perfect suspects but my premarital agreement and contentious divorce made the authorities rather one-sided."

"And still, they arrested Madeline. Worst of all is that once those sheriffs' offices have made up their minds, it's like taking off old wallpaper—nearly impossible."

Lila let out a long breath, put her elbows on the table, and propped her head against her closed fists. "Listen, I don't know you, but you seem honest. Honest and genuinely concerned about vindicating your fellow winery owner. I need someone on my side, too. If your friend is released, I'm next in line. Look, I know what I'm about to ask is going to sound fishy, especially since you've only just met me, but is there any way we can work together to find out who really did that son-of-a-gun in? You have a vested interest and I have a reputation to keep as well. And right now, it's on the line."

I couldn't believe what I heard and given the expression on Theo's face, neither could he. Then, Lila stood and walked to the counter. "I need another latte. Please, talk it over with each other. I have contacts, too, and maybe we can find the real murderer."

"Didn't see that coming," Theo said. "What do you think?"

"Even if she's the best liar in the state, better to have her in front of us than at our backs." I glanced at Lila by the counter. "I say yes. Let's do it."

"My sentiments exactly. But there's one snafu—Bradley."

"I know. That's why my stomach's been in a knot. Otherwise I would have gotten a cinnamon roll, too. I can't keep anything from him."

"You better hope it's not a conflict of interest for his firm."

"Heck with the firm. Pray it's not a conflict of interest for our relationship."

Chapter 28

"You need to tell Lila that Bradley's your boyfriend."

"How can I do that? I'm not supposed to know who her lawyer or law firm is."

"Good point. We'll ask her. Then you can act all surprised."

I rolled my eyes just as Lila returned to the table with another large latte.

"I practically live on this stuff," she said, putting it down on the table. "I haven't felt like eating much given all the goings-on."

Theo jumped into inquisition role with the smoothest segue ever. "That's why you have a legal firm to represent you. Let them get indigestion."

"Oh, I think I give them plenty. But then again, high-powered firms like Marvin Souza's in Geneva don't come cheap. But they're a family law firm, not criminal."

Suddenly I felt a jolt in my knee as Theo rammed it under the table with his, prompting me to speak. "Did you say Marvin Souza?"

Lila nodded. "Surely you must have heard of them. Especially living so close to Geneva."

Again, another knee knock. I shot Theo a look and quickly faced Lila. "Wow! Talk about coincidence. I'm dating someone in that firm— Bradley Jamison. He's in Manhattan right now on business but is expected back this weekend."

I didn't want to get too specific and wondered if I should have said anything at all, even with Theo's less-than-subtle insistence.

"Oh no." Lila moved the latte closer to her. "He's the lawyer who has been working on my divorce. So much for digging into my ex's affairs with you. What I really need to do is follow the money trail but I can't because all of Stanley's information is on his laptop, and for all I know the sheriff's office has confiscated it."

"What about backup files? You know, thumb drives. Would he have stashed one of those somewhere?"

"I never thought of that. If he did, it would be in his office. In Syracuse. I suppose I could get in. It's not breaking and entering if all you do is enter."

Oh my gosh! I love this woman. She thinks like I do!

"Besides, I know where my ex kept a spare key."

A spare key. That takes all the fun out.

"Um, if you find out anything, would you let me know? And we'll do the same with you. After all, we're both in the business of exonerating someone."

Lila smiled and wrote her name, cell number, and email on a napkin. I handed her a Two Witches business card and wrote my cell number on the back.

"Good meeting you, Norrie and Theo. Expect to hear from me. I need all the help I can get. Too bad my law firm doesn't add criminal law to its list."

We stood and told her to keep us posted but it wasn't until we were back in my car when Theo spoke freely. "Think we can trust her? That almost seemed too easy. Who opens up like that? Especially if you think you might be charged with murder."

"Desperate people, that's who. The question I have is, why does she feel so desperate?"

"Time for that chat with your boyfriend, huh?"

"Hope he understands the concept of coincidence."

As soon as we got back to Penn Yan, I texted Bradley. *Have something to share about Lila with you.*

He texted back, *Flying back late tonight. Will text when I land at nine forty three.*

I replied, *Drive over here before you go home.*

And then, *Absolutely.* Followed by kissy emojis.

I wondered how kissy they'd be once I told him what Theo and I had been up to, but frankly, I was grasping at too many straws and had to find some concrete evidence regarding Stanley's death. After all, didn't homicide trump sabotage, refrigerator raiding, and Avery's threatening note that was so far down the list that I had all but forgotten about it?

It was early afternoon when I returned to Two Witches and the Saturday crowd was going strong. I guess a midweek snowstorm followed by a prediction for another "event" had a way of compelling wine tasters to get off their duffs and start imbibing before they found themselves in winter lockdown again.

"How was your morning venture?" Cammy asked when I stepped into the tasting area. She looked up from her table of five and I gave her the thumbs-up. "Very fruitful. Tell you later."

Then I hustled back to my office to check emails and anything else that landed in there. On my computer screen, Lizzie had left a yellow Post-it that said, "Call Godfrey Klein. He stopped in."

I immediately scoured my work area for any *tokens* he or the entomology department might have gifted me. So far, so good. Only a crusty earwig in my desk and that one had been around for months. A gold star for neatness was one award that would elude me. I picked up the phone and reached Godfrey on the second ring.

"Hey, sorry I missed you. I was having breakfast in Skaneateles with Theo."

"That's pretty far to go for breakfast. What were you really doing?"

I told him about the possible Lila-Norwood connection and how Theo and I set out to do some information gathering only to be solicited by Lila herself to share any info about her late husband's dealings.

"Think you can trust her?" he asked.

"Funny, Theo asked the same thing. I don't know. But it's an opportunity we don't want to miss. Will keep you posted. Anyway, what's up with you?"

"I stopped in on my way back from a pest control check at a winery in Himrod. I needed to let you know about something. We got word from a colleague at the University of Kentucky in Lexington regarding a break-in at one of their labs. That university, by the way, is well known for its research programs in insect molecular biology, and genetics."

I rolled my eyes and stared off into space as Godfrey continued to ramble.

"Like our lab, they study DNA sequencing too, only they have not managed to extract cockroach DNA. As I mentioned earlier, it's a coveted substance. Make sure yours is safely secured."

"Oh, no worries there. No one's breaking down the doors for future generations of roaches. It's safe and sound in my basement refrigerator." *Unless we have a power outage in the summer and then, bye-bye roaches.*

"Good. Keep it that way. The U of K was working on extracting roach DNA as well. Only a small network of entomologists in our department is aware of it and we want to keep it that way."

"Understood. No worries."

"Great. I'm looking forward to the seminar and dinner. Exciting, isn't it?"

Like watching mosquitos hovering over a swamp.

"For sure."

"Be careful with your prying. I'm the one who has to report to Francine and Jason."

"I'm always careful."

He chortled and I laughed as well.

No sooner did my chat with Godfrey end, when Lizzie rapped on the doorjamb. "Norrie, it's Madeline. She's home on house arrest. Needed to speak with you immediately. Said your cell phone was busy and she couldn't wait."

"Thanks." I picked up the winery line and before I could say a word, Madeline spoke. "You were right. About picking up gossip from my pod mates. One of them told me she knew who was responsible for the traminette tampering but didn't have a name."

"Um, that's not very helpful. What *did* she tell you?"

"That it's someone who works for a competing winery on another lake."

"Even less helpful. That could be anyone. Did she mention which lake? There are eleven of them! Eleven. And most have wineries."

"Well, no, she didn't, but at least I know it was a competitor."

"Madeline, that was always in the forefront. Is there any way you could glean more information from your cell I mean, *pod* mate?"

"Shartrese was released on bail and I don't have her contact information."

"I see. Okay, well, we'll keep that in mind. What did your lawyers say?"

"Since the arraignment was already held, expect a trial date to be set. Norrie, I've been charged on circumstantial evidence. Eyewitness reports of me threatening Stanley don't equate with murder. And we still don't have the results on that meat thermometer they confiscated."

"Hold tight. I'm sure it won't be as bad as you think."

"No. It will be worse."

Chapter 29

When I got off the phone with Madeline, I knew I had to move on my two-tiered trap to finger Stanley's killer and find out who sabotaged those wine barrels. I wasn't sure if there was any connection between the two, but I figured that if so, it would eventually fall in place.

I sent Theo a fast text. *Want to talk about two-tiered plan over chicken wings at Uncle Joe's in Geneva? Ask Don. Bradley won't get in until ten-ish.*

Twenty seconds later, *Only if you're buying.*

It's a deal.

The remainder of the day was as perfunctory as could get. Customers in. Customers out. People stocking up on wine. People flipping out over predicted ice storm. All in all, it meant good business, especially if we'd find ourselves closed during the week as a result of the storm.

At a little before four, Glenda pulled me aside from stocking shelves and showed me a fragrant cloth bag that smelled oddly familiar. It dangled from a slim rope chain and I knew what was coming. "Um, is this some talisman you and Zenora want me to wear?"

Glenda pressed the bag into the palm of my hand. "You can wear it around your neck, or put it in your pocket. Your preference. Zenora sensed grave danger. Grave. The sage and basil will protect you."

They'll also make me stink like I just came off a three-day trail ride with no shower.

"That was very thoughtful of Zenora." I took the bag and raced back to my office before Glenda had the chance to offer up any more protection treasures. Thankfully, everyone was so caught up in final tastings, cleaning up, and getting things in order for the next day that any further conversation about "the dreaded harm" that hovered over me would have to wait for another day. Or, another century if I was lucky.

I told Cammy that I'd have to fill her in about Lila in the morning when we'd have a bit more time. "Sundays always start slow," I said. "We can get caught up then. Besides, I'll have more to tell you once Theo, Don and I commiserate tonight."

She put down the dishcloth that was in her hand. "Commiserate, huh? I know what that means. You and Theo have come up with a loosely thought-out plan that would rattle the senses of most rational people. Am I on the right track?"

"On the right track, but the train hasn't arrived yet."

"Let me know when it gets to the station." She winked and picked up the dishcloth. Then she smiled. "Good thing Bradley's coming in tonight. At least there'll be one voice of reason in your house."

I smiled back. "You're forgetting Charlie."

At a little before seven, Theo, Don and I placed our orders at Uncle Joe's. Buffalo chicken wings, Parmesan-crusted chicken wings, and garlic bread. I'd have to make it a point to walk the dog a whole lot more if I wanted to stay in shape.

"Okay," Don said to me as he wiped his lips and reached for another wing. "What plan did you have in mind?"

I glanced around the comfy Italian restaurant with its red and white checkered tablecloths and made sure no one was in earshot. "The first trap is for the wine sabotage at our place and Madeline's. I think we should call Joel Margolis from the *Finger Lakes Times* to do a write-up on our traminette that would be bound to attract the attention of the saboteur."

"What kind of write-up?" Theo eyeballed the wings and reached for one of the drumstick ones.

"A feature that focuses on Two Witches and how our winemakers tasted the wine-in-progress and were ecstatic at what they found. Flavors so intense that the end product would rival anything they'd ever produced."

Don gasped. "You can't do that. It's sheer fabrication."

"Consider it a fishing lure. Something that will compel our culprit to make sure we're unable to produce our wine."

"So, in other words, put Two Witches on notice that someone's going to return to the scene of the crime."

I nodded. "If Joel writes as well as he claims to, it will be like holding a biscuit out in front of a dog. Whoever is behind this won't let it go."

Theo looked at Don, then at me. "You'd have to have major surveillance twenty-four-seven, both inside and out. It's a really dangerous plan."

"Every plan carries risks. Plus, I can set it up so that our crew takes turns on guard duty."

At that point, Don all but choked on a wing. "Franz will be bellowing in German from now until Easter. And which lucky crew members do you propose to do that?"

"The vineyard and tasting crew. Well, maybe not Glenda. She's likely to put a spell on whoever shows up or burn a sage stick in front of them."

"What other plans did you have in mind?"

"Here's the best part. If we catch the culprit in the act, we can move to Tier Two. Have Zenora show up to confront them about Stanley's death and see if they were responsible. One look at her and the fear factor will take over."

"I have the fear factor already," Don said, "and we haven't even gotten to dessert."

Theo wiped his chin and leaned forward. "I'd be curious to see if Joel is willing to do that article."

"All he'll be doing is interviewing and quoting me. I'm the one on the line. And speaking of Joel, he was supposed to call me but sent a text instead. Said his power was out. Look, if we don't get to the bottom of this, Madeline may go to jail and whoever is out there will make sure our wine goes down the drain."

Don grabbed a large piece of the garlic bread. "All I can say is, I'm glad Francine and Jason are off somewhere chasing down bugs."

I gave his shoulder a pat. "Don't worry. It's just a news article."

"And the Boston Tea Party was just a rowdy get-together."

Nonetheless, Theo and Don gave my idea a passive okay and I told them I'd call Joel in the morning.

"What about Bradley?" Theo asked.

"I'll run it by him in the morning. He'll be too exhausted to think tonight. And I still have to mention the Lila thing."

The guys looked at each other. "And to think," Don said, "all I have to do is pick out a dessert."

• • •

True to his word, and decent road conditions, Bradley got to my house at ten fifty. With a slight stubble and even slighter mussed hair, it was hard to resist rushing over and planting a kiss on his lips. Same was said for Charlie, who rubbed against Bradley's knee and got petted in return.

"I need to travel more often," he said. "The welcome back is so worth it!"

"Are you hungry?"

"Just for sleep and being with you."

"I better be first in that order."

He pulled me close and the next kiss was even longer. I made us hot chocolates and took out a box of shortbread cookies. When we finished the last crumb, we walked upstairs to the bedroom. That's when I told him about the encounter Theo and I had with Lila.

"Lila's our client but I'm not so sure I'd get into bed with her. Figuratively. Not literally." I saw a faint blush on his cheeks and smiled as he continued. "Lila isn't exactly as she may seem when it comes to being up-front and honest. We've caught her in a few exaggerations and fabrications when it came to drawing up her divorce. Glad she didn't try talking you into doing anything you'd regret. Like sneaking into her ex's place of business."

This time I was the one who felt the heat rising in my cheeks. "Um, she almost did but when I told her about our relationship she backed off. Funny, but she didn't even know Theo or me and yet told us more than most people share with their closest friends."

"Yeah, that's the thing about Lila. She's a master when it comes to drawing people into her web. Like I said, good thing the conversation didn't go any further."

"More or less. We sort of agreed we'd share information but nothing specific."

"Good. Keep it that way." Bradley yawned and his eyelids started to close.

"Come on, let's get some sleep. Everything else can wait until morning."

Or until I figure out how to introduce the two-tiered plan.

As we walked into the bedroom, Bradley gave my shoulder a squeeze. "Have you thought about contacting that reporter from the *Finger Lakes Times*? If he were to do a write-up on your traminette, it could lure that culprit out into the open and pave a way to find out if the vandalism was related to Stanley's murder. Then again, it's not without risks. I shouldn't have even mentioned it."

"Oh yes you should! Absolutely! Because I had the same idea but wasn't sure how to tell you. But Theo and Don will help and I'm sure our crew will as well. What's the old adage? Safety in numbers?"

"And a well-crafted plan with a fail-safe in place."

"Good. Let's figure it out over breakfast. I can hardly keep my eyes open."

"One more thing. No matter what, we've got to keep Zenora as far away from this as possible."

"Aargh. I know. But she's like a homing pigeon when it comes to this stuff. A homing pigeon with a penchant for herbs, chants, and who knows what."

"Yeah. It's the 'who knows what' that concerns me." Bradley looked up and rolled his eyes.

"You and the entire teaching staff at Uris Library. Come on, let's sleep on it."

Chapter 30

When Bradley headed home the next morning, we had agreed that I'd call Joel Margolis, meet with him, and convince him to write the article. Then, once published in the newspaper, set up an after-hours surveillance team to monitor the outdoor barrels as well as the entry into our production area where most of the wine fermented.

"Given this person's tenacity," Bradley said, "that feature story should lure him out of the woodwork and back to Two Witches in no time. Too bad you can't have a sheriff's deputy in the wings."

"Does Grizzly Gary breathing down my neck count?"

He tousled my hair and gave me a kiss before taking off. Then, I reached for my cell phone and wasted no time calling Joel.

"Hey," I said, "sorry it's so early on a Sunday but I have a favor to ask you."

"Can you ask me over coffee? I was just on my way to the Starbucks on Hamilton Street."

"No problem. Give me twenty-five minutes and I'll see you over there. And don't wait on that first cup for me."

"Good, because it sounds as if I'll need my brain in gear if you're asking me for a favor so early on a Sunday."

"It's a small favor."

"That's how they all start out." He laughed and I could picture his dimples fanning out.

"Consider it an opportunity. See you pronto."

I dabbed a bit of blush on my cheeks and some liner before checking my hair. Then I grabbed my scarf and jacket. At least the weather was clear, albeit cold, but not the frigid cold it had been. Fine for now but a surefire warning that with another slight "warm-up" that ice storm was sure to get here.

Joel was already seated in the far corner past the counter. He had two cups in front of him and handed me one. "Winter blend with cream. Hope that's okay."

"Love this stuff. Thanks."

I sat and loosened my scarf. "Really appreciate you meeting with me."

"Actually, *you're* the one who's meeting with me. I was on my way here before you called." Then he laughed and those dimples danced on his face. Cammy was right. I needed to figure out what was going on in my head before I ever make commitments.

"Things are not looking good for Madeline. In fact, they couldn't look worse. And both sheriffs' offices are moving at a glacial pace. She'll go to trial for something she didn't do."

"How can I help?"

"If you were to write a feature article about our traminette, and explain how exquisite it's going to be, that would be the bait to draw out our vandal and catch him in the act of tampering again. Face it, whoever it was, that person wanted to make sure Madeline's wine and ours were off the market."

"And you think that this article would compel them to give the tampering another shot?"

"For sure."

"And how will this help you exonerate Madeline?"

"Stanley's body was found by her traminette barrel. The person responsible may indeed be the wine saboteur. If we can draw him or her out, we can trap them into confessing."

"How do you propose to do that?"

I bit my lower lip and reached for my coffee. "Um, that's the part that needs some tweaking."

"You mean some *planning*."

"Yeah, well, that, too."

Joel paused and stared at his coffee cup. "Give me a minute. I need more coffee if I'm going to commit to anything."

He stood and walked to the counter, then turned to me. "Did you need more coffee, too?"

I nodded and he nodded back.

When he returned, he handed me a scone and a fresh cup of Winter Blend. "It goes better with a cranberry scone."

"That's nice of you. Next coffee and treat are on me." *Uh-oh.*

"I'll hold you to it."

I went on to explain that basically all he would be doing is highlighting our traminette with quotes from me and my staff. His reputation wouldn't be on the line, ours would. At the end of our chat, he had agreed to speak with his editor and get back to me tomorrow.

"I'll call or text you in the afternoon. Mornings are haywire. Especially Mondays."

"No problem."

"Great. I'll do my best to convince him. Besides, people are always interested in wine around here. You *do* realize I'll be up all night writing it."

I smiled. "It won't go unappreciated." Then I quickly added, "I mean, thanks and the next coffee's on me."

He winked. "It'll be sooner than you think."

From Starbucks I drove home to take care of Charlie and then over to the tasting room to help with the morning setup. I finally had a chance to get Cammy up to date. Surprisingly, she was not fazed about part one in my two-tiered trap.

"It's good publicity, no matter what," she said. "Although I think you should run this by Franz. You know how he gets."

"I'll tell him it's a promo story that might result in an arrest."

"Always a great way to begin the day. Is he working now?"

"Uh-huh. Those winemakers never leave their labs for long. Always checking on something. I'll let you know how he takes it."

Twenty minutes later, I had my answer. Mostly in German. *"Gott im Himmel! Ach du meine Güte!"* I explained that the combination of our in-house security surveillance coupled with our volunteer guard duty would make it impossible for anyone to get near the wine barrels. Still, he wasn't too sure. It was only when I told him that we might use Zenora that he seemed to relax. I could have sworn he said something about scaring the daylights out of people but it was in German and English so I wasn't too sure.

Now it was a waiting game. Like everything else. If Joel got the okay, I had no idea when the story would surface. And timing was everything. At least we had a pretty clear forecast for that ice storm. It was to begin in the Great Lakes as a slow mover and make its way to us by the end of the week. That meant six days if I was lucky. Otherwise, it wouldn't be until the following week when the two-tiered plan would get underway.

With nothing else to do except serve wine to patrons and sneak in screenplay work, I passed the time without incident until the following day. Bradley had to get organized for his full week of work so we agreed to have dinner at my place on Tuesday. He'd pick up barbequed ribs from Wegmans and I'd take care of the side dishes. Yay! I could get used to that kind of eating.

When five thirty finally rolled around, I was glad to trek back home, turn up the heat and crash on the couch with Charlie. Little did I realize that my waiting game was about to end the next morning when I got to work.

• • •

Lizzie was already buried in paperwork at the register when I breezed in on Monday, and the rest of the staff was every which way and that as they got set up. I waved hello and darted into my office, not sure if I should remind Joel or leave things alone. As it turned out, Joel's story took second place to the email that popped up on my screen.

It was from the Yates County Public Safety Office and for a minute I thought it might be one of those "cease and desist" letters from Grizzly Gary to me, but instead it was an official lab report from the county that had been forwarded to me.

I recognized the form having seen one of those before. It dealt with chain of custody, securing evidence, and a whole lot of rigmarole relating to the sample in question. In this case it was the blood found on Madeline's meat thermometer in her winery kitchen. But how that report wafted its way to me was anyone's guess.

I bypassed cells, enzymes, protein, and water, looking instead for the one thing that mattered—the blood type. It was O positive and from what I remembered in high school biology, it was one of two common types. The other being A positive. The question remained— was it Stanley's blood? If not, then whose?

I phoned Madeline under the pretense of asking her if she'd heard anything about the lab report and then segued into finding out that she was O positive. Not exactly encouraging, but not discouraging either. Stanley Hurst could have been O positive as well. Unfortunately, the lab report only dealt with the meat thermometer and not the victim.

"I wish those deputies would find out something," she said. "It could get me off the hook. Pray Stanley's blood was A or B or anything but O."

Oops. That train left the station.

"I'm sure your lawyer will know once the county provides the report to him."

"This is beyond unnerving. I can't sleep. I can't focus. I won't even be able to conduct the next WOW meeting."

I froze in my tracks and mumbled something about skipping it because no one can conduct that meeting as well as she could. *And no one wants to touch it!*

Madeline thanked me for my concern and told me she'd keep me posted. Then I took a closer look at the email and without wasting a second, phoned Gladys Pipp.

Her voice was upbeat and pleasant as always. "Oh, Norrie, I was just about to phone you. Kindly disregard the email you received from this office. I meant to forward it to Deputy Hickman, who's in Benton at the moment, but must have clicked your address by mistake. It's only a few letters apart."

"Thanks, Gladys. I appreciate it."

"Oh, anytime dear."

"Um, would you happen to have received the reports on the facial imprint at my house and the object Eugene found? Oh, and the fingerprints from my refrigerator?"

Her voice got lower and I strained to hear. "I really shouldn't be disclosing this so keep it under wraps. The first and second pieces of evidence are still under analysis."

"What about the fingerprints?"

"Partials. Under analysis. But we did receive a very detailed report from the entomology department regarding the tarp analysis. I'd read it to you but I can't pronounce any of the words."

"No worries. The forensic scientist is a friend of mine."

"Yes, I seem to recall that. Anyway, you have a nice day and be sure to stock up. They predict that storm by week's end."

"I will. You too. And thanks again."

I glanced at the time on my computer and debated whether or not to phone Joel, but as if the machine could read my mind, my cell phone pinged with a text message from him. *It's a go! Interview u 2 nite at dinner?*

I texted back, *Tim Hortons ok?*

Dinner at a restaurant, even for business, could be misconstrued. But Tim Hortons with its bright lights and constant family traffic could only mean one thing—food and coffee. I had set the two-tiered plan in motion and there was no backing down.

Chapter 31

A few seconds later I received a text from Joel with a smiley emoji and the word *yes*. Then, *is 7 OK?*

I texted back with another smiley and a *Yes*.

That being done, I left my office in search of Cammy, who was in the storeroom gathering more wine for our racks.

"Everything's cascading around me but I think I'm on the right track," I said. Before she could eke out a hello, I told her about Bradley being okay with my two-tiered plan, and the fact I was meeting with Joel tonight. Then, I backtracked and filled her in about the email that had serendipitously landed on my desk. Although, truth be known, I was positive it was intentional on Gladys's part.

"Too bad you can't find out about Stanley's blood type. That would narrow things down."

"I could if I were willing to take the chance and get into Eugene's lab. But it's too iffy. Tried it before and barely escaped before getting caught."

"Maybe the right conversation with Clarence. You know, fish it out of him without having him realize it."

"I think that's a skill set I don't have. Then again, it's worth a try."

Cammy smiled and reached for a bottle of Chardonnay that she added to the rolling cart in front of her. "Tell me more about your two-tiered plan. I have a feeling all of us are going to get roped into it."

I grinned. "Roped is such a strong word. More like coaxed or bribed."

"Oh, brother."

I rubbed the back of my neck and proceeded to tell her why Joel and I were having dinner at Tim Hortons.

"Had you named any other restaurant, I would have been certain it was social and not business. But Tim Hortons? I think the Geneva Hockey Team has dinner there after games. Hope you don't run into them."

"Ew. It's at seven. Joel got the green light from his editor to run the story and has to hustle if we expect it to go into the Wednesday community section."

"And then what?"

"Then the real surveillance begins. Hopefully our crew will agree to take turns with the stakeout. On the clock for sure."

Suddenly I realized I had left the storeroom door open and Glenda walked in. "What's this about a stakeout? Are you setting a trap for the killer?"

"I, uh, um . . ."

"Norrie's having a feature story written about our traminette in order to lure the saboteur out. There's a possibility he or she is our killer."

"Perfect plan! Simply perfect!" Glenda fluffed her holographic hair, exposing earrings that resembled a cuttlefish being devoured by a bird. "Zenora and I can use her luring chant to compel that heinous person to return to the scene of the crime."

Cammy put another Chardonnay bottle on her cart and looked at Glenda. "Does Zenora have a chant to get him or her to fess up?"

"Not a chant, exactly. More like a high-pitched noise that resonates in one's ears for hours after the initial exposure."

I held up my hands and widened my eyes. "No chant. No Zenora. We'll be fine. Totally fine. Just surveillance, that's all. And a quick call to the sheriff's office if the culprit returns here."

Glenda shook her head, bouncing those earrings around. "It's far too dangerous to leave it with only surveillance. Zenora has recently learned a spiderweb chant that's bound to slow down the culprit."

"Spiderweb?" I didn't like where this was going but I'd already opened the door and I wasn't referring to the one into the storeroom.

Glenda waved her arms in the air as if conjuring spirits and looked directly at Cammy and me. "You know, a net! That saboteur will be caught in the trami*nette*, so to speak. And with no way out."

All I could picture was a can of Spider Silly String Spray and I had to clamp my lips together to keep from laughing. "Um, could you be more specific?"

"It's a chant that's meant to attract insects that will swarm over the person, thus trapping them in place."

"Glenda," I said. "It's January. There are no flying insects." *Or Godfrey would be all over this!*

She stood perfectly still and spoke slowly. "There *will* be once Zenora recites the chant."

Wonderful. Terrific. Just what we need.

"Actually, what I had in mind was more of a cell phone photo of the perpetrator in the act. But hey, flying insects? What the heck."

"I knew you'd understand." Glenda turned and left the storeroom seconds before Cammy and I burst out laughing. "I have tears in my eyes picturing this."

"I have tears in my eyes period! I can't possibly let those two anywhere near our surveillance."

"Maybe you won't have to. Maybe Clarence will come through about Stanley's blood type and it will prove Madeline wasn't the killer."

"But it won't point a finger at whoever tampered with our wine barrels."

"Aargh. I suppose you're right. Maybe you and Theo need to come up with a three-tiered plan."

"Three?"

"Yeah. A third tier to keep Glenda and Zenora away."

I sent Bradley a text informing him that Joel's feature would be in Wednesday's paper and that he'd interview me for quotes. What I didn't mention was the where and when. Then again, it was only Tim Hortons.

With a slow afternoon and five hours away from seeing Joel, I took Cammy's advice and phoned the sheriff's office requesting to speak with Clarence Eustice.

"Clarence? It's Norrie Ellington from Two Witches Winery."

"Were you trying to place a call to Deputy Hickman? We have a new receptionist who is just learning our phone system."

"No, I can have this conversation with you."

"Good, because the deputy took an early lunch."

Better yet.

"Actually, I really wanted to have this conversation with Eugene, but knowing how nervous he gets around me, I thought someone else might be able to answer my questions. Not that Eugene wouldn't. In fact, he might have mentioned something of the sort when he dusted my refrigerator for prints, but why upset the guy? Do you know if the results are in?"

"Give me a minute. I need to pull up the report on my computer."

I clenched my fingers and held my breath.

"Nothing definitive, I'm afraid. Partial prints on the fridge and nothing viable on that facial imprint. Keep in mind, what you see on TV isn't a genuine reflection of what forensic labs are capable of doing."

"I understand. It's not like blood type that any junior high science student couldn't do with a kit. So I imagine that Stanley's blood type has already been established. In fact, I might even have overheard Deputy Hickman mentioning it to his secretary. What was it? Oh yes, O negative."

"You mean O positive."

"I suppose. That's pretty common, isn't it?"

"Around thirty-seven percent."

"Eugene owes you a thank-you for not having to speak with me."

"I'll be sure to let him know. Is there anything else I can assist you with?"

"Nope. Please let me know if those partials point to someone."

"I'll make a note of it. Have a good day."

"Woo-hoo," I shrieked from my office as I charged out of there all but bumping into Cammy, who was now stocking the wine racks. "I did it! I did it! Clarence told me Stanley's blood type—O positive."

Then I caught my breath. "Drat. That's Madeline's type, too. Of course, it's a common blood type, but I was hoping Stanley's would be something else so that lousy meat thermometer could be dismissed as evidence."

"Drat, indeed. That means your two-tiered plan will be swinging into action, huh?"

"Faster than you think. We need to run this by our tasting room crew and see who wants to sign on."

"I imagine everyone. Sam's always in need of extra cash, Glenda already has her own plan in place, and I'll be there just for the heck of it. That leaves Roger and Lizzie. And you know Lizzie. If it's after eight p.m., she'll be asleep. And isn't Roger on some historical reenactment board that meets Thursday nights?"

"Yeah. The Spanish-American War. Go figure."

"That leaves what? Five of us if we count Zenora."

"Theo will do it. Not sure about Don, but now we're up to six. I hate to ask Emma and Fred since they get here at four thirty most days to start baking."

"Six of us will manage."

"Wait! I forgot Bradley. Make it seven."

"You sure?"

"Oh yeah. He's a real Hardy Boy when it comes to this stuff. Just like Theo. While you're stocking shelves, I'll go around and let the crew know about our plan. Hopefully they'll all agree to it and we can make a surveillance schedule for Thursday night. Good thing that storm's not due to start until Friday."

"Hopefully the saboteur and killer turn out to be the same person and we can all celebrate when we're iced in."

"Absolutely."

So much for positive thinking . . .

Chapter 32

Cammy and I agreed it would be best to have everyone work in "stakeout pairs" for two-and-a-half-hour shifts beginning at six thirty. That would mean four shifts beginning at six thirty at night and ending at four thirty the next morning when the vineyard crew arrived.

Theo opted for taking the two a.m. shift since he's up anyway by four and, according to him, "What's another two hours?"

Glenda was insistent she and Zenora join Theo because three a.m. is apparently some sort of witching hour. Don't ask. Thankfully, I rarely do.

Sam said he'd take two shifts since he was used to pulling all-nighters and would start at nine. Cammy would join Sam for the nine slot and Bradley and I would start the ball rolling at six thirty.

I told everyone we'd have thermoses of hot chocolate and coffee for them as well as some pastries and cookies. Since Two Witches held many outdoor events, thermoses were easier for coffee and we had an abundance. As for the pastries, Emma and Fred were more than happy to bake lots of them.

"This is beginning to sound better and better," Sam said. "Almost like a Boy Scout winter campout but without having to start our own fire." He had just finished up with a group of four people and was headed to the bistro for his lunch break. "Uh, not that I'm running the show, but do you think we ought to have a quick meeting so everyone knows what to do?"

"You're right," I said. "I have an awful habit of thinking that because something is clear in my head, it'll be clear to everyone else. I'll ask our crew to stay an extra few minutes to go over the plan. That way, if we need to make changes, we've got a few extra days. And thanks, Sam. Lately my mind is all over the place."

He smiled and walked toward the bistro.

• • •

In the next two days, our tasting room staff spent more time coming up with scenarios for netting and trapping the culprit than descriptions for the wines they were introducing to patrons. And with each minute, the anticipation grew. Suddenly, everyone pictured him or herself as the next Sam Spade. Well, everyone except Glenda. Frankly, whatever or whoever she pictured in her mind, I didn't want to know.

When Thursday afternoon finally rolled around, I was positive whoever messed with our wine barrel would reappear. My dinner interview with Joel paid off. His article in Wednesday's paper pretty much cinched it as far as I was concerned. Not outright accolades, but detailed and strong descriptions of a wine that had every promise of knocking one's socks off. I figured that the person who sabotaged Madeline's traminette and tried to do the same with ours wanted to make sure those wines never made it to the bottling room.

Oddly enough, John was on board with my plan. Mainly because he didn't figure anyone would show up so close to Friday's ice storm. But Travis, one of his vineyard workers, did. And Travis said he'd assist with the "Midnight Stakeout" because things had gotten way too boring in Penn Yan. We paired him up with Sam for the long nine-to-two shifts.

As four p.m. drew near, Cammy rapped on my office door and I motioned her inside.

"Hey," she said, "my weather app says that ice storm is supposed to start midmorning tomorrow but look outside."

I walked over to the small window in my office with its narrow view of our barn and the lake. "Yeah, looks like sprinkles of rain and maybe a bit of sleet."

"Freezing rain, you think?"

"Could be. It did warm up earlier this afternoon before it got to be really cold again. But I thought that an arctic blast was fueling a snowstorm that was supposed to turn into freezing rain later tomorrow."

"Me too. But the weather people have gotten it wrong before."

I shuddered. "Let's hope they didn't this time or we'll be the ones literally trapped in the traminette."

Cammy stared out the window. "Yeah. Rain and sleet. I suppose nothing to write home about. What time is Bradley coming over?"

"Early. Said he'd be at my house by five. I'm bringing home some sandwiches from the bistro and then we'll be on guard duty by six thirty."

"I'm doing the same. I'll stick around here until then. Got a good book to read and also put in an order for a giant BLT club and potato salad. I'll lock up and walk over to the production building."

"You can always join Bradley and me."

"You guys barely get enough time together. I'll be fine. The peace and quiet will do me good."

"Okay, catch you in a bit."

Roger offered his apologies for not being able to participate and Lizzie said if we needed to get in touch, she'd unmute her phone. I thanked both of them and sent Joel a text informing him of our plan. His response was the same as Lizzie's, but I texted back that we'd be okay. Then he sent a second text, *Do you need additional volunteers?* I couldn't tap those tiny keyboard letters fast enough. *Thanks but we are fine. Got tasting room and vineyard crew people.* I neglected to mention that we didn't have the full roster, but the last thing I needed was an awkward situation between Bradley and Joel. Even though the only interaction Joel and I had were conversations over coffee and sandwiches.

When it got to be five thirty, everyone with the exception of Cammy hustled out of there. The rain fluctuated from liquid to sleet but nothing that warranted a change in plans. Bradley and I wolfed down the tasty roast beef sandwiches on ciabatta bread and made sure that we had two giant thermoses of hot coffee for our stakeout. Then we were off to meet Cammy at the production building. Earlier, I had dropped Charlie off with Don since I didn't want the dog to get stuck in the house if the ice storm meant we would be trapped at the winery.

Cammy was already at the side door when Bradley and I pulled up in his car. He parked in the side lot and minutes later, the three of us made ourselves as comfortable as we could in the outer room with its old cushioned chairs and side tables. I could picture Franz sitting in one of them perseverating over a batch of wine with Alan or Herbert.

"If I were that perpetrator, I'd be showing up tonight too," Cammy said as she shifted in her chair. "That article all but awarded our soon-to-be traminette best wine of the year without even tasting it. Face it, with a storm threatening us tomorrow, he or she would want to get this over with before we got socked in with more snow."

"What? More snow? Who said anything about more snow?" I looked at Bradley and then back to Cammy.

"Whenever there's an ice storm, it's always followed by snow," she said and laughed. "Boy, you've been in Manhattan too long."

Not long enough.

Bradley stood and stretched before plopping back in his chair. "Two things we haven't talked about—mode of transportation for the guy or gal, and means of entry. If the person has any brains in his head, he wouldn't drive directly up here. The outdoor surveillance would catch him. That leaves a few possibilities—park behind the Grey Egret and walk or have someone drop him or her off at the base of the road with a set time for pickup."

"Hang on. I'll call Theo and Don and ask if they have surveillance back there." I pulled out my phone and tapped the number. Seconds later, I got my answer from Don, "Nope, but it's scheduled for later this month with Top View Security. After what happened to you and Madeline, we figured it was the smart thing to do."

I sighed. "Guess that answers that. Anyway, what matters is how they plan on breaking in. We've got to make sure that only the night-lights are on in this room so they don't see us. Even with the blinds pulled, someone can still see movement from the window."

"No time like the present. I'm flipping off the switch." Bradley walked to the door and in an instant we were engulfed in darkness, with the exception of a few floor night-lights, one of which was an old Disney princess light that used to be in Francine's bedroom.

For the next two and a half hours we kept our voices low and consumed scads of pastries and cups of coffee before we realized the implications that Bradley pointed out. "We'd better slow down or someone might hear a toilet flush."

Next, we fixated ourselves on social media and pointed out hilarious gifs to each other. "It's almost nine," Cammy said. "Sam and Travis should be here any second." Just then, there was a knock on the side door and we heard Sam's voice. "It's only us!"

Like it or not, I was on edge. "In here. Keep your voices low. Did you guys see anything on your way over?"

"You mean *felt* anything," Sam said. "Only rain and sleet. Oh, and a bit of wind. Are we supposed to get wind?"

"Who knows." I looked at the weather app for Penn Yan and it said "wintry conditions, pending ice storm."

Travis walked toward us. "We'll be okay if you guys want to take off."

Just then, a gust of wind rattled the building and all of us jumped. So much for a little wind. Then, within seconds, another gust. And another. I looked at Cammy. "Those are heavy wind gusts. Maybe you're better off waiting until it dies down."

Before she could answer, the wind did. And this time with a force that made me second-guess my timing.

"Yeah, maybe you're right," she said. "I always carry a change of clothes in my car in case I get stuck somewhere. Unfortunately, it's usually at one of my aunt's houses."

All of us laughed and in that instant, our cell phone weather alerts went off. *From the National Weather Service—wind, rain, icy conditions in effect for Ontario, Yates, and Seneca counties beginning at 6:30 and expected to last throughout the night. Stay off the roads. Rain changing to ice.*

"Great," Travis mumbled. "Now they tell us. They had all week. That storm wasn't supposed to start until sometime tomorrow."

I went over to the window and looked out. In the distance I could see the lights from the Grey Egret and lots of precipitation dancing all around. "I hate to say this, but I'm beginning to have second thoughts about that culprit returning tonight."

"I'm not," Travis said. "It's the perfect time. No one would expect it."

I bit my lip and hoped he was right. Then I remembered the old adage—Be careful what you wish for. And as it turned out, that old adage was right.

Chapter 33

If Cammy had any thoughts whatsoever about driving home, the relentless wind coupled with a driving rain that was more sleet than rain assured her that she'd be spending the night with us in the winery production building.

"Good thing we came stocked with supplies," I said. "Bradley and I weren't about to take any chances. We brought Cheetos, potato chips, pretzels, candy bars, and Oreos. Oh, and some Catalina Crunch health food snacks that Francine had in the pantry."

"Yep, way better than a Boy Scout winter retreat," Sam said, "except for your sister's health food stuff."

For the next few hours, we checked our cell phones, posted on Facebook, and texted people we hadn't talked to in weeks. Don called Theo with updates from the TV news sources but it was the same stuff we had on our phone alerts.

"We can always call this off," I said, "and head over to my house."

"Or ours," Theo added. "It's closer and downhill. By the way, think Alvin will be okay?"

"For sure." Travis sauntered to the window and stared. "I piled up tons of hay and double-checked that his water supply was heated. Besides, that goat seems to enjoy the brisk winds."

One thirty rolled around before we knew it but still no sign of our perpetrator. Then, the unmistakable sound of a door inside the tank room that creaked open.

"I made sure all the doors we locked," I said. "I thought our culprit would get in through one of the sliding windows."

"Oh no," Cammy said. "I may have left it unlocked when I let Sam and Travis in. Shh! It could be them. Glenda and Zenora won't be here for another half hour. *If* they make it at all."

We remained motionless and held our breath for what seemed like ages. Then, out of nowhere, the worst wind ever and within seconds, the room went black.

Great. The power must be out.

The only sound were footsteps on the concrete floor and it was obvious it was more than one person.

"Shh," I said. "We've got company. All of us need to walk into the tank room with our cell phone flashlights on."

"Then what?" Sam asked.

Unfortunately, I hadn't worked that out in my plan. I took a breath and whispered to Bradley, "Maybe fan out and try to surround them?"

He whispered back, "I don't think we have another choice."

I kept my voice low and hoped I couldn't be heard in the tank room. "Fan out and move in. We'll surround them. And try not to bump into anything." *Or Franz will never get over it!*

The wind really whistled in the tank room. It wasn't as insulated as the outer office and I swore the temperature had dropped by ten degrees. To make matters worse, there were no windows in there so any outdoor lights from the Grey Egret or our building weren't visible. Also, the roof was one of those tin roofs that echoed every single sound the rain and sleet made.

As I moved closer to the center of the room, I could discern an aroma of pine and musk. Had to be someone's aftershave. I poked Bradley, who was to the left of me, and said, "I think it's men. Or at least one man. I can smell his aftershave."

"Yeah, real musky. Almost too musky. Some guys really overdo it."

We moved our flashlight beams up, down, left, and right but didn't see anyone. In fact, the only thing we saw were everyone else's flashlight beams all over the place. It was a mini-strobe light show but without the disco music.

Sam approached us and elbowed me. "They must be hiding behind one of the tanks. We should circle around the first line where the big vats are and then keep going, huh?"

At this point, we could have circled the globe. I was pretty sure that whoever was in here had seen our flashlight beams and had gotten out the same way they got in. Through an unlocked door.

"Psst!" I called out. "Cammy, Travis, and Theo, you guys circle behind the smaller vats, and Sam, Bradley and I will go behind the big ones. Shout if you see anyone. Maybe the element of surprise will stun them."

By now the wind had become downright ferocious and the pitter-patter of rain and sleet on the roof was more like a jackhammer than an ice storm. And then, without notice, a piercing yowl caused Sam and Theo to drop their cell phones. I held my phone to the ground but Bradley accidently bumped into me and my phone joined Sam's and Theo's.

Meanwhile, Cammy was on her own at the other side of the tank room, and seconds later I heard a crash. "They're getting away," she shouted. "Rush to the door."

"We can't even find the door," I yelled back.

Then, another voice, "We brought glow sticks. We'll catch them. Good thing we got here early."

Glow sticks? Early? Oh my gosh—it's Glenda and Zenora!

"Glenda? Is that you?" My voice literally bounced off the walls.

"Yes! Where did that killer go? Zenora's luring spell must have worked."

"It's not the killer, or culprit. Or wine vandal. It's just us! We thought you and Zenora were the perpetrators."

Just then, the lights came on, but flickered, illuminating Zenora's long wooly cape. It gave her a strange appearance of a Neanderthal dressed for an eighteenth-century dinner party. I later found out it was a cashmere cape made out of wool from Mongolian goats. Don't ask.

"Patience, all," she said. She outstretched her arms like Moses holding back the Red Sea. "I feel great power with my luring spell. It will attract our villain like an outdoor porch light attracts moths."

I swallowed what little moisture I had left in my mouth as Sam and Theo bent down to pick up our phones. "Um, good thought. So, how were the roads? We didn't think you'd make it."

"Oh, we didn't drive." Zenora adjusted her cape and glanced at Glenda. "A friend of mine is a snowplow operator for Yates County. We met up with him in Geneva and since he had to salt Route 14, he dropped us off at the base of your road. It's kind of frowned upon but we told him how urgent the situation was."

Fantastic. It'll be a regular campout with Glenda and Zenora here all night as well.

"I see. So, uh, getting back to my question, how are the roads?"

"No traffic," Glenda said. "But the salt truck didn't seem to have a problem."

Of course not. It's the salt truck!

"Well, everyone," I said, "I think we can safely say our venture tonight was a complete flop."

And in that second, the lights went out again, accompanied by a howling wind that sounded like coyotes seconds after a fresh kill.

"The air tells me something different," Zenora said. "It's thick with anticipation."

Theo bumped me and whispered, "Like Carly Simon." Thankfully, no one else heard. I cleared my throat and sighed. "Okay, it's almost two and we might as well stick it out. I mean, it's not as if we can do anything else at this point."

"Might as well retreat to the outer office and see what ensues." Bradley pointed his flashlight and the others turned theirs on as well. Once back in the office, we tore into the pile of junk food as well as the supply of bottled waters that were in the small office fridge.

"Did anyone lock the door behind Glenda and Zenora?" I asked. "Because I didn't."

Cammy finished chomping on something and answered, "All taken care of. The dead bolt kept sticking but the bottom lock underneath it is all set."

"At least it's something," Bradley said. "But I wager if anyone is that determined to get in here on a night like this, no lock is going to deter them."

Under ordinary circumstances, Bradley's comment wouldn't have made any of us bat an eyelash, but sitting in the darkness with only our cell phone screens lit up, it was as eerie as could be. So eerie that I actually shuddered and tightened the scarf I had draped around my neck.

When we were done crunching and munching, albeit quietly, Glenda put her finger to her lips. "I think I heard something."

"It's only the wind," Cammy said, but before she finished the word *wind*, we heard the unmistakable sound of a door crashing open. *Of all the times for that dead bolt to get stuck.*

We wanted to catch the culprit in the act, but *as* they were trying to break in, not once they did.

"Same plan as before?" Sam asked.

"Give it a second. Then, we should all run in shouting. Shouting so loud as to terrify whoever it is."

"They'll run out and we won't be able to catch them on the slippery ice," Cammy said.

Theo immediately responded. "They'll slip, too. Makes it real easy."

"No sense waiting." Bradley's voice was clear and determined.

"Let's do it!" I let out a shriek that got muffled with everyone else's, and next thing I knew we elbowed, bumped, and collided with each other as we charged to the tank room like the Rough Riders during the Spanish-American War. Roger would have been proud.

And while the Rough Riders most likely carried bayonets, we carried our cell phones that were either jostled or clenched in our hands without paying attention to the flashlight feature. Beams shot out everywhere like strobe lights and the eight of us ran about the room willy-nilly in search of our intruder.

The howling wind didn't help any, and neither did the relentless sound of ice hitting the metal roof. Still, we persevered. Some of us got knocked into the stainless-steel tanks in the dark while others ran in circles.

Then, the most unexpected thing. Someone's flashlight beam hit the bottom of Zenora's face and made her long, angular features take on a ghoulish appearance. I remember doing something like that at summer camp as we held flashlights under our chins during ghost stories around the campfire.

She must have seen or felt something because she called out, "I will curse that scourge to the end of time in a hellish fire!"

Sam, who was inches from me, choked back a laugh and whispered, "Too bad she can't try out for a part in *Macbeth*."

Then Zenora again. "Cease! Before it's too late."

I was about to join Sam with a laugh of my own when suddenly a man called out, "Get her away! Get that witch away from me!"

In seconds, we all raced to the sound of his voice, bumping shoulders, arms and legs. That's when something hit the ground and broke, scattering its pieces all over the place. I prayed it wasn't a piece of valuable winemaking equipment.

Next thing we knew, some of us tripped over whatever it was and landed on the floor. Myself included. But that didn't deter the rest of our crew.

"I've got him!" Bradley shouted. And then, "Rats! This guy knows how to fight. He landed a kick to my shin and got away."

"He just kicked me too!" Theo yelled. "Someone please move your flashlight beams!"

As if on cue, we all did, only to figure out that Bradley and Theo had been fighting each other in the dark. Worse yet, whoever Zenora scared had bolted out of there the same way he got in—through the door he busted open.

Chapter 34

"I'm calling the sheriff's office. Not that they can get here, but still, they need to know that a killer just escaped from our production building."

"And I'm calling Don," Theo said. "He needs to be on the lookout."

Then Zenora, "I'm summoning him back with the luring spell."

Wonderful. A repeat performance in the dark.

"No! No luring spell. I think we've had enough luring. At least we know one thing—our plan worked. Whoever that guy was, he risked everything tonight to sabotage our wine. And no one does a thing like that if they weren't in the wine business themselves. They want their traminette to succeed at all costs. Including eliminating the competition."

I raised my voice since keeping quiet no longer mattered. "He couldn't have gotten far. It's too dangerous to walk, so that leaves what? A snowmobile? Most likely he's got a buddy close by waiting for him. If that darn wind would stop, I'd bet we'd hear it."

With my flashlight pointed down as I tapped the sheriff's office, I saw what caused some of us to stumble and fall. Scattered on the floor were similar sized and shaped wood chips.

"Oak chips! Oak chips for fermentation!" Theo bent down and picked up a few. "Yep. Unmistakable fragrance. Oak chips, all right. That guy knew exactly what to do."

"So do I." I tapped the number and waited. "The sheriff's line is busy. Figures."

"Or it's dead," Cammy said. "That happens during storms. Do you have a cell number?"

"Aragh. Yes. Grizzly Gary's."

"Might as well do it," Bradley said. "He'll find out soon enough. Best to hear from you."

Then Theo's phone pinged and it was a text from Don. *I'm on it! Heavy duty flashlight and boots with snow cleats.*

"Don's going after him," Theo announced. "I'd better get out there!"

"Not without us!" Bradley was already across the room and nearing the door with me hot on his heels.

"Don't start the party without me!" Sam sounded as if a giant keg was being brought into the room.

Cammy, who stood near Sam a few minutes ago, echoed the same thing while Glenda and Zenora vowed to "encircle the intruder and hold him down with their thoughts." Yep, their thoughts . . .

Theo pushed the door open further and we all exited into the cold, icy night. Pellets of sleet hit my face as I tried to keep my flashlight beam focused on the area between our production building and the Grey Egret. Hazy lights from Don and Theo's place made the landscape look like something out of *Wuthering Heights*.

Suddenly, I heard a familiar sound—Charlie's hound-dog howl, and it was close.

"He must have gotten outside when Don opened the door," Theo said. "I hope he doesn't bolt."

"Me either, but he thrives on excitement and loves to be around people. He probably thinks this is a party."

The wind was even more ferocious outside, making it difficult to tell where our voices were coming from. But the dog's howl echoed and got louder as we continued downhill. Then, a voice that wasn't Don's. "Call your dog off! He's about to rip my face apart! I'm on the ground and he's on top of me!"

"Stay still," I screamed, "or he's liable to sink his teeth into a cheek." *Or lick you to death, whichever comes first.*

"Charlie wouldn't—" But Sam didn't get to finish his question, when Cammy and Theo answered with a resounding *No!*

"Shh, that's only for our perpetrator's benefit," I whispered. "Let him think that Plott hound is a Rottweiler."

We continued to where we heard the man's voice but fanned out in case the wind had played tricks on us. I pulled my scarf even tighter and chastised myself for leaving my gloves in the outer office.

About fifteen yards away, I could make out Don's silhouette. The beam from his flashlight was aimed down, so while he had a clear view of the intruder's face, we had nothing but a hazy one. Still, we had managed to wrangle the guy and that was all that mattered at the moment.

With the exception of Glenda and Zenora, we rushed the scene, slipping, yanking on each other, and cursing the icy rain. Instead of joining our fracas, those two created a fracas of their own—a strange musical yowl that sounded as if a fresh kill had been made. Zenora later informed me it was a *spiritual reckoning* for our culprit.

Don had replaced Charlie by the time we reached them halfway between his house and our property. I got a good look at the man's face but didn't recognize him. Late forties maybe? Stubble and a black wool cap. I didn't take any chances. I whipped out my phone and took three photos, just to be sure.

"The sheriff's office is sending someone," I lied. "Even in these road conditions. So you're not going anywhere."

"The spirits have turned their backs on you, too," Zenora added, "and darkness will befall you."

Sam kicked my ankle and mouthed, "In case she hasn't noticed, darkness is here already."

I choked back a laugh.

"It will be a relief to the sheriffs' offices in Ontario and Yates counties," I said, "knowing that we've caught Stanley Hurst's killer."

"What???" The man sat up but didn't move. "I didn't kill anyone! I'll admit that I tried to break into your wine production building but—"

"You didn't *try*, you busted through the door," Cammy said. "And who's to say you're not lying about committing murder."

"Okay, fine. I did break in. And I was the one responsible for ruining your other vat of traminette, but I swear on my life, I did *not* kill Stanley Hurst and I'll be able to prove it. At least I hope my lawyers can. I was, um, uh, engaged in tampering with another winery's barrel around the time of the murder."

"And pray tell, how do you know what time that was?" I asked.

"Because it's been all over the news. Besides, I had no gripe with the guy. I don't own any property that would suffer on account of his high-rise development."

"But your other business would have taken a backseat due to Billsburrow's traminette and ours. Isn't that so?" I wasn't about to let the guy wheedle his way out of anything.

"I'm not proud of it, but yeah, it's true. I have an interest in a winery in Chester, Virginia, and your traminette would have knocked us out of the market."

"So you came up to the Finger Lakes to make sure that didn't happen?"

"I have family here."

"Nothing like combining nefarious business with a family get-together," Theo said.

"You're Audrey Killion's son, right?" Don leaned closer to the guy and didn't budge.

"I'm one of them, yeah. But she had nothing to do with the wine tampering. She has no issue with the wineries. Not like—"

And in that instant, the piercing sound of sirens split the cold night air.

"I called the sheriff's office and got through," Don said.

No way around it. It was only a matter of minutes before I'd be on the hot seat with the local deputy and not our intruder.

"Don't think of making a run for it, because our statewide facial recognition system is flawless." *Just don't talk with Eugene.* "And speaking of facial recognition, they'll find yours on my door pane!"

"Huh? What are you talking about?"

"You know very well. What were you doing sneaking around my house and ferreting through my refrigerator? What were you expecting to find?"

"Your refrigerator? I have no idea what you're talking about. I don't even know who you are or where you live."

"Norrie Ellington. Co-owner of Two Witches and I live in the white farmhouse up the driveway from our winery."

"Listen, I confessed to what I did. Plain and simple. But breaking into someone's refrigerator? Sounds more like what a homeless person would do. Trust me. I get enough to eat."

"I'll believe it when the lab report comes out."

Theo nudged me and whispered, "I don't think he's your peeping Tom." Then he took a step toward the man. "Tell us who you've got waiting for you."

"No one. I came on my own. My snowmobile is behind the barn over there."

In spite of the driving sleet and cold temperatures, I was on overdrive, and with it, my adrenaline pumped like crazy. Cammy tapped my shoulder and asked, "What are you going to tell Grizzly Gary?"

"I'll know as soon as it comes out of my mouth."

Just then, a sheriff's vehicle pulled up to the side of the driveway that separated the Grey Egret from Two Witches. Two doors slammed, followed by the familiar figure of Deputy Hickman, illuminated by the distant lighting and the moon. With him was another deputy I didn't recognize.

"Miss Ellington!" His voice boomed like a canon. "If I were a betting man, I would be a millionaire. Not a single doubt in my mind you'd be leading this, this . . . oh good heavens, I hardly know what to call it!"

"Call it apprehending a murderer! We caught Stanley Hurst's killer. It's the same man who sabotaged the wine barrels here and at Billsburrow."

"I didn't kill anyone! No one! I'm innocent! I'm not a murderer."

The deputy sauntered over to where the man remained on the ground and took out a pad and pen. "Then suppose you tell me how you got here."

Just then, Zenora answered. "By the spiritual forces of the winter moon and my luring spell."

Deputy Hickman turned to me. "Just *how much* drinking have you folks been doing?"

I explained as best as I could about my two-tiered plan when he looked at the other deputy. "You getting any of this down? It's almost dawn on one of the most dangerous road-condition nights in the county's history, and here we are in the middle of a Marx Brothers movie."

Then he focused his attention on our captive. "I need your name, address, and a brief recount of this situation. You didn't wind up on the icy ground for the fun of it."

"I'm Benjamin Killion and my family owns a bakery on this road." He then went on to explain that while he was fully responsible for the damages done to our wineries, he had nothing whatsoever to do with Stanley's demise.

Deputy Hickman read him his rights, cuffed him and put him in the backseat of his vehicle. "We'll need to wait it out until the salt truck returns. Only reason we were able to get this far was because we radioed the county and followed one of their salt trucks." Then he motioned to his partner. "Rick, phone the county and find out when the salt truck will make its next loop. Meantime, we can sit tight in the car."

Next, he directed his attention to all of us. "I'll need statements from each of you. Given the precarious road conditions, I am not summoning you to the sheriff's office. Email us your write-ups with complete contact information. Lamentably, Miss Ellington knows how to reach us."

I gulped and smiled as the two deputies hauled off Benjamin and got into their vehicle.

"I'd call that a partial success," Theo said. "Now all we need to do is catch the actual killer."

"Or a cold." Don sneezed. "Come on. Plenty of hot coffee at the house and a toasty fire. Got plenty of blankets too so you can all camp out in the living room."

"And you'll be safe from the evil that lurks," Glenda said. "We brought plenty of crushed sage."

I did a mental eye roll as we trekked downhill to Don and Theo's place. There, waiting on the steps, was Charlie, who'd probably had enough excitement for the night.

Chapter 35

No surprise that the county roads were closed the next day along with schools and businesses. Fortunately, the temperature rose and the closure was lifted for a brief while by early afternoon. It allowed Cammy, Glenda, Zenora, Sam, and Travis to get home before another deep freeze with accompanying rain was expected.

Bradley, Charlie, and I returned to my house to wait out the rest of the storm.

"I can't believe it wasn't him," I moaned to Bradley as I heated up some tea. "I was so certain."

He put his arm around mine and pulled me close. "You did an amazing job. Frankly, I wasn't so sure we'd get this far."

"I suppose. One down. Two to go."

While Bradley got the mugs out for our tea, I phoned Madeline to give her the good news about our saboteur, but it was a far cry from lifting her mood. "You shouldn't have taken such a chance, Norrie, but I'm glad you caught that scoundrel. At least we can hold out hope for some remuneration. Still, it doesn't do a thing for getting me off the hook as far as Stanley's murder is concerned."

"They only have circumstantial evidence."

"I think that's all they'll need. I suppose I'll need to relinquish my role as organizer for our WOW group."

Not if I can help it!

"All of the evidence isn't in yet. Besides, Bradley, Theo and I will come up with another plan."

"You've already put yourself in danger. Please don't do it again on my account. My attorney is a good one and I'm sure he'll fight long and hard for me."

"We all will."

When I got off the phone, I was more determined than ever to move on to the next tier in my plan/trap. I sat at the kitchen table and cupped my hands around the hot mug of ginger spice tea. "Remember when Benjamin said his mother wasn't involved in the traminette tampering?"

Bradley blew on his mug and set it down. "Uh-huh. Frankly, I don't believe she was either. I mean, what on earth would be in it for her? She runs a small, albeit burgeoning, bakery with another son, and had no beef with the wine industry."

"True, but she had an issue with the high-rise. It would have cost her a tremendous loss of business."

"Still not motive enough. It would mean a loss of revenue for lots of lakeside businesses. Including yours."

"Ugh. I know. But here's the thing—When Benjamin told us his mother didn't have an issue with the wineries, he said, 'Not like—' and got cut off. I think he was about to say 'Not like Stanley Hurst. Look, maybe it's pure speculation on my part, but I think we need to put Audrey Killion to the test and find out if she was behind the murder."

"What about the others? The yes votes who could have been bribed or blackmailed?"

I shook my head. "Nothing on Diane Oftspringer, although I'd recommend some budget counseling. And nothing on Michael Antonacci or Avery Pullman. At least nothing I could find. Oh, and by the way, I still think Avery wrote his own threatening note."

"Yeah. That wouldn't surprise me. What about Victor Dahl? You and Theo found something in his email, right?"

"A message that said 'One down, one to go.' And then something about 'doing it' or the 'milk will run dry.'"

"Could be a threat. Or not. Maybe it had to do with milking those cows. Maybe they got new equipment that required a change in the procedure."

"I'll check in with Gladys Pipp once the offices are open. If anyone would know, it would be her."

Bradley laughed. "Boy, it didn't take you long to figure out the shortest distance between two points."

"Hey, someone around here needed to!"

"Okay, so what devious trap for Audrey did you plan to set this time?"

"I'm not sure. We'll need to mull it over. Theo told me that when he checked out the bakery, he didn't see any sort of impaler and that Audrey told him her natural treatment for pantry pests worked. Still, she could have lied. Those little buggers on the tarp that covered Stanley's body could have come from there. I was hoping to find out more from Godfrey at that cockroach banquet but I'd better call him sooner."

"Well, right now we've got plenty of time on our hands. My office will be closed for the next few days, so we might as well begin brainstorming the second tier."

I stood, put my arms around his neck, and gave him a kiss on his cheek.

"Keep that up and we won't get to brainstorm."

I smiled. "Work before pleasure." Then I handed Bradley one of the small notepads I had on the kitchen counter and took one for myself. "If I remember correctly from college, it's about *quantity* over *quality*. At least at first. That means anything goes."

For the next forty or so minutes, we came up with scenarios that would make Quentin Tarantino proud. They would also drive Deputy Hickman into a new career, which might not be such a bad idea, come to think of it.

Finally, we landed on two possibilities. Both of which would have to wait until the ice freeze that had taken over the county disappeared. The tricky part would be the timing since another snowstorm was sure to follow. At least according to Cammy, who's usually right when it comes to weather predictions.

"I'm good with both of these," I said, "but maybe we should see what Theo thinks. For sure, he'll want to be part of it."

Without waiting for an answer, I tapped Theo's number and told him what Bradley and I had in mind.

"You want me to what?? That's worse than landing in manure. What's your next brainchild?"

I took a breath and articulated every word. "It's the classic distraction and action scenario. You know, where one person distracts the suspect while the other sneaks around for evidence."

"I suppose I'm going to be the distractor while you're going to be the actor? So to speak."

"That would make sense since you and Audrey have already chatted. You could pick up where you left off or yak about something else. Meanwhile, I'll see if I can get into the back of her bakery and hunt around for pantry pests. I'll scoop them into an envelope and then get Godfrey to have a look-see."

"Hmm, compared to your other exploits, this one doesn't sound too bad. Okay, when?"

"How about this afternoon? We can't afford to wait and right now the temperature is above freezing. At least for the next two hours. We'll be on the clock for sure. Plus, Bradley can join us and help you keep Audrey otherwise occupied."

"Fine. Come on down. Don will be more than pleased. And yes, it was an acerbic comment for sure."

"Tell him you'll bring back some goodies."

"I'll have to or he'll lock me out."

I made a quick call to Godfrey and got a response I never expected. Apparently bugs weren't the only thing found on that tarp.

"Are you sure?" I asked.

"Uh-huh. Even had the culinary lab test it."

"Cornell has a culinary lab?"

"Food Science, Norrie. Food Science."

"Wow. So, what did the foodies find?"

"There was some type of dried jam or jelly on it. Elderberry."

"Oh my gosh! Oh my gosh! Just like the stuff they found on our wine barrel. It makes sense and points a finger at the same time. Benjamin would have visited his mother's bakery or even helped out.

Easy to transfer that sticky stuff. It doesn't really point a finger at her for the murder but it certainly points in her general direction."

"Please tell me you're not about to do something you'll regret."

"Only if I get caught." I proceeded to give him the rundown on our plan, especially if it went south and we found ourselves in need of bail money.

"Not funny, Norrie. But keep me posted one way or the other."

"For sure."

Ten minutes later, Bradley and I picked up Theo and headed down the lake to Audrey's bakery. Road traffic was light and steady considering the wet highway with icy patches. In two hours, it would be a skating rink.

"What if the bakery is closed?" Theo asked. "We never thought of that."

I glanced in the rearview mirror to the backseat. "Somehow, I think she'll open. Lots of customers will want breads and the like. Chances are she has enough in stock."

Bradley turned his head to Theo. "I just googled the bakery. It'll be open until five. Looks like it's a *go*, folks!"

Sure enough, when I pulled into their parking lot, four cars were already there. I gave Bradley a nudge and briefly turned my head to Theo. "The more distractions, the better. I'll do the sneaking and the two of you can ask all sorts of questions. Plus, she'll want to talk since you're buying baked goods."

As we approached the door to the bakery, we noticed she or her son had thrown sand on the steps instead of salt. Yep, environmental concern and all of that, I mused. There were two people at the counter and a third milling around the shelves when we went inside. Only Audrey was there. An awful thought sprang to mind and I tired to ignore it. What if the son was in the storeroom? Then what?

I'd always operated by the seat of my pants but this was one seat I didn't want to mess up. I crossed my fingers he was elsewhere and looked around for a door that led to a back room. Meanwhile, the guys stood behind the other customers and waited. When I located the only door in the shop, other than the entrance, I glanced over to make sure Audrey was preoccupied. Then, I rushed inside.

Thankfully the room, with pantry shelves that ran floor to ceiling on three sides, was empty. Or at least that's what I thought. I stepped inside, prepared to look in the back of the shelves that housed flour, cornmeal, and other bug-inviting products. But just as I pulled a small envelope from my pocket, something behind me clattered and I froze. Only two words sprang to mind—*bail bondsman.*

Chapter 36

Excuses, explanations, and apologies filled my head as I spun around to confront whoever it was who'd discovered me. It was only when I glanced down and saw a large tabby cat that I was able to breathe normally again.

I let out a slow breath and walked to the wall that housed assorted flours. As quietly as I could, I moved them around in order to get to the back of the shelves, where I was positive I'd find some of the culprits. No luck. No luck whatsoever. I also checked the trash, but all I saw were crumbled notes, as if someone had an incomplete English assignment in there.

The cornmeal section was next and still no bugs. Then I noticed some large barrels with linen sack bags inside. I opened the lid to the first one and sure enough, icky black insects were in the flour mix. I scooped a few of them and dropped them into the envelope. Then I did the same with the barrel next to it. Weevils? It didn't matter. All that mattered was that these insects match the ones found on that tarp.

Then, as I was about to leave, I noticed Audrey's canned goods— the same mason jars my sister used. No surprise. Nothing tastes like homemade jams and jellies when used on cookies and pastries. I perused the assortment for a split second and there it was—elderberry! Audrey mentioned something about having raspberry bushes and a strawberry patch when she talked with Theo, but not elderberry. Still, there it was, the evidence of homemade canning!

By now, I was more than certain Stanley's murderess was a few feet away happily selling cheesecakes and babka. I could wait for Godfrey to make the final determination, or . . . I could speed up the process. I grabbed my iPhone and googled "pantry pests," determined to find the Latin name so when I confronted Audrey, I'd have some validity.

Seconds later, I exited from the storeroom and walked to the front counter. Bradley and Theo had just approached, their arms filled with breads and cakes.

"Excuse me," I said to Audrey, "I'm a winery owner who works with the entomology department at Cornell and it appears we have matched your (*Oh please let me come up with a name*) Granious blantanous weevils to the ones found on the tarp that covered Stanley Hurst."

"What? That's impossible! My bakery doesn't have pantry pests. I use natural herbs to prevent their infestation."

I shook my head. "Apparently it didn't work. You may want to check your storeroom."

"You were in my storeroom?"

"I didn't have to go in there," I lied. "I can spot the little buggers from here."

In a flash, I crouched down and shook a few pests from the envelope into my hand. "See for yourself!"

By now, the other customers had left and we were the only ones there.

Audrey's face turned red and she furrowed her brow. "I don't remember any entomologists getting samples here."

"My notes say they did. They spoke with a Benjamin Killion who was in here. It must have been at a time when you stepped out."

"Fine. Suppose they did. A weevil is a weevil. Just like a roach is a roach."

Don't tell that to Godfrey.

"Ah-hah! That's what you think. We match skin thickness, color, antennae length and shape as well as the kind of feces they produce." I pictured Godfrey laughing his head off at the feces remark, but to my knowledge, I was spot-on with the other stuff.

"And," I added, "the department isolated dried elderberry jam on the tarp. If they were to match it with your homemade jellies, I dare say it would be all the evidence they need!"

I expected Audrey to break down and confess, but instead she reached under the counter and aimed a gun directly at my face. A gun! The one thing I never imagined would have happened.

"Go ahead, shoot," Bradley said. "What's the worst you can do, get us soaking wet?"

"It's a water pistol?" And thank goodness my boyfriend didn't set me up to be the next victim.

He laughed. "Uh-huh! My nephews have the same ones. Realistic, huh?"

"A little too realistic if you ask me." Theo let out a slow breath and I thought we'd be in the clear.

Then, out of nowhere, the other son appeared behind the guys and it looked as if the gun he held in his hand wasn't loaded with water. He nudged Bradley and whispered, "We have lots of extra tarps in the storeroom."

Then, out of shear lunacy, I poured the contents of my envelope into my hand and threw it in his face. "These are stinging roaches from an inspection down the road. At first you won't feel a thing, but in ten minutes, you'll be fighting for your breath."

The momentary shock was enough to get him to drop his gun and rub his eyes with both hands. Theo snatched the gun and Bradley grabbed the guy by his wrists. I thought it would be all over but it was only the beginning.

Audrey flew out from behind the counter holding a long skewer stick that she raised directly at my chest. Instinctively, I ducked, allowing Theo to elbow her under the arm. But the momentary blow didn't last long. Audrey still held fast to the skewer and attempted to plunge it into Theo's torso. With no weapons of my own, I did the only thing I could—land a few punches to Audrey's back, resulting in what could be best described as a schoolyard fight.

Meanwhile, Bradley had the gun aimed at Audrey's son and wasn't about to move. Then, all of a sudden, I heard him yell, "Alexa! Dial the Grey Egret in Penn Yan! Ask for Don. Say the word *emergency*." The virtual assistant that was shelved behind the counter did as

Bradley commanded, and as soon as Don got to the phone, all of us spoke at once.

"Get help!"

"Alexa can't call 911!"

The sound of Theo, Audrey and me crashing into shelves and knocking over baked goods was enough for Don to reply, "On it!" and get off the phone.

At some point, I thought Audrey would tire of fending off Theo and me, but having a sharp skewer in her hand must have given her a sense of bravado because that wacky woman wouldn't quit. Worse yet, she knew how to fight.

And while I was out of breath, she apparently was not. Then, at some point in our melee, I spied homemade cider in those plastic half-gallon bottles. Leaving Theo to ward off the MMA fighter-of-the-year, I unscrewed the cap and poured it all over Audrey's head. As she hurried to wipe her eyes, she let go of the skewer and Theo kicked it across the room. Luckily, Bradley was able to pick it up while still pointing the gun at Audrey's son.

Suddenly the room got still and we stood like a tableau, only we weren't acting out a scene from history, we were simply exhausted. It was little wonder that when two sheriff's deputies entered the bakery a few minutes later, they thought Bradley had held us hostage.

"Drop your weapon! Now!" one of them shouted.

Bradley immediately did as asked and replied, "It's not my weapon. I confiscated it from the man in front of me who tried to kill me."

Audrey's son narrowed his brow and grumbled, "I was only trying to scare him."

Then, the second deputy glanced at Theo, Audrey, and me. "You all look as if you've been fighting off racoons, or worse."

I took a breath and wiped the sweaty hair from my brow. "Not racoons—Stanley Hurst's murderess and I can prove it. See that skewer on the floor? One just like it is the murder weapon. Have Eugene in your lab match it up to the actual wound dimensions and you'll find out the killer is Audrey Killion."

"The woman is out of her mind," Audrey said. "Lots of bakers use skewers for small cupcakes as a special bakery item."

"But lots of bakers don't have pantry pests that match up to the ones found on that tarp Stanley was wrapped in. Oh, and don't let me forget the elderberry jam. Which, by the way, created quite the mess on our stainless-steel barrel."

The younger of the two deputies turned to his partner. "Do you have any idea what she's talking about? One minute murder, then the next, jam on stainless-steel."

At that point Theo filled them in and added his own take. "Audrey couldn't have pulled off that murder on her own. At the very least, she needed help moving the body from the scene of the crime to its dumping spot at Billsburrow Winery." Then he pointed to her son. "Look no further. I think you'll find her accomplice a few feet from you. And the gun is his, too!"

Then the son looked at his mother. "Mom, I think we should—"

"Don't you say another word," she snapped. Then she glared at the deputies. "You won't be able to prove anything."

"Murder carries a life sentence," I said, before turning to Bradley and whispering, "It does, doesn't it?"

"Nonetheless," the older deputy said to Audrey, "although this is not official evidence, given the circumstances, I'm bringing both of you in for questioning. And expect to stay there for a while. The road is icing up and the county will be closing it down within the hour."

Then, out of the blue, her son blurted out, "I'm not about to serve a life sentence for something I didn't do. All you said was that someone died in your bakery and you didn't want to have that blemish on the business so we needed to move the body and that it would be easily found at a winery."

"Ah-ha!" I fixed a look at Audrey and the words flew out of my mouth. "So you did murder Stanley, after all. Pure cold-blooded murder."

Her eyes welled up and her voice trembled. "It wasn't murder. Well, not cold-blooded murder. That awful man came into my bakery to gloat over the fact that his high-rise would be built. Didn't care a whit about anyone's lakeside business. Even made some snarky remarks about our mom-and-pop bakery and said no one would care if it went out of business. Well, *I* cared and my family cared, but he wouldn't stop antagonizing me. Finally, when he said my scones tasted as if they were baked in Pompeii at the time of the volcano, I guess I lost it. I was holding a cupcake skewer to create those trendy desserts and all of sudden, I stabbed him in the chest. I thought I'd just wound him, but apparently, I hit a vein. Or an artery. Or whatever kills a person right away."

The deputies read Audrey her rights and cuffed her. Then, they did the same with her son. I motioned to Bradley and Theo as I started for the door.

"Well, I suppose you don't need us here any longer. We best be on our way. Your office can thank me later."

The same deputy shook his head. "Not so fast. I'll need to see your IDs and have you write down your contact information. Expect a visit when the roads are safe."

I gulped. "Deputy Hickman?"

Both deputies nodded and my stomach tightened.

"Think they'll be able to make that arrest stick?" I asked Bradley and Theo once we were back in the car and on our way home. "After all, she can say she was forced into a confession."

"They'll put a firecracker under Eugene for sure to hasten the evidence match-up," Theo answered. "Which should really endear you to him." Then he burst out laughing.

"And if Godfrey can provide a perfect pest link, it'll cinch it!"

Bradley reached over and gave my arm a squeeze. "Leave this part to the sheriff's office. I'd say Madeline will be in the clear soon enough. As will my client, thank goodness. There's only so much of Lila Stratington-Hurst one can take. She'll be happy with the news once I speak with her."

The icy spots in the road multiplied as I got closer to Two Witches Hill. Theo leaned over at least half a dozen times directing me to go slower.

"Okay, okay, we're almost there. I wanted to get home before all those icy spots turned into one big ice-skating rink."

"I can't believe you pushed it to the grand finale," he said. "I just thought we were gathering information and having a tête-à-tête with Audrey."

"Um, yeah. So did I. Until all the pieces came together. Then I figured I'd better act fast while we had the chance."

Bradley reached for my arm again. "We can sleep well tonight. You can chalk up two mysteries solved. No more tossing and turning."

"You're wrong," I said. "There's Avery's note and that email from Dahl Farms. But the scariest mystery is still out there. Who on earth snooped around my house and got into my refrigerator? And more importantly, why? I'm never going to get a decent night's sleep until we find the culprit."

Theo bumped my shoulder. "You ought to ask the sheriff's office for a salaried position."

Then Bradley laughed. "She's lucky they don't offer her a cell for interference."

Chapter 37

I couldn't wait to share the news with everyone the following morning, but thanks to that ungodly early morning farm report, they all knew. Along with the fact that all county roads were closed until further notice, along with schools and most business. The term *ice-skating rink* was bantered around by more newscasters than anyone imagined.

"I've got to call Joel at the *Finger Lakes Times* and give him the exclusive details. It's the least I can do," I said to Bradley as we drank our coffee. "Funny, but up until I got into that storeroom, I had a few doubts. After all, one would think that developer from Ithaca, Norwood Peltz, would have a good motive. Revenge is always on the list. But something kept pushing me to Audrey. Instinct maybe? Anyway, I really need to share this with Joel."

He looked up and crinkled his nose. "I'd wait with details until Deputy Hickman speaks with you. Last thing you need is to undermine the arrest. Just tell him you'll provide all of that later."

I nodded and tapped Joel's number. He, too, had gotten the gist of things from the farm report but was thrilled that he'd have an exclusive feature story. "It's the least I can do," I told him. "You've given me so much info as well." He asked about coffee sometime and I said, "Sure, when the dust settles." *Things are spinning enough as is and when I'm with Bradley, I want to be with Bradley.*

Then I mentioned Avery's note and the creep who broke into my house. "If you hear anything, let me know."

"You'll probably find out before I do, but hey, maybe one of those two mysteries will lead to another article. Talk to you soon, Norrie."

Bradley came up from behind and kissed me on the neck. "Finally, we have a whole day together and can lounge about and channel surf."

"Or, we can poke around the internet for my stalker. I'm thinking it's got to be a woman given the black fingernail and diamond earring. Ew, that makes it even creepier for some reason. Geez, I wish Eugene would hurry up but he'll be way too busy with the new evidence on Audrey. And speaking of which, I got a good look at her fingernails—French manicure. Besides, it would have been preposterous for her to sneak around my house. But ever since I was told about the black nail, I've been looking at everyone's hands!"

"And to think we'd get a reprieve," he said and laughed. "Okay, how about we fry up bacon and eggs, make toast and then get serious about internet searches for similar behaviors in the area."

"Works for me!"

The home-cooked breakfast after yesterday's escapade was the epitome of comfort food. But the comfort didn't last long. No sooner had I wiped the toast crumbs from the sides of my mouth when the landline rang and I could see the caller was Zenora.

"Norrie! I had the most horrid premonition yesterday but our phone lines were down due to the ice. Are you all right?"

"I'm fine. Absolutely fine. What did you see?" *Oh, why do I ask these things? What's wrong with me?*

"Someone tried to stab you with the tip of a javelin. Or at least that's how it appeared. Visions aren't always clear."

"That's it? The javelin?"

"No, it was an odd juxtaposition of things. I saw cookies, and cakes, and breads, and pastries. But most of all, I saw you in danger."

Oh my gosh! Maybe her visions have more validity than I thought.

"Um, well, actually, Bradley, Theo, and I caught Stanley's killer. It was Audrey from the bakeshop down the lake and she did try to stab me with one of those skewers for cupcakes."

"Oh, dear. I could have warned you. But Norrie, that wasn't the only vision I had. I saw you surrounded by a crowd of people with a madman intent on harming you."

Wonderful. Just what I need.

"Do you know where? When? Who the madman was?"

"I'm sorry. Everything is filmy and foggy. It requires skill and interpretation. But you need to be on guard. Avoid crowds."

And madmen.

"Thanks, Zenora, I appreciate it. And tell Glenda hi and that I'll see her tomorrow. The temperature is expected to rise overnight and the ice will melt."

"Yes, I saw that as well." Then she chuckled. "On the Weather Channel."

"I heard that," Bradley said. "I wouldn't give it too much validity, but being on guard is always good advice."

When we finished with the breakfast dishes, we sat on the couch and I booted up my laptop. The next hour was spent goggling "stalker reports" in Yates, Ontario, and Seneca counties. Surprisingly, and frighteningly, we got lots of hits. Most were from college campuses but a few mentioned houses in Geneva, Waterloo, Seneca Falls, and Penn Yan.

Of those, only three mentioned things that weren't related to looking into bedrooms. In Waterloo, the lead line read, "Man seen peering into windows. Homeowner reported her bathroom soaps had been stolen and that the suspect most likely got in from the bathroom window. Suspect never apprehended."

In Canandaigua, the line read, "Stalker admits to crawling in through basement and emptying bathroom trash that contained toenail clippings. Suspect apprehended. Admitted to a fetish for toenails."

"Ew!" I shrieked after Bradley read the line out loud. "That's positively disgusting. Worse yet, who knows what my refrigerator raider was after?"

"Then you're not going to like this last one and it was in Penn Yan. A few months ago. Hmm, surprising Deputy Hickman didn't mention anything. Then again, they've been looking into a murder."

"What does it say?" I braced myself for the worst.

"Woman arrested for stalking coworker and breaking into his house."

"That's no so unusual."

"I didn't finish. It reads, 'Suspect confessed to removing hair from coworker's brush to make a voodoo doll."

"Ick! You're right. That's worse than the other two. At least I don't think anyone can make a Voodoo doll out of the contents in my refrigerator. Still, it's creepy. Does it say if these crazies were released?"

"Uh-huh. Misdemeanors. Most likely their lawyers pleaded down. Fines, counseling, whatever. Listen, I don't think any of them is your guy or gal."

"Me either. Now what?"

"You have your staff keep their eyes and ears open and ask the WOW folks to do the same. Hearsay travels fast and some of it has validity."

"I suppose we can jump to Avery's note and the Dahl Farms email. I know they don't have anything to do with me, but it's an itch that needs scratching."

"Or a new plot for one of your screenplays?"

I smiled. "Only if there's romance involved."

Bradley pulled out his cell phone and looked at his notes.

"You actually use that app?"

"Yep. Easier than losing scrap paper all the time. Hold on a sec. Okay, here it is. The note that Avery received said, 'Shame on you for crushing the wine industry. Watch your step. You'll be the next victim.' It would seem logical that it came from one of the wineries, but it could be a setup."

"It said 'crushing the wine industry'? Those exact words? Because I don't remember without going back to my notes."

"Those exact words, yeah."

"Oh my gosh! I know who wrote it! Chalk up another charge for Audrey Killion, although it pales in comparison with murder."

"What do you mean?"

"When I was in the storeroom at her bakery and rooting all around, I glanced at her trash in there. Lots of crumpled notes. I remember the word *crushing* but didn't give it a thought. Maybe it was the draft version of Avery's note. Why not? Audrey was furious at him but needed to implicate someone else. Hang on!"

I immediately dialed the sheriff's office and was thrilled that Gladys Pipp answered. I'd forgotten she lived a few houses down from there and could walk if everyone had salted the sidewalks. And knowing Gladys, she probably called her neighbors to make sure they did.

"Norrie! Please tell me you're all right. I heard about yesterday from at least three deputies. Can you imagine? That nice lady from the bakery on the lake. It just goes to show you, you never know. Oh my goodness, I'm rambling on. Deputy Hickman would have my head. Thank goodness he's on the other side of the building at the lockup."

"I'm fine, Gladys, but I think I know who was responsible for Avery Pullman's threatening note. When I was at that bakery yesterday, I went into their storeroom and in the trash were lots of crumpled papers. I saw one with the word *crushing*. This might be a long shot but maybe it was a draft of the actual note. If so, Audrey or her son must have written it to give Avery a message while implicating one of the wineries. Deputy Hickman needs to check it out. The thing is, if he knows it's my suggestion, he'll ignore it."

"Maybe not. But it doesn't matter. The sheriff's office sent a forensics crew to her bakery to see if they could find the actual murder weapon. I'm sure they'll check the trash. In fact, I'll do one better. I'll message them and reiterate that the office wants any possible evidence that might link her or her son to the other recent crimes."

"You're the best! Next time I'm in town, I'll drop by with more jellies and jam!"

"Watch out." Bradley grinned when I ended the call. "Next thing you know, they'll be offering you the job as chief deputy sheriff."

I choked back a laugh. "Now if we can only decipher that cryptic 'Slip slop, better watch your cows' message Theo and I found on Victor Dahl's computer."

"That could have been anything."

"I know, but it still plagues me. Maybe Victor wasn't responsible for Stanley's death, but he might have been into something that involved the guy. Remember, the Diamante truck was seen at Dahl Farms on more than one occasion and I doubt it was for buying milk."

"I take back what I said about a sheriff's deputy position, you need to be writing hardboiled murder mysteries!"

"Don't tell Renee that! Oh my gosh! Renee! I've got to get that paranormal cozy screenplay finished up!"

"Can you write and smooch on the couch at the same time?"

"I can always try!"

Chapter 38

The sudden realization that I had let my screenwriting lapse hit me like a snowball in the face. Needless to say, Bradley and I spent the day nestled in the house, while I wrote and he made a valiant attempt at baking both pizza and cookies!

The neat thing about writing screenplays is the dialogue, and since Bradley was there, I was able to run the lines by him.

"Does this mean I get to co-author it?" he asked.

"Only if you want to deal with Renee."

By evening, I was well on my way to meeting my deadline but no closer to solving the last two nagging mysteries. We turned in early since both of us had busy days ahead playing catch-up.

"Next Friday is that entomology dinner, isn't it?" I detected a small grin on his face.

"Aargh. Don't remind me. A room full of scientists intent on talking about cockroaches. I can't think of anything worse. Not even those stink beetles that infested that convent a while back. I can't believe Godfrey talked me into it."

"He's a good friend and I love the idea he keeps an eye on you. Maybe the evening will turn out to be more exciting than you bargained for."

"Yeah. They'll talk about house flies or something equally gross."

As offhand comments go, Bradley hit the nail on the head. Only it had nothing to do with disgusting insect-related conversations. *That* would have been a blessing compared to the evening I had to endure.

• • •

The next morning, Bradley headed out early. First home and then to his office to sift through "the nightmare of paperwork and emails." We agreed to celebrate our victory of nabbing Stanley's killer by having dinner at Port of Call the following Saturday night. We also agreed to ask Theo and Don to join us.

At a little before nine, I got a call from a very elated Madeline. "I'm a free woman! A free woman! The sheriff's office nabbed Stanley's killer and you'll never guess who it turned out to be!"

"Well, if the truth be known—"

"It was Audrey Killion and her younger son. Can you imagine? Deputy Eustis stopped by first thing with the details! I'm a free woman! I imagine all of this will be in detail in tomorrow's newspaper and on the TV stations today. All we got were ribbons on the bottom of the screen yesterday. Then again, we weren't exactly glued to the TV."

"I know. Same here."

"What a witch that woman is. She deserves to have the entire Encyclopedia Britannica thrown at her. Not just a book!"

Too bad it's not in print.

I decided not to tell Madeline who really trapped Audrey. I figured that news would surface soon enough. "She literally killed two birds with one stone before getting caught," I said. "Ridding herself of the one person who could jeopardize her business and framing one of us. I still wonder about the blood on your meat thermometer, though. Maybe Audrey's son snuck in."

"Oh, goodness. I was about to tell you. It was Melissa's. My tasting room manager. When she told me what she thought happened, I informed Deputy Hickman but he pooh-poohed it."

"Pooh-poohed what?"

"Melissa remembered cutting her wrist on that sharp can opener we have by the kitchen drawers. She didn't realize it at the time, but droplets of her blood landed on that meat thermometer in the open drawer. And she has the same common blood type as me. And the late Stanley. Anyway, it's inconsequential now. I'm a free woman! I'm a free woman!"

"That's wonderful news. Wonderful."

"I'm afraid we'll have to postpone our next WOW meeting because I have eons of work to catch up on. I hope everyone will understand."

"Understand?" They'll be giving each other high fives and jumping up and down.

"They will. I mean, we will. I will. Everyone will. Take as much time as you need." *Six months sounds good.*

"Thanks. And thanks for believing me!"

The winery continued to buzz with the news of Audrey's arrest when I arrived there shortly after ten. Lizzie was the first to greet me with, "They interrupted the farm report with more details of Audrey Killion's arrest. Did you hear it? Imagine that. Such an ordinary woman."

"Madeline called me this morning. She's holding a 'get out of jail free card,' although she really *is* out of the Ontario County lockup."

Then Cammy and Glenda raced over. "That entire family should be behind bars," Cammy said. "Imagine. First the older son with the wine tampering and then his younger brother and mother with murder."

"They haven't convicted her yet," I said.

Glenda fluffed her holographic hair, revealing a lighter shade of orange underneath. "Zenora predicted as much. But it's not over. Not by a long shot."

"What do you mean? Audrey confessed. I know. I was there."

And then I realized what I had said. "Shh. Not a word or we'll be swamped with gossips and busybodies once news spreads. Deputy Hickman even held off before he finally had to inform the public."

I told both of them about the trek I made with Bradley and Theo, and how I was determined to eke out a confession from Audrey.

"You're lucky she didn't impale you with her cupcake shish kabob."

"Oh, she tried. Believe me, she tried."

Then Roger ambled over and told us he was really glad Stanley's killer got caught. He mumbled something about enemy spies and the French and Indian War before Sam showed up and pretty much said the same thing Cammy did.

"At least we know who was responsible for our wine loss," I said.

"Two Witches has an attorney in Penn Yan who'll deal with it."

Then I looked at Glenda. "Can Zenora be more specific? You know, about her next premonition."

"They come in waves."

Fantastic. Waves. Like a tidal storm waiting to be unleashed.

"Okay. Thanks. If she gets swept under, let me know, will you?"

Glenda nodded and went back to her tasting room table, followed by Roger and Sam.

"Hey," Cammy said. "Isn't that cockroach dinner at the Scandling Center in Geneva coming up soon?"

"I'm afraid so. Godfrey said the food will be marvelous and I'm sure he's right. It's the conversations that will make me lose my appetite. Especially if there's a presentation."

"Try to daydream. That's what I do when I have to attend things like that. Or listen to a really boring sermon. Shh! You didn't hear that from me!"

"Your secret's safe!"

I made sure that Emma and Fred, along with Franz and John, knew exactly what had happened. Naturally, they were all one step ahead of me. Franz mumbled about the quality of the Cab-Franc and that we might have to use it in a blend. But at least he was thankful our traminette had been spared. Unlike Madeline's.

John made sure our surveillance was beefed up, and asked if I wanted to have the same done to the farmhouse. "I hate to say it, Norrie, but life on Seneca Lake isn't the same as when your parents ran the winery."

"Ugh. I suppose you're right. Yeah, go ahead. It's not as if Charlie's a Rottweiler."

"By the way, did you see the ribbon that's been at the bottom of all the Sunday newscasts? It reads, 'Yates County Sheriff's Office Arrests Woman for Murder of Developer Stanley Hurst.'"

"Ugh. No. What else did it say?"

"You won't like it. It read, 'Deputy Gary Hickman credited for his stellar investigation.'"

"Stellar investigation? He couldn't find a missing sock! I don't believe it! I did all the work! All of it! Well, maybe not the forensics, but still . . ."

"Let it go, Norrie. A murderess is behind bars, and her vandalizing son isn't far behind."

"I suppose. Anyway, I'm not done yet. I've got a food stalker to catch and a cryptic email to figure out."

"Do it at home. On your laptop. Much safer. Then again, I have to remember who I'm talking to."

"Don't worry. I think all the real excitement is done." Then I caught myself. Never say things like that. They immediately put a jinx on everything. At least according to Glenda and Zenora.

Chapter 39

Murders around Seneca Lake aren't all that common, even if I had seen my share. Naturally, Audrey's arrest was all the customers talked about for the next week. And Joel's insightful feature story in Wednesday's *Finger Lakes Times* only fueled the fire. So much for talking about wine. When Friday finally rolled around, I left a little before four to take care of Charlie and get ready for the dinner. At least I had the rest of the weekend to spend with Bradley, even if we were about to do some more sleuthing on the Victor Dahl email.

I told Godfrey I'd meet him at six forty-five in plenty of time for the seven p.m. dinner. I figured we wouldn't be getting to the food until seven thirty or even seven forty-five with all the introductions and speeches. Luckily Francine's closet had an abundance of winter dresses in my size. Unfortunately, none were my style. I did the next best thing. I found black slacks and a long cowl-neck tunic that looked spectacular. Besides, knowing that entomology crew, their eyes would turn at a double antennae insect rather than a twentysomething screenwriter.

The temperature hovered around freezing but the roads were clear and the next storm wasn't expected until midweek. I arrived at the Scandling Center at six forty and found a decent parking space. At least a foot or more from the nearest car. Since I drove Francine's Subaru and not my old Toyota, the last thing I needed was to scratch or dent it. Then I hoofed my way to the entrance, thankful I'd worn suede calf-length dress boots. I tried not to think about roaches but it was like trying to ignore an itch in an inconvenient place. Little did I know that roaches would be the last thing on my mind in just a matter of hours.

Godfrey was at the door and gave me a hug. "I'm so glad you're my plus one tonight. It's going to be an exciting evening for sure. We've got incredible speakers with wonderful videos and presentations, including the noted entomologist from the University of Kentucky, Parker Somber."

I did a mental eye roll and smiled as Godfrey continued. "Parker Somber's been in the area for a few weeks, speaking at different college campuses."

"Sounds, uh, interesting."

"Oh, it is. It *is*. Come on, let's go to our table and I'll introduce you to the entomologists you haven't met. Alex Bollinger and Arvin Pincus will also be there."

"With their wives or girlfriends?"

"No, they're both single."

No surprise there.

The banquet room at Scandling was nothing less than spectacular. It had been decorated with tasteful flowers and gorgeous garlands. A cash bar and an appetizer buffet table flanked the side and back wall.

"I understand the canapes are really tasty. Arvin's made three trips already. He likes to arrive early."

No wonder.

The round tables housed six to eight people and I was glad I knew Alex. Godfrey introduced me to Judith Einswinger, an entomologist who focused on winged pests, and Claudia something whose last name I didn't quite catch. According to Godfrey, Claudia was a noted expert on gnats and recently had a major article published in *Entomology Today.*

"You've got to try the stuffed grape leaves," Claudia said. "I can't quite place the filling but it's delicious."

Godfrey wasted no time ushering me to the appetizers. "Relax There are no insects being served."

"I know, but still . . ." I selected a few cheeses and crackers as well as the mini-croissants and fried mushrooms before returning to the table. Judith and Arvin were discussing the Pacific dampwood termite that apparently swarmed into people's yards and houses in Sunset, California. I shuddered and turned instead to Claudia, who had just consumed a meatball and remarked how similar it tasted to the ground crickets she ate while in Bali.

Yep. Can't go wrong with cheese and crackers.

Godfrey placed his dish of assorted delicacies on the table and dove in. "In a few minutes, Margaret Smith, the director of Cornell University Experiment Station, will welcome us and then turn the program over to the conference chair, Patrick Tingley. This is so exciting. So many noted speakers!"

I bumped his elbow and whispered, "I thought you said we weren't going to listen to lots of boring speeches."

"Not boring. Fascinating."

Like reading the ingredients on a can of Raid.

I put another carrot in my mouth and turned back to the Dampwood Termite discussion, only now it had morphed into someone's research study that Judith and Arvin thought lacked viable scientific evidence.

Meanwhile, Alex and Godfrey talked about the Ithaca roach infestation and how they could better track the movements of those disgusting insects. Then, true to Godfrey's word, someone introduced Margaret and she expressed her "ultimate joy" at hosting this conference. Short and sweet. Hallelujah!

Then Patrick Tingley welcomed us and told us to enjoy the slide presentation as we began our meal. Next thing I knew, horrific images of flying, nesting, and crawling bugs filled the two giant screens in the room just as my Caesar salad was served.

Alex leaned over and asked me how things were going at the winery since he'd heard about the wine tampering. I told him we only had moderate damages that hopefully we could recoup, unlike Madeline who lost her specialty wine.

The subject of Stanley's murder also came up with Alex and Arvin crediting the Yates County Sheriff's Office. I wanted to gag. Then, I told them about my refrigerator raider and how he or she got in from the outside cellar door.

"That's pretty unsettling," Alex said. "Did you ever get that door replaced?"

"As a matter of fact, I did. Home Depot in Geneva installed a primed cellar door a few days later. In between the storms. It locks like a charm and no one can get in."

"Lunatics and nutcases always find a way," Arvin said. "You should consider an alarm system or camera surveillance."

"My vineyard manager, John, is one step ahead of you. He's getting surveillance installed this coming week. Believe me, I've been going to sleep with a can of wasp spray by my bed if an intruder shows up."

We finished our salads just as the lobster bisque showed up, along with Dr. Justantine Lourango, a highly esteemed entomologist from Peru. He took the podium to provide us with a "little chat" about screwworms that burrow under the skin. By the time he finished, I itched all over.

Then, the main course arrived. I had ordered the eggplant and zucchini and it looked marvelous. Spinelli's had done an incredible job with the food, but having to look up and see enormous screens with icky insects wasn't exactly the most enticing way to enjoy a meal. Unless of course you were one of the entomologists. They were in their glory with each full-colored photo.

Another entomologist spoke briefly about some endangered insect but I was too busy trying to enjoy my meal. Then, when the main course was over, the keynote speaker was introduced. Dr. Parker Somber from the University of Kentucky. Godfrey had told me about him so I prepared myself for a snooze fest.

What Godfrey didn't tell me was that Dr. Somber looked to be in his early thirties and quite the millennial. Tight-fitting jeans, blue shirt and a gray winter casual coat that pulled the entire outfit together. Maybe it wouldn't be such a snooze fest after all.

I watched as Dr. Somber used a laser light to focus on the anatomy of some hideous insect from the *Formicidae*. It looked like an ant on steroids, but in a flash I noticed something else.

The laser light beam reflected back and when he turned his head, I could see a diamond stud earring. A zillion what-ifs raced through my head. I remembered Godfrey telling me that Dr. Somber was in the area giving lectures at the colleges, putting him here at the time of my stalker discovery.

I took a breath and clasped my hands. Lots of men wear a studded earring and just because this guy did, there was no reason to jump to such a crazy conclusion. I fiddled with my dessert fork and tried to focus on what they'd serve.

It didn't matter. There was only one thing I could do—find out if he had a chipped black nail on one or more of his fingers. I knew it was kind of a vogue thing to have one black pinkie nail, but until I could get up close and personal, I'd never know.

"Will Dr. Somber be sticking around after his presentation?" I asked Godfrey.

"No. He has a plane to catch in an hour. Why? Are you finding this interesting?"

"Very."

I glanced around the room and calculated my options. Then, out of sheer determination and a bit of madness, I stood and announced, "Can you go over the formaldehyde again? I think there's a discrepancy." And with that, I charged to the stage before Godfrey could stop me.

In the back of my mind I thought, *What's the worst thing that could happen?*

And then it did.

Chapter 40

As I rushed to the stage, I heard at least half a dozen entomologists shout out, *"Formicidae!"* and I could hear the sound of rushing footsteps behind me. I had to act fast. Wasting no time, I stormed up the steps to the stage and reached for Dr. Somber's laser pointer, hoping he'd hang on to it long enough for me to check out his fingernails. I could always claim temporary insanity.

Sure enough, he latched on to the laser pointer like Charlie with a dead rabbit carcass in his mouth. That gave me enough time to eyeball his right hand, all the while thinking, *What if it's on his left?*

Still, I couldn't get a close enough look. That left me no alternative but to grab his wrist and pull the hand closer to me, causing him to drop the pointer at the same time I dropped my jaw.

"Security!" he shouted. "Someone call Security!"

"Yes," I screamed. "And call the Yates County Sheriff's Office along with Ontario's! This man is a stalker who broke into my house and I can prove it!" *Eugene better have figured out the DNA on that fingernail or I'm dead in the water.*

Then I looked directly at Dr. Somber, narrowed my eyes and spoke. Luckily, the microphone was turned on so the entire audience got to hear me. "What the heck were you rooting around in my refrigerator for? And I know it was you! The forensic techs found part of your chipped black nail, which incidentally isn't my favorite fashion statement, but hey, evidence is evidence. Oh, and speaking of which, you must have been really perturbed to have lost your diamond stud. Replacements are costly."

Dr. Somber immediately put his left hand to his ear but didn't say a word.

"Ah-hah! I'm right, aren't I?"

But before he could answer, which in retrospect I doubted he would, four members of the audience and a security officer rushed up the steps. Unfortunately, they chose not to detain the reputable Dr.

Somber, but instead focused their attention on me.

I yelled at the top of my lungs. "Call the sheriff's office and ask for Deputy Gary Hickman. Yates County. Yates!!!"

Then, off to the side of the stage, I heard Patrick Tingley address the audience, telling them to be patient while the "unforeseeable situation on stage gets resolved." Then I heard him say something about sending an apology to the University of Kentucky and that's when it hit me! I knew exactly why the notable Dr. Somber was in my house.

I usually let the stuff Godfrey tells me blow over my head, but I remembered something about that university in Lexington. They studied DNA sequencing too, only they hadn't managed to extract any from a cockroach. Somehow Dr. Somber must have found out that I was gifted a sample and thought it easier to steal it from my possession than risk going after a sample in one of the Experiment Station labs.

"You were after cockroach DNA from my house, weren't you?" I said to Dr. Somber. "How'd you know I had it? Did you plant a mole in Cornell's lab? It doesn't matter. You're going to be arrested for breaking and entering. And for ruining my sleep. And busting a lock. And . . ."

At that point, Dr. Somber stepped away from the podium and said, "My apologies. I'm going to miss my flight and my Uber must be outside by now. I'll post study notes on my website for all of you."

Study notes my patootie!

He bolted stage left, leaving me no recourse. I rushed him like an NFL linebacker and pounced on him, throwing all of my weight on his back. It caught him off guard and he fell forward. That's when I literally remained on top of him until I felt two strong arms pulling me off.

"Don't let him get away! Call Eugene from the Yates County Forensics Office. Or Deputy Clarence Eustis if you can't reach Deputy Hickman. Heck, call someone! I can prove Dr. Somber attempted to steal a priceless treasure from my possession."

Not as priceless as a chocolate diamond or a Renoir, but as insects go, it's top of the line apparently.

By now, Dr. Somber was down the stairs and halfway through the banquet area. I broke free from my detainer and lit after the entomologist like nobody's business. All those days forcing myself to take a morning run with Charlie finally paid off.

I bumped into tables, I crashed into guests and I knocked over a tray of what I think were chocolate mousse desserts. Darn! Behind me I could hear Godfrey, Alex, and Arvin shouting but I kept running. Dr. Somber was only a few feet ahead of me and I didn't want those feet to turn into yards.

He exited the banquet room and charged toward the coat closet. Duh! I should have realized he'd have a winter coat and a bag stashed there. Unlike me. I'd thrown my coat over my chair when I got inside.

I watched him reach for a long black coat and in that instant, I rushed him, causing him to topple over, along with assorted coats and jackets. As he scrambled to get up and out of there, I yelled, "You owe me for damages, buddy! Food that had to be tossed because ink stuff got on it from the dusting of prints. And a broken lock from my basement door. I plan to collect every last cent! Oh. Don't let me forget the chocolate mousse dessert that I missed. You owe me for that, too!" I was like a madwoman who had lost all of her faculties. Words spewed out of my mouth like steam from a geyser. Maybe it was the tension from the past few days or maybe the realization that this guy had violated my privacy and my sense of security. No matter. I was completely unglued. Nevertheless, I was determined to prevent him from leaving the building and getting into that Uber.

Dr. Somber shook off the three or four coats from his back and that's when I grabbed a handful more from the hangers and threw them at him. Then, in a most unprecedented move, I turned and raced out the building. It was a long shot but I had to take it.

I flew down the steps to the front entrance, where I knew his Uber ride would be waiting. Sure enough, a dark SUV had pulled to the curb and I opened the passenger door. "Drive away!" I shouted to the dark-haired woman seated behind the wheel. "Your passenger is about to be arrested for stalking, breaking and entering, and invasion of privacy. Nice way of saying, he's off-kilter and who knows what he'll do. I'm with the campus safety patrol. Sheriff deputies are on their way. Cross Parker Somber off your list and drive off while you can."

Meanwhile, I heard Dr. Somber's voice. "Hold my ride! Hold my ride!"

The woman behind the wheel hadn't budged and I was positive the guy would get away with everything. I seriously doubted the Yates County Sheriff's Office would compel the state of Kentucky to send him back to New York.

Turning my neck slightly, I could see Dr. Somber a yard or less away. "Now!" I shouted. "Did you know there were over three thousand assaults reported to Uber this past year from drivers? Because I do. It was on the news." *At least I think it was three thousand.*

With that, the woman pulled away from the curb and shouted, "I don't get paid enough for this." Seconds later I saw her taillights as she turned right to get back to Main Street.

"You're crazy, lady," Dr. Somber said as he raced toward me. The words came out between gasps for breath. "If I miss my flight, you'll be the one paying for my next ticket."

"Tell me the truth. You were after that roach DNA. How did you know I had it? What database did you rob? Breaking and entering is one thing, but tampering with a university database carries a stiffer sentence. Intellectual theft and all that goes with it. Come to think of it, Dr. Godfrey Klein has a good friend at that university. An administrator." *More or less.* "You'll be lucky if they let you mop the floors at the University of Kentucky."

"I didn't hack into a database. While I toured the entomology labs I saw a list of gifts that the university bestowed on its valued patrons. Your name and address were on top and I couldn't believe my eyes when it said, 'Blattaria DNA.'"

"So you couldn't resist?"

"Hey, no real harm was done. And where the heck are you storing it? The DNA will lose its—"

"Shelf life?" *And I hope it's a short one.*

"Efficacy, if it isn't refrigerated."

"Oh, trust me. It's refrigerated, all right. In a small fridge in our basement that you walked right past." *Even though it was covered with rags or towels or whatever else was on hand.* "You were inches away from your precious treasure and you blew it."

"I wouldn't say that." And then, without warning, Dr. Somber reached into his pant pocket and pulled out a small taser. "One wrong move and I won't be able to release my grip. The electric shock will do more than render you unconscious."

I looked past him, hoping to see Godfrey or anyone for that matter, but then I realized they never knew I went into the coat room. That meant they were looking for us elsewhere. Like the entrance on the other side of the building. Rats!!

If I made a move, he'd be inches from me and with an arm held out, that taser would hit me worse than a bullet.

"What do you want?"

"You're going to drive me to the airport, but first, we're going to make a little stop at your place to pick up what I should have found the first time around."

"DNA sounds so fragile. Sure I couldn't interest you in some award-winning wine?"

"Don't be cute, Miss Ellington. Walk me to your car and don't try any funny stuff."

I did as he said, but when we reached Francine's car, instead of pushing the open button on my fob, I pushed the siren and immediately regretted not bringing earplugs. The sound was worse than deafening. So much for the fob repair. It was ear-piercing and thunderous. The frat houses near the Scandling Center emptied immediately with throngs of boys rushing into the street.

"Is that an air-raid drill? Or an emergency shelter-in-place?" someone shouted.

The siren was relentless. No matter how hard I pushed the knob, it refused to stop. I remembered the mechanic telling me I'd have to start the car to get the noise to quit and that he expedited a new key fob for delivery since the repair was "iffy." *You think?*

Then, off to my left, I saw Godfrey and Alex charging toward us with Arvin running at least ten paces behind them. The only thing I didn't see was Deputy Hickman, and for the first time, I regretted it.

Chapter 41

Dr. Somber held the taser in front of me and directed me to open the driver's side door. "Start it once you get in. And no funny stuff. I'm leaning right over you. And if you make a move to pull out, it will be your last."

I put my right foot inside the car and that's when I heard a voice that startled me. "It's a good thing I refilled my antianxiety medicine, Miss Ellington. The sheriff's office texted me, insisting I get over here immediately. *Immediately.*" Eugene! He stood directly behind Dr. Somber, no idea that the man was a raving lunatic. "Like I said, Miss Ellington, this better be important because you pulled me away from my Dungeons & Dragons game. I'll have you know the webmaster was not pleased."

Dungeons & Dragons? Webmaster? Is that what Eugene does for fun? I thought those games went out in the eighties.

Then he realized I was held hostage by Dr. Somber. Next thing I knew, Eugene gave the doctor a swift kick on the back of the guy's knee, causing him to drop the taser. I snatched it in a nanosecond and threw it across the icy pavement.

"What did you do that for?" Eugene asked.

"I was afraid I'd tase myself. Grab him! Grab that guy!"

Eugene grasped Dr. Somber's arm but the man shook him loose and began to run.

"Come on, Eugene. Hurry! That's the intruder who got into my basement. Black fingernail and all."

Next thing I knew, the cavalry had come. Godfrey, Alex, Arvin, and a few others from the banquet. Also, two security officers. One charged after Dr. Somber while the other held up his palm and told me not to move.

"I'm not the bad guy. It's Dr. Somber. He broke into my house, and Eugene here can prove it. He works for the Yates County Sheriff's Office. He's a forensic scientist or something like that."

"I can't very well prove anything, Miss Ellington, until I compare samples. And my title is Forensic Science Technician. I specialize in laboratory analysis."

The security officer glanced at Eugene and directed both of us back to the Scandling Center.

"But what about Dr. Somber? They're not going to let him get away with anything, are they?" I whined.

"Turn around and see for yourself. My partner detained him and we're waiting for our county sheriff's office to respond."

As Eugene and I walked back to the building, he kept mumbling about missing his D & D game and how the mere mention of my name has caused him to get hives.

"I'm sorry, Eugene, really I am, but you need to look on the bright side. You'll be nabbing a bona fide criminal. Now, what was it you needed?"

"A sample of that man's skin, or bodily liquid for a comparative analysis."

"No problem. I take it you analyzed the fingernail in question, right?"

"Yes."

"You're in luck. When I reached for his laser pointer, I accidently scraped some of his skin under my fingernail. Get a toothpick, or a Q-tip or a paper clip, and help yourself."

Eugene turned to the security officer. "Would you mind if I went back to my car to retrieve my kit?"

"Make it quick. We'll wait here."

Eugene hurried back and sighed. "I should have kept my cell phone off. Clarence got a call from Deputy Hickman and he, in turn, called me. Deputy Hickman is at a family get-together in Victor. He's expected back in the morning."

Thank God for small favors.

I held out my hand and he used a small pointy instrument to remove the debris from under my finger. Then he put it in a vial.

"I'll need to run an analysis in my lab and that will take a few hours," he told the security officer. Then, to me, "The only reason any of this is happening is because the deputy on duty called Gladys Pipp because he wasn't sure what was going on."

There isn't enough jam in the world to thank you, Gladys.

The security officer motioned to Eugene. "Why don't you go on ahead and Miss Ellington and I will go back inside the building."

Eugene wasted no time leaving the scene, just as I heard sirens coming from down the block. Yep, Ontario County sent its crew. The security officer and I stood for a moment and watched as two deputies approached the crowd that had Dr. Somber cornered.

"I'm not sure what's going on, Miss, but I hope for your sake whatever that lab tech compares will be a match."

"It will be." *It had better be or I'll be joining Francine in the Philippines.*

I was escorted back into the Scandling Center and had to wait in the security office.

"Would you mind checking the entomology dinner and see if you can bring me my chocolate mousse?" I asked. "It's the only reason I came."

The officer laughed and made a phone call. A few minutes later, a server knocked on the door with two desserts. At least something went right. As for Dr. Somber, it was anyone's guess.

"Do you have any idea what's going on with the man who tried to abduct me?" I asked.

"Abduct you? We thought you were chasing *him*."

"Uh, yeah. Until I got too close. Then things kind of changed in a split second." I then told him everything that had happened, beginning with the break-in at my house.

"It's understandable why you were so distraught," he said. "Still, there must have been a better alternative."

"Nope." I shook my head. "He had a plane to catch. It was now or never."

Just then, someone rapped on the door and I was relieved to see it was Godfrey. He nodded to the officer and stepped toward me. "Dr. Somber was taken to the Ontario County Sheriff's Office for questioning. I imagine you'll be next. For heaven's sake, Norrie, *what is going on?* You can't possibly think he was the one who broke into your house."

"He was. And Eugene's analysis will prove it." *Or Bradley will need to pull lots of strings to get me out of this one.*

Godfrey took a seat next to me and I explained exactly how I had reached my determination regarding the esteemed entomologist.

"I hate to say it," Godfrey said, "but what you're accusing him of isn't all that far-fetched in my field. In the late nineties, someone from the University of Pennsylvania was caught breaking into a lab at the University of California, Davis, in order to steal a specific sample of varroa mites. Very deadly to bees. At first, no one would believe it, but then, a plane ticket was discovered and the scientist was arrested."

"See? And roach DNA must be worth more than mites."

A few minutes later, two Yates County deputies and one from Ontario County walked into the security office. I was asked to provide a detailed written statement and was given a pen and a pad. Nothing like old-school.

"Now what happens?" I asked them.

"You're fortunate you have friends in the sheriff's office, Miss Ellington," one of the Yates County deputies said. "We were directed to get a statement and inform you that Deputy Hickman will be paying you a visit at your home first thing in the morning."

I might as well buy him his own coffee mug.

"Thank you. I guess that means I'm free to go."

"Free, but remain at home or at your winery. Those were Deputy Hickman's orders."

I nodded, smiled and stood as they left the room. Next, I turned to Godfrey. "I'm really sorry about messing up the end of that mesmerizing discourse on whatever Dr. Somber droned on about.

Please let everyone know."

"Do you want me to drive you home and you can pick up your car tomorrow?"

"Nah, I'll be fine."

"Text me when you're home. Okay?"

"Sure. And thanks again. The food was amazing."

The drive home was uneventful and I couldn't wait to call Bradley and fill him in. Like Godfrey, he was stunned at my overly exuberant reaction once I was certain the intruder was Dr. Somber and the motive was crystal clear.

"I'm just glad you're in one piece, hon. That guy could've really hurt you."

"It retrospect, you're right, but I had adrenaline on my side."

"Now what happens?"

"I wait with baited breath for Eugene's analysis. And ask you for those names of criminal defense attorneys."

"I don't think you'll need to worry in that regard. Seems it would be a college campus issue and the worst they can do is send you a letter of reprimand or even go as far as to ban you from their campus for a while."

"Good to know."

"Listen, I know we planned on dinner at Port of Call a week from tomorrow, but how about you and I getting together with Theo and Don sooner. Maybe Uncle Joe's for pizza this week? I came across some rather telling information about Lila and I think it might interest you, considering your barnyard sleuthing with Theo."

"Did she confess to anything while you were here?"

"No, not yet. I'll tell you more when I see you. Ask the guys if Tuesday or Wednesday would work for them."

"Will do. Theo and Don will never turn down pizza, especially from Uncle Joe's."

When our call ended, I texted Theo. *Positive intruder is hotshot entomologist. Eugene running lab work. I may be banned from Hobart campus if I am wrong. Long story.*

Five minutes later, my cell phone buzzed with Theo's call and I told him about my night at the cockroach banquet.

"Seriously?" he said. "You got on stage to look at the man's fingernails?"

"How else was I going to nab him?"

"Maybe by notifying the Yates County Sheriff's Office."

"No time."

"You've got a knack, Norrie. That's for sure."

"Keep your fingers crossed Eugene finds a match or I'll never be able to set foot in Geneva again."

"It's winter. Wear a ski mask."

I asked him about pizza at Uncle Joe's and after conferring with Don, we decided on Tuesday. In Don's words, "Why wait for a good thing?" Then I texted Bradley, let Charlie out and headed up to bed. As usual, the dog beat me to it and nabbed a spot near my pillow.

In spite of being on edge over the lab results, I fell fast asleep as soon as my head hit the pillow. If bad news was going to be delivered to me in the morning, at least I'd be wide awake to hear it.

Chapter 42

I don't remember being this anxious about anything since the SAT results. At a little past five the next morning, I bolted out of bed and did something I never thought I would. I turned on the radio and listened to the farm report. Commodities, price index, dairy, blah, blah . . . And then, a special announcement from the Yates County Sheriff's Office.

Forget throwing on jeans and going downstairs for coffee. I turned up the volume and sat on the bed. *This better not be some stupid road closure or worse yet, someone's cows getting loose again.*

At first I couldn't believe what I heard, but the program host repeated what he said. "Breaking news from the Yates County Sheriff's Office. An arrest has been made in regard to a local break-in at someone's home. Sheriff's deputies, in conjunction with the forensic office, are credited for their swift action and comprehensive approach to crime solving. This is the second such crime that the office has solved in the past few weeks."

"Swift action and comprehensive approach? Second such crime?" Unbelievable! I did all the legwork. *All* of it! Not to mention risking my own life and limb with that roach-DNA-seeking entomologist!

And why didn't Eugene call me? Unless the local break-in wasn't my house. Drat! I immediately raced to grab the cell phone and see if I missed his text. Sure enough, there it was—*Skin cells viable. Genetic profiles confirmed. Ran 40 DNA segments for alleles. Amplified variations. Peaks fell at same l to r position. Eugene.*

I reread the text at least three times. He might as well have written it in Arabic. None of it made sense. Was it a match or was Deputy Hickman about to read me the riot act in a few hours?

I googled the word *alleles* but that didn't help much. It meant variations. I knew what peaks were, but what they represented was anyone's guess. *Thank you, Eugene.*

Rather than bother anyone at the sheriff's office, I did the next best thing. Or at least I thought it was at the time. I called Zenora. After all, she was a research librarian at an Ivy League school. I figured she must know how to make sense of the text. In retrospect, I should have had that first cup of coffee to clear out my brain.

"Norrie! You're alive! You're breathing!"

"Uh, yeah." *Otherwise I would not have been able to call you.*

"Oh, Norrie! You know what this means, don't you?"

"No idea."

"My ancient chant worked. I saw you surrounded by winged insects and one particularly venomous one whose stinger pierced your arm. The ancient chant, in conjunction with burning sage and lavender, had to be sung before it was too late. And fear not, no one knew where the aroma of burnt smoke emanated from."

"You chanted and burnt stuff in your office? In the library?"

"The vision came upon me while I was cataloging some English sonnets. Fortunately, yesterday was Friday, and not many students were in the building after four. I daresay, no one noticed."

"What about the smoke detectors?"

"Oh, I disabled them weeks ago during our All-Hallows' Eve celebration."

Of course. *Why oh why do I continue to ask these things?*

"Zenora, I need you to focus for a minute. Do you know how to make sense out of a text from a forensic lab? I can't get past the technical jargon."

"Text it to me. I need to see the words in print. Then give me a few minutes."

"Thanks. Shall do."

I ended the call and immediately forwarded her Eugene's exact message. Less than ten minutes later, she called back.

"The variables matched because the peaks fell at the same left to right position."

"Um, could you put that in words a kindergartner might under-stand?"

"The samples matched."

"They did? That's what it said? They matched!" And why didn't Eugene say that? He speaks English.

"Yes."

"Zenora, how were you able to research it so quickly?"

"I have databases no one even knows exists. It's my job security. Well, *that* and my spiritual outreach to the realms beyond our tangible presence."

And all this time I thought Eugene's text was impossible to cypher.

"Uh, thanks. Thanks a lot, Zenora. I appreciate it."

"The looming darkness above your head is fading. You can bask in the knowledge that the ancients have listened to my chant."

"Uh, again, thanks. Really."

I got off the phone before Zenora told me to ingest a horrid herb, or worse yet, bathe myself in something unthinkable. If she was right, then it *was* my house on that farm report.

I scurried to get dressed and then texted Bradley, Godfrey, and Theo in the same thread. *Caught farm report. Got text from Eugene. Got translation from Zenora. Yes, Zenora. It's a match! Dr. Somber was the refrigerator raider. Wanted the roach DNA.*

Then, I sent another text. This time to Joel. I told him that I had a new feature story for him and he called a few minutes later. "How about I drop by your winery this afternoon and you can fill me in?" he asked. "Unless you can take a break and meet for coffee. All roads are clear."

I texted back, *Busy Saturday. Stop by. We can chat in our bistro.*

Joel sent a thumbs-up emoji and I grinned. Seconds later, I had a K-cup in the Keurig and Charlie's kibble filled.

When I got to Two Witches at a little past ten, the first thing I asked Lizzie was if Deputy Hickman was waiting for me.

"Oh, I didn't know you were expecting him."

"I'm not. Well, it's not an appointment or anything. I sort of created a minor ruckus at the Scandling Center last night when I nailed the stalker who got into my house."

"What?" Cammy asked. She stood a few feet away and overheard me.

"Might as well call Glenda over. I can see her straining to listen as she's filling a wine rack. Besides, Zenora probably told her."

"Zenora was there?"

"Aargh. This may take some explaining."

In the next three minutes, I told Lizzie, Cammy, and Glenda what had taken place. "It's okay to let Sam and Roger know. Also Emma and Fred."

"Do you think anyone will press charges?" Cammy widened her eyes.

"They should lock Dr. Somber up for a century!"

"Not Dr. Somber, *you!*"

"Nah. It's a college issue."

"It's a good thing the spirits were aligned and Zenora was able to chant you through safety." Glenda wrapped her fingers around a large amulet of a hideous bird creature that she wore around her neck.

"Uh, yeah. Great singing, er . . . I mean chanting."

As it turned out, I got a phone call from Grizzly Gary in lieu of a visit. *Keep that chanting up, Zenora.*

Dr. Parker Somber confessed to everything and agreed to pay restitution for any damages, including the cost of my new basement doors. So far, a terrific way to start the weekend. With the wine tampering, Stanley's murder, and the break-in at my house finally solved, I could get back to that pesky screenplay before I found myself kicked to the curb by Renee.

I called Franz and John and gave them the good news as well. Godfrey, who was concerned about my behavior as well as my safety, dropped by at a little before noon. We chatted in my office over hot bacon and cheese paninis.

"You really had me scared, Norrie," he said. "But I trusted your instincts. Although not necessarily your recklessness. Anyway, our entire office is shocked and dismayed about Dr. Somber's attempted theft."

"Um, that brings me to asking a favor of you. Possessing that invaluable DNA cockroach specimen is far too risky for me. Think of all the other greedy and nefarious entomologists who want to get their hands on it. How about if the Experiment Station stores it in a nice, safe place for me? I can even stop by and visit it from time to time. What do you say?"

"That's a good idea. If you can break away for a few minutes, I'll pick it up. All I need is a small cooler."

"Absolutely! And Godfrey, I'm really sorry about interrupting that spellbinding dinner."

"No worries. You can attend the spring banquet. We'll be hosting a symposium on dung beetles and Dr. Olga Rominsky from Texas A&M will be the guest speaker."

All I could do was nod.

Chapter 43

As I swirled the spaghetti on my fork Tuesday night at Uncle Joe's, I told Bradley, Theo and Don how relieved I was that I didn't have to meet with Deputy Hickman. The statement I completed on Friday night was all they needed.

"I sent Eugene a gift," I said. "Had it delivered to the Yates County Sheriff's Office."

"Wine? Food?" Don asked.

"Nope. Tickets to Comic-Con in New York City next October. Even paid for two nights at a hotel. It was the least I could do. He can play Dungeons & Dragons all he wants."

"Wow. That was really nice of you."

"Not really. It's more of an insurance policy. The way things are going, I may need to keep Eugene on retainer."

Don laughed and reached for a slice of garlic bread.

"Okay, folks, I'll make everyone's evening complete," Bradley said. "A while back when Norrie told me about her escapade with Theo at Dahl Farms, I couldn't stop laughing. And when she mentioned a cryptic email they found on Victor Dahl's computer, I never imagined I'd be the one to decipher it."

"Huh?" I dropped my fork and bits of the marinara sauce spattered on my shirt. "What do you mean? How?"

"I met with Lila Stratington-Hurst to go over Stanley's will and that's when she confessed to having an affair with Justin Dahl, Victor's grandson. They met each other on an online dating site. Anyway, it seems a clause in that will specified that if she cheated on Stanley, the will would be null and void. So, she wondered if there was any way that anyone could prove it, especially Victor, who had warned his grandson to steer clear of her."

My jaw literally dropped and I motioned for him to continue.

"She thought that if she was able to send him an anonymous email, he would be too distracted with a possible threat and not focus on her."

"Oh my gosh! So that means the Diamante truck that was observed at Dahl Farms was driven by Lila, not Stanley." I dipped my napkin in my water and tried to wipe off the marina splatter.

"It would appear that way," Bradley said. "Hey, does this mean I get to become the next Hardy Boy?" He elbowed Theo and the two of them broke up laughing before Theo could finally respond.

"Only if you're willing to drive home covered with cow manure or worse. Those are the risks we amateur sleuths take."

"Ah, but think of the rewards." I grinned like the Cheshire Cat.

"What rewards?" Theo furrowed his brow.

"We don't have to run the WOW meetings!"

Epilogue

Joel Margolis's feature story was so well crafted and so well received that in conjunction with his first feature about Stanley Hurst's murder, he received a promotion and a bonus in pay. He offered to take me out for dinner at Belhurst or Geneva on the Lake, but I declined. I told him I valued his friendship but was committed to my current relationship. We agreed to meet for coffee once in a while and keep each other posted regarding the goings-on in our area.

The best news of all came from the Town of Benton Planning Board. Due to Stanley's unfortunate passing, the high-rise proposal had been rescinded by its current owner, Lila Stratington-Hurst. Instead, she put the property up for sale again and started a bidding war that Madeline won. We'd have a traminette vineyard on Seneca Lake and not a mini-Manhattan.

I finally finished the screenplay for the paranormal cozy and held my breath for whatever whimsy came next from Renee. As it turned out, the studios were now interested in urban romance with a focus on "flawed characters who are redeemed by love." I did at least ten mental eye rolls when she gave me the news.

The Seneca Lake Wine Trail sent us a reminder about their new St. Patrick's Day weekend event entitled "Leprechauns, Shamrocks, and Wine." They made no mention of murders and I held my breath they'd be right.

About the Author

Ann I. Goldfarb

New York native Ann I. Goldfarb spent most of her life in education, first as a classroom teacher and later as a middle school principal and professional staff developer. Writing as J. C. Eaton, along with her husband, James Clapp, she has authored the Sophie Kimball Mysteries, the Wine Trail Mysteries, the Charcuterie Shop Mysteries, and the Marcie Rayner Mysteries. In addition, Ann has nine published YA time travel mysteries under her own name. Visit the websites at: www.jceatonmysteries.com and www.timetravelmysteries.com

James E. Clapp

When James E. Clapp retired as the tasting room manager for a large upstate New York winery, he never imagined he'd be coauthoring cozy mysteries with his wife, Ann I. Goldfarb. His first novel, *Booked 4 Murder*, was released in June 2017, followed by ten other books in the series and three other series. Nonfiction in the form of informational brochures and workshop materials treating the winery industry were his forte, along with an extensive background and experience in construction that started with his service in the U.S. Navy and included vocational school classroom teaching. Visit the website at www.jceatonmysteries.com

Made in United States
Troutdale, OR
10/31/2023

14168569R00159